THE CONTORTIONIST

HARROW FAIRE: BOOK ONE

KATHRYN ANN KINGSLEY

Copyright © 2020 by Kathryn Ann Kingsley

First Print Edition: September 2020

ISBN-13: 979-8-68242-934-9

ASIN: B08FHCWRP2

KATHRYN ANN KINGSLEY

All rights reserved.

No part of this book may be reproduced in any form or by any electronic or mechanical means, including information storage and retrieval systems, without written permission from the author, except for the use of brief quotations in a book review.

This is a work of fiction. Names, characters, places, and incidents either are the product of the author's imagination or are used fictitiously, and any resemblance to locales, events, business establishments, or actual persons —living or dead—is entirely coincidental.

FOREWORD

I have always loved the circus. I've always adored a carnival. There's a certain kind of magic that comes along with them. By design, they are a little ephemeral, a little fantastical, and a little to the left of reality. Strange animals, strange costumes, and sometimes even stranger people.

My family has been in the circus since the Vaudeville days. Flyers, aerialists, wing-walkers, tightrope artists, and even one "Almost-Human Gorilla." I've even dabbled in trapeze and silks myself. I taught myself how to handle a bullwhip for my days playing a ringmaster for a local ghost tour. (Note—I don't recommend teaching yourself how to use a bullwhip. It stings.)

I suppose it was only a matter of time before I combined my two loves—circus and horror—into a series. They go so well together, don't they?

Because whether it's the freakshows, or the clowns, or the mirrored funhouses of a carnival, there's an inherently eerie quality to the traveling acts of yore. It always begs for a story that's somehow deeper, somehow more sinister… somehow alive.

Foreword

Thank you to Kristin, my best friend and hobby circus buddy, who looked at a flying trapeze rig stuffed inside a Jordan's Furniture in Massachusetts and, when I said, "Hey, let's put ourselves in traction," she shrugged and replied, "Sure."

Real friends proof your explicit chapters. Better friends let you talk them into doing crazy shit.

Thank you to my friends and fans, Michelle, Sylvia, "Ziph," Aza, Amanda, and all the rest, for cheering me on as I write. Thank you to my husband, Evan, for putting up with the hours and hours it takes to create something like this. And thank you to you, readers, for coming along for the ride.

I hope you enjoy Harrow Faire as much as I enjoyed writing it.

Welcome.

Enjoy your stay.

You might just never leave.

THE FAMILY

0. ~~The Contortionist~~ *Vacant.*
1. The Magician
2. The Flyer
3. The Aerialist
4. The Ringmaster
5. The Catcher
6. The Twins
7. The Zookeeper
8. The Strongman
9. The Bearded Lady
10. The Juggler
11. The Firebreather
12. The Rigger
13. The Clown
14. The Seamstress
15. The Puppeteer
16. The Soothsayer
17. The Diva
18. The Barker
19. The Mechanic
20. The Maestro
21. Mr. Harrow

1

Human souls are worthless.

If souls are the currency of hell, then the devil himself has become the victim of inflation.

Souls carry no value. It isn't the fabric of the animation in which a person is borne. A soul is merely the gangue around the valuable ore in the rock. It is that personality that the soul carries like a basket of eggs to the market, trudged there by a vessel of flesh.

Seity.

That is where power is to be found. In memories, in choices, in the uniqueness to which the soul bears witness. The smell of grandmother's cookies. The order in which one puts on one's socks in the morning. The memory of exchanged vows at an altar. These are what carry true value.

It's a shame people are too foolish to value these things. Is it not the tragedy of the elderly when they can no longer remember who they once were? Do we heed these warnings of loss?

No.

Humanity is too eager to toss away that which they deem ordinary without ever realizing what it was that they had.

Surrounded by ourselves, we think such things are commonplace. Worse yet, we think of our memories as monotonous. Not simply abundant, but boring.

It makes the job of taking it all away so much easier.
Welcome to my Faire.
The fee won't be too high for you, I promise.
You won't even notice when it's gone.

-M. L. Harrow

Harrow Faire sat neglected and abandoned.

The dilapidated towers of wood scaffolding stabbed at the sky like bony fingers reaching out of the dirt. Broken and burnt bulbs sat in rusted sockets and had not illuminated the night sky in decades. Rafters and structures were tilted and bent, collapsing under age, and rot, and time.

It was the skeletal remainder of a carnival—a reminder of the laughter and joy that once was. Carriages with flaking paint that once bore colorful swirls, smiles, or terrifying faces had not budged in decades. No music had come from the abandoned hurdy gurdy machines. No air had pumped through the pipe organs.

Harrow Faire sat neglected and abandoned.

Right up until the moment that it didn't.

Sitting on the edge of a large lake in New Hampshire, it had been called the Coney Island of the North. Which was kind of insulting, seeing as it had been there first. But for a long time, located on the old railways that ran up to the mountains and through into Canada, it had been just as popular as the boardwalk attractions of New York City.

But the bizarre combination of the traveling circus and a

permanent fairground attraction had long since lost the war with time.

Cora had been driving past Harrow Faire for as long as she could remember. She grew up in the area, and now she passed it every day on the way to work and back. Before that, as a teenager, she prowled the skeletal remains with her friends. She had even come with her father from time to time to explore the urban ruins. He was always encouraging her to get into "safe trouble." Whatever that meant.

But those days of adventure had long since passed. Her life was far more mundane now. Nine to five, she sat at the counter at the local bank. She was a teller. A standard, boring job in a standard, boring town. The most interesting thing that had happened in the past few years was a sinkhole in the center of town that had eaten half a hardware store.

That's what passed for entertainment in Glendale, New Hampshire.

A freaking sinkhole.

Working at the bank wasn't a fun gig, it wasn't an interesting gig, but it paid the mortgage on her little condo. There were two kinds of homes one could find dotted around the lake that bordered the town. The multi-million-dollar summer mansions owned by the rich, and the crappy places where everybody else lived. She was firmly in the latter category.

She had driven past the Faire a thousand times. Because of that, she made it a clear mile down the road before she realized something was out of place. It was a solid two minutes before her mind processed what she had seen.

Wait.

What the fiddly-fuck did I just see?

She pulled over to the side of the road. Checking the

clock, she had half an hour before she had to be at the bank. She was always early, and she figured she could skate in a little closer to nine, just this once.

Cora used the front of someone's driveway to turn around and head back toward the Faire. Sure enough, when she approached, the Faire was no longer the one she recognized. Her eyes hadn't been playing tricks on her.

Not that she understood what she was looking at, however.

The gate to the parking lot, with its three wooden swords stabbing upward, holding the sign that declared its name in scrolling hand-painted text, had always been locked. A sign dangling from the doors had always boldly professed that trespassers would be prosecuted.

Not that it had ever kept the teenagers out. There wasn't much else for the local kids to do, except drink, get high, or bum around abandoned places. Or all three. It was generally both. Cora never really partook of the drugs or alcohol, but she *loved* the abandoned places. And since the nearby mills had all been shut down in the early part of the twentieth century, there were plenty to explore. She would take her dad's camera and head out into the darkness or early morning hours and come back with some amazing photos to show for it.

"Locks only keep out the honest" was a motto her dad always used to say to her, usually while he was cutting the padlock on some abandoned building so he could take her in to look around. Poking around old places made for a weird father-daughter hobby, but it was still bonding time.

Besides, he was a famous photographer—well, as famous as a photojournalist could be, anyway—and she had always planned to follow in his footsteps. People knew her father's photos, even if they didn't know his name, and she wanted to make him proud. He had taken her into the abandoned Faire many, many times, teaching her how to shoot in low light and how to frame the shot just so.

And how to dodge the local police.

Sadly, she grew out of the age where it was acceptable to get chased out of some long-empty church or institutional building by the cops. Not to mention, she wasn't as bouncy as she used to be. She always used to sprain her ankles, twist things, or what-have-you. But as a child, it didn't lead to days or weeks of pain, physical therapy, or time on crutches.

She *hated* crutches.

But as she aged, even just into her twenties, the idea of climbing through a window was far more daunting than it had been before.

Since her chronic illness issues had started, she had to give up most of her hobbies and her job as a photographer. Oh, she could still wander around a park and take photos of flowers, or architecture, or things like that. But her real passion and her specialty had been covering more dynamic things. Live events. Concerts, weddings, or even better—news. Most people never would have suspected that photographers had to do a lot of running and ducking and crouching to get into the right spot at the right time. But it was part of the gig.

Now she sat at a desk all day instead. She missed picking up gigs for the local newspaper or heading down to Boston and Portsmouth to cover big events or parades as a freelance stringer.

But the fond memories of ducking behind old tents or hiding in the bones of a ride, laughing and giggling alongside her father, played through her head as she pulled into the large parking lot of the Faire. She stopped close to its open gate. She could see well enough from there, and something made her nervous to go any closer.

She knew this park.

And it had never scared her before.

Now, she wasn't staring at a weathered sign with faded and peeling paint. She wasn't staring at the locked gate and rusty chain. The notice declaring legal woe upon any who set foot inside the fairgrounds was gone.

The metal was no longer rusted. The paint was no longer peeling. It was all...brand new. It looked like it had just been installed. She parked her car, stopped the engine, and climbed out.

"Grand Reopening! Tonight!" read the painted drop cloth that hung from the brand-new entry sign. But it wasn't just the sign that looked new. Looking past the gate to the ticket booth and beyond, she stared in shocked silence. She stood there like she was gaping at Godzilla.

Harrow Faire wasn't abandoned anymore.

The tilted, dilapidated structures had been straightened. The paint was fresh. The light sockets that had been missing most of their bulbs had been fixed and replaced. The signs were bright and legible. All the rot and wear had simply... been erased.

But nothing looked modern, either. It all looked vintage, like a careful restoration of the original park. It was a style that just wasn't done anymore.

Who had done it? When? And how? And...*why?* It wasn't like there was a lot of business up in bumble-fuck-nowhere New Hampshire.

How did I miss this? How the hell did I drive past this every day and not see people working on it? I know my mind wanders when I drive, but this is a new level of oblivious.

The Contortionist

There was no other explanation for the restored park. She must simply be that dense.

"Hello, there!"

Cora shrieked and jumped a foot in the air, whirling to face the sudden voice. She hadn't seen the man on the ladder behind the entrance sign over the parking lot gate. He looked like he had just finished hanging up the banner.

He was climbing down and waved at her with a friendly smile. "Sorry, sorry. Didn't mean to startle you."

"It's okay." She smiled warily back at him. The man seemed perfectly fine, but something about him seemed... somehow odd. He was handsome. There was nothing obviously unusual about him. But he was dressed in clothing that looked like it dated from the forties. He had a white shirt and wore black suspenders over it that held up a pair of trousers stained with paint. He was broad at the shoulders and had an easy, casual flair about him. Even with the weird dated outfit. "When did all this happen?" She gestured at the Faire.

"Huh?"

"I swear this place was still abandoned yesterday."

"Oh!" He laughed. "Eh, time flies, doesn't it?" He shrugged. When he walked up to her car, he took a moment to look it over with a broad smile on his face. She wasn't sure why. It was a beat-up old Ford Focus. "Nice car."

"Thanks?" She chuckled. What a weird man. Maybe he was hitting on her. That was the only reason anybody would complement her ugly-ass car.

"I'm Jack." He reached out to shake her hand and realized his own was covered in paint. He wiped it off, looked at his palm, then, seeing that it was all still there because it was dry, shrugged and held it out again.

"Cora." She smiled and shook his hand. She wasn't

surprised at how firm the gesture was, what with the muscles the guy was sporting. "Nice to meet you."

"You too! You should come to the Faire tonight. See the shows. Ride the rides. Eat the terrible fried food. I mean—well, the food's honestly great, but it's terrible for you." Jack scratched the back of his neck.

"I love pretty much any food whose method of delivery's a stick." Cora shook her head with a smile and looked out at the park. The signage had all been redone in careful hand-painted curling letters. She could see the Ferris wheel rotating slowly. "Who paid for all this?"

"Oh? Mr. Harrow, of course." She looked back at the guy like he had grown a second head. He looked confused at best. "What?"

"Mr. Harrow? The guy who used to own the park?"

"Who else?"

"I'm assuming he's been dead for, like, a hundred years."

"Well, yes, but his estate still exists." Jack smiled helpfully. Now *she* felt like the moron. "Things got hung up in legal battles when the last of his kids died. But now the funds got freed up, and here we are."

It must have taken millions of dollars to restore the park. She honestly couldn't believe what she was looking at. She swore it had been abandoned just yesterday. This kind of work would take months, if not years, and there would have been articles in the paper about it.

Not just *poof*.

Maybe she had simply missed it. She ran her hand over her face. That must be it. That was the only option. Seriously, the only option.

She looked back over to Jack. He seemed like a nice guy. She was surprised she didn't recognize him—Glendale was a small-ass town. But he probably was brought in from else-

The Contortionist

where to do the work. It wasn't like there was a cadre of restoration specialists hanging out in Nowhere, New Hampshire. Maybe he was a theatre guy from New York or something.

"Are you coming tonight?" He smiled hopefully.

Nothing interesting happened in Nowhere, New Hampshire. So, how could she resist? "Yeah. I think that sounds like fun."

"Bring some friends! I'll be working in the big top all night, but if I see you, I'll wave at you from the rigging. I run the lines." He scratched at his short dark hair with stubby fingernails. He clearly worked with his hands all day. "Nice to meet you, Cora."

"You too, Jack. Have a good one."

He walked away with another casual wave. She climbed back into her car. Shutting the door, she winced in pain. She had woken up with a dislocated wrist, and it was still sore. Such was the joy of Ehlers-Danlos syndrome, she supposed. Her muscles and tendons were hypermobile.

Sure, she was super bendy, but it wasn't as fun as it sounded. It meant that some days she felt like a ragdoll whose stitching was coming undone.

After putting the joint back where it belonged that morning, she had just taken some Naproxen and gone about her day. It happened more often than not. Nothing ruined a day like waking up to play the new game of "that was fine last night…"

All the way to work, she was lost in thought and cruised along on autopilot. She got her coffee from the breakroom, and nearly missed saying hello to half her coworkers. She couldn't stop thinking about Harrow Faire.

Weird. This whole thing is just so weird.

Luckily, her job was mind-numbingly routine. It always

was. She could just phone it in, coast through, and do just fine. *Overqualified,* her boss called her. But there wasn't much else to do in the small town. No promotions were available in the tiny branch, and there weren't many other prospects.

So, she was happy to pay her mortgage and go on with her life. Just like most people, she supposed. She had wanted to move to Boston or New York, or even settle for Portland, before she had to give up photography.

But with her chronic pain, she couldn't lug the equipment anymore. Not even for weddings. It had just become too much.

She couldn't do a lot of things anymore.

At lunch, she searched for news articles about Harrow Faire reopening. She came back empty-handed. Just Wikipedia pages and old photographs. She asked her coworkers—who were lovely people, but all had thirty-plus years on her and were all just as boring as the job itself—and came up just as empty. None of them had even noticed it had been restored.

The Faire didn't even have a damn website. *Everybody has a website. Everybody's dog has its own website at this point.* Not even a Facebook page. Weird.

She texted her friends who still lived in town. Trent, Lisa, and Emily. The four of them had grown up together, and they were all too stupid to leave. Trent had landed a job as the event coordinator for Castle in the Clouds on the north side of the lake, so he was pretty much set. Lisa was a housewife now with two kids and working on more. Emily was still pining after Trent, working alongside him at the historic mansion, seemingly unable to accept the fact that Trent was not into her. Or ladies in general.

When Cora told them in text about Harrow Faire

reopening, Lisa didn't believe her, and neither did Trent. But Emily—always being the pragmatic one—had gone to investigate since she had the morning off. She texted back with a photo twenty minutes later of the same restored gate and grand reopening sign Cora had seen.

It was quickly settled. They were going right after they all got out of work. Trent worked until seven, but they'd be clear after that.

Cora smiled. She was excited.

She couldn't remember the last time she went out on the town with all her friends. Especially anything as weird and silly as going to a carnival. It wasn't the biggest park in New England, but it was still going to be fun. She'd have to get a bag of cotton candy and leave it out to let it get stale. It was always better stale. She didn't care what people said.

She dazed her way through the rest of the day—not like anybody noticed—and was eager to pack it up and go home. Standing from her desk, she held back a cringe again. Sitting at a desk all day sucked, but everything else sucked worse.

Living with constant pain was a gradient. Either it hurt, or it hurt worse. Physical therapy helped, insomuch as it kept her joints from randomly dislocating. Less frequently, anyway.

Heading home, she showered, fed her fish, and made herself a salad to tide her over until she got to the Faire with her friends. She was probably going to eat her weight in funnel cake and other fried bullshit, so she should take it easy.

Hopefully, they sold alcohol. She knew she drank too much. She wasn't an alcoholic, not by any means, but a drink a night was probably not a great way to live. But that, coupled with the medical marijuana she was allowed to smoke, kept the pain, and her life, vaguely tolerable.

Six thirty, and she climbed into her car to head to the Faire. To her surprise, the parking lot was packed. For a company with seemingly zero marketing budget, they seemed to be doing just fine for themselves. She parked in the first spot she could find and headed to the ticket booth. Not seeing anyone she recognized, she texted her friends.

The smell of popcorn and spun sugar filled the air. She could hear laughter and the sound of rides clanking. The hurdy gurdy and pipe organs of all the rides made for a cacophony that joined the other perfectly archetypical sounds of a circus.

It brought back every memory of every fair she had ever been to. This place had been abandoned even when she was little, but all fairs more or less sounded and smelled the same. She remembered holding on to her dad's hand as he led her through the rows of games designed to con people out of a dollar. The giant toys she always wanted to win but knew she never would. She remembered screaming on all the old rides, getting lost in the rickety funhouse, and staring at her distorted reflection in mirrors.

She wondered if everybody had all the same memories of places like this. But Harrow Faire seemed like a lot more than just the standard carnival—they had circus tents. The ads on the fencing of the ticket booth, painted like old sideshow posters, promised tightrope acts, flying trapeze, monsters and animals, a bearded lady, and more. It was dizzying. It was like a traveling circus had humped a theme park and Harrow Faire was its bizarre, mutant offspring.

Oddly, it looked like there were two entrances. One normal one—a series of turnstiles that *ka-chunked* as people passed through them—and a second one that was a giant painted face of a skull, with a gaping jaw for a door. Over it, the sign read *"The Dark Path Awaits,"* but nothing else. No explanation as to why there was a second way in. The second entrance wasn't nearly as busy, but she saw a few people trail into it, chuckling and shaking their heads as if unsure about what they were getting themselves into.

Her phone buzzed. Looking down at the screen, she sighed. Trent and Emily were late because an event ran over. Lisa was stuck with a sick kid and couldn't make it.

Typical.

This was why they never went out anymore.

"Hello there, pretty lady, want to come inside? Or do you just like lingering in the parking lot?"

She looked up at the sound of the voice. A man stood in the ticket booth, leaning on the counter, grinning at her.

The booth was painted in gold and crimson stripes. Flashing lightbulbs overhead that were meant to draw the eye and became dizzying after too long.

The man who had spoken, like his set dressing, was old-fashioned. He looked...there was no nice way of putting it. He looked like a sleazebag from the 1920s. His brown hair was slicked back, carefully combed and gelled into a pomaded dome. He even had a narrow mustache that would have been fashionable a hundred years ago. He'd be attractive, if she thought she could trust the fucker as far as she could throw him.

He had his chin on his hand and his elbow on the counter, and he was smiling at her like there wasn't anybody else in line. There were other people running the rest of the counter, and he seemed content to ignore the pileup of humans and talk to her where she stood off to the side.

"I'm just waiting for my friends."

"You might as well go in without them. No sense waiting

out here where there's nothing but my handsome face to look at." He waggled a finger toward her phone. "You have one of those thingamajigs, don't you? Makes it very easy to find people nowadays. Go on in and tell them where you are when they get here."

He even talked like someone from an old movie. What was that accent called? Transatlantic. That was it. A fake accent that people put on to make themselves sound posh on the silver screen or on the radio. It went with the scenery; she'd give him that. Along with his insistence that he didn't know what a phone was called.

The park must have hired interactive actors. She tried not to snicker. "I gotta give you props for sticking with the theme." She smirked. "I'm betting five dollars you own one of these." She held up her phone toward him.

"I love a quick buck. That's a deal!" He cackled and slapped his hand on the counter. "Not sure when you'll pay up or how I'll prove it, but I like a bargain where I see one. And I'll tell you what, pretty lady—I'll make you an offer. See, there are two ways to get into Harrow Faire." He gestured at the two gates, the normal one to his right and the morbid one to his left.

"I noticed."

"And you didn't ask me why?" He put a palm to his chest. "I'm insulted." He stepped out from behind the booth, swinging the little door open and letting it latch behind him. He was wearing a striped suit that matched the ticket booth's gold and red stripes. He walked up to her with a grin. He was smooth—too smooth. Like an old...*hah*. Like an old carnival barker. And that was exactly what he was, she realized.

"I honestly didn't notice you."

He gasped and clutched his heart. "Oh, the pain!"

The Contortionist

She laughed at his melodrama and shook her head. "Okay, okay. What's with the second entrance?"

"That's where we let people in without any money changing hands. That is, if we like them." His smile became thinner. Less natural.

"You let them in for free?"

"Oh, I never said *that.*"

She looked at the skull-painted gate and shot him a raised eyebrow. "See, I'm coming up with options for what the hell you're talking about, and all of them are dirty. So... I'm going to need more than that."

The man laughed hard. "No! No. Nothing salacious. Nothing so mundane." He waved his hand dismissively. "No, we just take a tiny piece of your seity instead."

"Seity?"

"Individuality, my dear! A little bit of what makes you—well—*you.*" Now he was launching into a speech he had clearly given a thousand times. Or at least he had practiced it enough to make it sound that way. "Maybe it's how you brush your hair in the morning. Or the memory of the way the crust on momma's apple pie crunches. Or what radio station you like to listen to in the morning."

"You're saying you'll steal a piece of my soul?" She snickered. "Come on."

"Nothing so trite. Souls are cheap. Billions of them out there, right? A personality—now, *that* is a commodity. Because what is a soul with no individuality? A battery in a car, that's all." The man was still smiling. It wasn't a friendly expression. If he was trying to be creepy, he was nailing it. "Don't worry, it's only a tiny piece. Only a smidge. You won't even notice it's gone...I promise."

"You said you only offer it to the ones you like. Why?"

"Why eat a hot dog when you can have a steak? We pick

the ones that burn hot. The ones with a lot of personality to go around. And you..." He reached out and picked up a strand of her long dark hair. She yanked her head away from him and shot him a glare. He lifted his palm as if to say he was sorry. "You burn bright. Brightest I've seen in a long, long time."

"I'm nobody interesting."

"No, I think your life turned you into nobody interesting." He shrugged. "So, take your pick. Walk through the Dark Path, and we take a tiny piece of you, or pay the normal fee."

Cora narrowed her eyes at him. "You're trying to freak me out, and I'm not even sure why. Publicity stunt?"

"Ah, yes. The skeptical type. I love the skeptics. So much fun to watch them break down when everything they thought was a lie is suddenly true." He took a step back from her. "No, Cora Glass, we take a piece of you for a good cause—to keep our own fires burning."

"I—What—" she stammered. "Wait. Do I know you?"

"We've never met. You'd remember me." He smiled.

Now she was getting nervous. "Did you, like...find me on Google or something?"

"I have no idea what half of those words mean." He grinned and climbed back into the booth and flopped down on his stool. "Take your pick! Go inside and spare your wallet—or prove that you might believe me and pay up in hard cash. Y'know. If you're scared."

Cora decided she didn't like this guy. He must be a con artist. They probably had a camera on her, and somebody was using facial recognition software and feeding information to him via an earbud. That had to be it.

There was no other possible explanation.

He was feeding her shit and trying to scare her. She'd go

home, talk about it on social media, and people would come see it for themselves. Mentalism was a fun illusion, but it was only that—an illusion.

And so was his stupid selling-a-piece-of-her-personality bunk.

She texted her friends that she was going inside and she'd meet them by the carousel when they arrived. Looking back up at the sleazebag, she smirked at him and got an equally snarky expression in response. "I think you're full of shit."

Daring her to do something was basically all a person had to do to guarantee she did it. She hated being afraid of things. She walked toward the skull-faced entrance.

"That I am, pretty lady, that I am," he called after her. "But don't say I didn't warn you when you can't remember your favorite color!"

Shaking her head, she muttered "asshole" under her breath and stepped through the weird gate. In an instant, she was plunged into total darkness. She put her hands out in front of her to keep from walking into a wall.

Silence surrounded her like a blanket as overwhelming as the nothingness around her. She couldn't even hear the sound of the carnival outside. She had followed a few other people through the gate, and there was no sign of them.

There was no sign of anything at all.

Until she heard a laugh.

It sent a shiver down her spine like someone had dumped ice cubes down the back of her shirt. Its laugh was eerie and disturbing; its voice was worse.

"Welcome to Harrow Faire."

2

CORA RAN.

She wasn't proud of it. It wasn't like it was the smartest thing to do—running full-tilt through the total darkness.

"Welcome to Harrow Faire."

The terrifying laugh had been one thing. The voice whispering in her ear was another. But when something touched her, that was the last straw.

Whatever had touched her hadn't been simply a hand on her shoulder, or a brush against her arm. The touch hadn't even been dirty. She probably would have preferred it that way. It felt like something had reached a hand into her heart and yanked. Something cold had pulled on a thread inside of her and unraveled a piece.

Like it was…taking something from her.

A piece of her soul. *Souls are cheap. A personality…now, that's a commodity.*

No! It was just nerves. This was just her being scared of someone jumping out of the black void and terrorizing her. It had to be. The guy at the ticket booth was full of shit.

So, why was she running?

The Contortionist

And why hadn't she *hit* anything yet?

She finally had to stop. It hurt too much to keep going. Everything ached. She didn't run on a treadmill for a reason. Her ankles were too loose, and she'd roll a joint and knock something out of place. Most of her joints were loose, floating in space, and it didn't take much for them to partially dislocate. And if she stepped wrong, she ran the risk of jamming a bone right onto the concrete.

That was all she needed—more time on crutches. Christ, she hated crutches. That was a chafing in the armpits she'd never get used to, and she dreaded it every time.

She doubled over, panting, resting her hands on her thighs. She reached for her phone to use the flashlight, but she must have lost it while running. "Damn it."

Her ankles were aching. She rolled her left one and felt the joint struggle to pop back into place. She wasn't quite sure if she got it back in there or not. She winced. It hurt. It always hurt. It was just a matter of how high the volume knob was set that day. Oh, joy. That was going to make the rest of the night so much fun. She was looking forward to explaining to her friends why she was going to have a limp for the rest of the night. *Well, I went in the spooky door, got spooked, and ran like a bitch in the darkness. And because I have super-wacky-fun-time joints, I now have to limp around like a seventy-year-old man for the rest of the week.*

Ehlers-Danlos Syndrome could go fuck a brick in hell. Seriously.

How big was this place, anyway? She had run in one direction for a solid fifteen or twenty seconds and hadn't hit a damn thing. She wasn't fast, but this place also couldn't be the size of a gym, either. When she straightened, she took a slow breath and finally felt her heart start to calm down.

She took a step forward—and bashed her nose into something.

"Ow! God damnit—" How had she managed to stop inches short of running into a wall? She wasn't that lucky.

The wall talked. "God?" A dark, twisted chuckle. "Where?"

She went rigid at the sound of the voice in the darkness. It wasn't something she had walked into, it was some*one*. She froze. It was a man, and that was all she could tell from his voice in the darkness. "Uh—hello?"

He didn't answer.

"Are you trapped in here, too? Do you know the way out?"

"The answer is yes to both of those things. But not in the way you're asking, I'm afraid." He laughed. It was more of a cackle, really. Vincent Price would have been proud. He sounded tall—the voice was coming from above her. And he also sounded…insane. There was a strange sharp-edged lilt to his words that paired along with a British accent.

"Can you help me get out of here?"

"And why would I want to do *that?*" Now there was danger in his voice. His tone dropped and became gravelly, sultry, and…no. Fear made the hair on her neck stand up. She was trapped in a dark place with a dangerous man she didn't know.

No. No, this wasn't happening.

Not again.

She took a step back from him.

She tried.

Suddenly, there was a wood wall at her back, and she hit it hard. It sounded hollow like plywood. But it couldn't possibly be there—she hadn't turned around. But she felt it, cutting off her path. She grunted at the impact.

"No running. Can't have you hurting yourself, now, can we?"

She screamed and could only hope someone could hear her. She broke off as hands cradled her face, holding her between gloved palms. Their touch was warm and shockingly tender. But they still sparked a deep and intrinsic terror.

Whoever it was shushed her. "There, now...take a deep breath."

Her hands flew to his wrists and tried to pull him away from her, but he didn't budge. She might as well have been moving a statue. "Don't touch me!"

"No, no, calm down. That's not what I'm after. Easy, now. I just can't have you running off again. Although that *was* fun to watch." He chuckled. "Maybe we'll do that again later. Nothing more entertaining than a good spot of terror!" Whoever he was, his tone was all over the map. One minute playful, the next, terrifying. "I have a question for you, darling..."

"Let me go—"

"Mmh, in a moment. I just want you to answer me something..."

"Please—Please don't—"

"What would you trade for the pain to go away?"

Her protests broke off. "W—what?"

The hands tilted her head back, as if turning her to look up at him. Whoever the madman was, he was *freaking tall*. "I can feel it in you. This sickness. Waking up every day in miserable pain. It took your life away from you—all your happiness and your joy. Drinking away your passion and leaving you the sorrow of your broken life and broken body. Being told there's no cure—being told to accept your new facts and move on. What would you trade—what would you give away—to make it never hurt again?"

How could he...who is he? Another mentalist trick? She couldn't promise that enough clever web searches wouldn't turn up the fact that she had a chronic illness. "I don't know what kind of stupid game you people think you're playing—"

"All the world's a game, and all the men and women merely playthings, darling. Everything in life—in death—in creation itself is just a round of chess. There are winners, and there are losers, and there are pawns on the board. I'm giving you a chance to take yourself out of the game. Do you understand me?"

No, she really didn't. "Let me go."

"I can take it all away. All your pain. All your suffering. You can wake up tomorrow without any of it."

She did her best to glare up at the darkness. It was clear he could see her, even if she couldn't see him. "I'm going to kick you in the nuts so hard they're going to get stuck in your throat if you don't fucking let me go *right now.*"

He cackled. "That's a good one! I love it." His hands left her face, and she shoved him. She might as well have been shoving another wall. "Now, now. Don't get feisty."

She stormed into the darkness. She didn't know where she was going.

"Other way, cupcake. Go left."

She snarled in frustration. But she obediently followed his instructions. "Asshole."

"Mmhm. I don't like that one as much. Not nearly as clever. Think about my offer, Cora."

"You want clever?" She turned in the darkness to face the voice. "Go fuck yourself with a pogo stick."

"Much better! Now, go on and enjoy your night. Your

The Contortionist

friends are looking for you. Come back and see me if you want to make a deal."

She whirled from the voice and...was standing at the exit. She was standing in the archway of a dark tunnel and staring at the carnival. She whirled to face the darkness again but could clearly see the black plywood walls that made up the space.

A space that hadn't been there before.

She struggled to grasp what she was looking at. "What the fuck?"

"You dropped this."

Cora screamed and jumped a foot in the air. Whipping around, she saw the sleazebag from the front counter—the one with the slicked-back hair and pencil mustache. He was leaning against the exit wall with one knee bent, his foot propped on the painted surface like he'd been waiting there all night. She could see the back side of the ticket booth and the turnstiles.

The corridor she had walked through couldn't be anything deeper than ten feet. But that wasn't possible.

None of it was possible.

The man was holding her phone out to her. She snatched it from him. The screen wasn't cracked; that was some good news. "What the hell was that?"

"Exactly what I told you, toots." He smiled. "Tell me something. What's your favorite color?"

She opened her mouth to answer and stopped.

She didn't know.

It was right there on the tip of her tongue. She knew it. She had to. She always had a favorite color—she had ever since she was a kid. Everybody had an answer to that question.

Didn't they?

But suddenly...she had nothing.

Her eyes went wide with slow, creeping fear, as the man laughed. "See?" He walked away from her. "Kids these days. They never listen."

She was shaking. She felt like she was sweating. She needed to sit down before she fainted. She walked—limped—to a bench and collapsed onto it, putting her head in her hands. What had just happened to her?

She had run through darkness in a straight line. There was no way the space was that big. There was no way she didn't hit the walls. Were they moving things around on her? Rearranging the space? Why?

And why couldn't she remember her fucking favorite color?

Panic. That's why. It's just panic. When you calm down, you'll remember. They're just inside your head, messing with you.

"Cora! There you are."

At least that was a voice she recognized. Looking up, she saw Trent and Emily. Relief welled in her. She smiled weakly. "Hey, guys."

"What the hell happened to you?" Trent furrowed his brow. He was dressed perfectly, like he always was. His blond hair was carefully done to look messy, even though she was sure he spent an hour working on making it sit *just so*. She never thought a guy could pull off skinny jeans until she met him. He had a casual flair, even if he was perfectly dressed. He turned heads of both genders and was proud of it. "You look like you're gonna throw up."

Cora and Trent had been friends since early grade school. He got picked on a lot for being "the weird little gay kid," and she was considered an outcast for reading as much as she did. So, they became fast friends and had been close ever since.

The Contortionist

"I don't know. I might hurl. Did you guys go through the freaky tunnel?" She pointed at the exit to whatever the hell she just walked out of.

"Huh? No." He shrugged. "They said we weren't allowed in. Said it was for 'the special ones,' whatever the fuck that means. Did you go through it?"

"Yeah..."

"Was it fun?" Emily smiled and tucked her hands into her oversized coat's pockets. She was a mousy creature. Amazingly intelligent, but too shy to do much with it. She was terrible at advocating for herself, and she liked to blend in as much as possible. Her dark hair was cropped short. She was very pretty, but always tried to hide it. She and Trent couldn't have been less alike. "Must have been something good if you're all freaked out. What was in there?"

"No, it was shit. And I don't even know if I can explain it. It was awful, and I don't recommend going through there if they offer. I think there was a guy in there trying to feel me up." Cora shook her head and stood.

"And you didn't take him up on the offer?" Trent groaned. "C'mon, Cora! You had your chance after all this time, and you said no?"

"I'm not gonna let some guy I don't know cop a feel in a pitch-black room." Cora glared at Trent.

"Psh. This is why you have less fun than me." He cracked a lopsided grin. "Just saying."

"Uh-huh. Sure." She shoved her phone back into her coat pocket. It was early spring, so there was still a bit of a chill in the air at night. "Let's just go. I want to forget about it."

"I wanna see the freaks." Emily shoved Trent's arm playfully. "I didn't think they were allowed to have freakshows anymore. I thought it wasn't P.C."

"Maybe they want to be there, so it's okay," Trent replied as the three of them headed off into the park. Well. They walked, and she limped. "I'd rather do the rides and then go see the strongman."

"I think you mean see the rides and *do* the strongman," Cora teased with a grin. "You just want to drool over some big, buff, half-naked guy." She smiled, trying to brush off all the weirdness that had just happened. It was all a trick. It was all just a clever setup. Some interactive theatre, modern-art bullshit. Now she had to put it behind her. There was funnel cake somewhere that needed to be eaten, after all.

"Guilty as charged. Besides, don't you? C'mon, Cora— you've been single for what…five years now?"

"Yeah, don't remind me." She shot Trent a look. It wasn't a topic she liked to talk about. Her relationship with her ex hadn't ended well, to say the least.

"Look, I'm not saying you have to date him. I'm just saying you probably want to ogle a big, buff pile of man-meat just as much as I do." Trent slung an arm around her shoulder and hugged her to his side, making her laugh. "Did you see the poster? C'mon."

"You realize the guy probably looks nothing like that," Emily chimed in.

Sensing victory, Trent went in for the kill. "Well, there's only one way to find out. I say we go howl at some sexy guy bending rebar around his neck." He was beaming. "Maybe he'll pick me up and hold me over his head."

"You're just hoping he picks you up, period." Cora rolled her eyes. Trent had always been a bit of a player—heading to Portland on the weekends to hit up the clubs. He was always begging Cora to go with him. After his constant pestering, she finally gave in. Once. And only once. She had

The Contortionist

stood there like an idiot and never went again. Emily went along frequently.

She couldn't imagine her mousy friend sitting in the corner of a dark bar, listening to the deafening music and watching as Trent flirted with everything that moved.

Honestly, she didn't know why Emily did it to herself. It was clear she was madly in love with Trent and had been since they were kids. But she was a grown adult, and she could make her own mistakes.

Lisa was the only one who had managed to find someone and pin them to the ground. Her husband Robert was a nice guy but never seemed to want to go out with them. And because of that, it meant that Lisa rarely went out either. Parental life seemed like a special level of Hell that Cora wanted nothing to do with.

"You hurt yourself again, Cor?" Trent asked, his brow furrowed in concern.

"Of course. Doesn't take much." She tried not to sound bitter about it. She shrugged and settled for sounding matter-of-fact. "I tripped over something in the dark tunnel thing and knocked my ankle out of whack." *No way in hell am I admitting I was running away.* "But I wouldn't mind sitting to watch a show. Let's grab some food and go see the silly strongman act."

"Sounds good, and—oh! Candy apples!" Trent abandoned her side to take an abrupt right turn. He was like a human raccoon. Any shiny object, and he was off like a rocket.

Emily and Cora laughed together, shaking their heads and walking after their friend. He was always a handful, and that was why they both loved him, if in different ways.

She limped along, and Emily slowed to fall in next to her. She knew it wasn't fun for her friends to put up with someone who was always injured. But there wasn't anything she could do about it.

If it wasn't her ankles, it was her knees. If it wasn't her knees, it was her hips. If it wasn't those, it was her wrists or her shoulders. They were always floating. Her tendons just couldn't do their fucking jobs for ten minutes. It was one thing, after another, after another.

"I can take it all away. All your pain. All your suffering. You can wake up tomorrow without any of it." That was what the creep had said. But he was lying. It was a trick. He wanted to sell her drugs, at best. At worst, he wanted to trade her something awful for said drugs.

"I'm sorry, Cor," Emily said gently, smiling in that sympathetic way a person used when they felt bad, but didn't quite understand. Chronic pain wasn't something people could really wrap their heads around unless they actually experienced it.

"It's fine. It is what it is." Most of all, Cora hated being the weak link. It wasn't her fault, but it didn't stop her from feeling guilty.

She tried to shove it all away. Tonight wasn't about feeling sorry for herself. It was about silly rides, goofy shows, and a whole lot of shitty food.

For once, she was going to try to have some fun.

―――

He watched her from the shadows with a smile. Although, to be fair, he was almost always smiling.

Madness was funny that way.

He supposed there were two ways to go. He could either be the kind of brooding flavor of nuts that sat in its tower

The Contortionist

and lurked, or he could be amused by it and the voices in his head. He preferred option B. At least it was entertaining.

Whistling to himself, he moved from the darkness and down the main fairway, idly spinning the end of his pocket watch around in a loop, wrapping it around one of his fingers, then changing directions when it ran out of length. He'd rather be winding a lock of Cora's long dark waves through his fingers, but he settled for the chain for now.

She had big, beautiful gray eyes. They seemed to change from dark to light as he watched. They had been brimming with wild terror and edged with some kind of dark and haunted memories. She was so full of pain—in her body and her mind—and it made her all the more delicious. He was going to savor this one.

He had stood there in the shadows and listened to Barker harass the poor girl. *"What's your favorite color?"* And she hadn't been able to answer. The fear on her face was stunning.

The answer was red.

Her favorite color had been red.

Right up to the moment when the Faire had taken it from her, and he had been the one who received it. It was such an odd thing to get used to—being fed little pieces of people by the Faire. He preferred to do things his own way. But many of those who were part of the Family that lived within the Faire weren't so lucky. Most of them couldn't rely on their own means to sustain themselves.

But him? His talents were *specific*.

When the sensation had hit him—that the Faire had harvested someone, and it had been given to him—he had come to see who had given him such a tasty morsel. It was his favorite color, too. Wasn't that charming? But that wasn't what had really pulled him out of his tent and away from his practice.

It was the flavor that went *along* with the red. He ran his gloved finger over his lips, as if he had actually tasted her. As if something might linger there, like wine on your lower lip after a sip. She warmed him in the same way. He tipped his hat to the man standing on the stage as the performer readied himself for another trick. "Evening, Firebreather."

"Screw off, Puppeteer." The other man glowered down at him.

He laughed. He didn't care. He was used to the insults, and he was too excited to be annoyed. He hadn't felt like this in a very long time, after all.

It was time to add to his family. Time to make a new doll. He hadn't crafted a new puppet in a very, very long time. He was beginning to wonder if the drive had left him altogether.

Oh, he still suffered from the hunger that drove them all to dance for the mortals and lure them in. He saw them streaming by like so many fish wandering down a stream. But it had been a long time since he had felt the need to put his lure in the water and try to catch one for himself.

He had begun to worry that his will had begun to leave him after all these years, as it happened to so many others. But his concerns were now swept away. He had just been uninspired by the fish, that was all. But that had changed the moment he saw her.

When he tasted her.

Now he was going to have the rest of her.

Oh, she'd play hard-to-get. The fish would dart and nibble the line. He would have to be patient to sink the hook just right in order to puncture through her flesh. But the lure he dumped into the waves in front of that particular tasty piece of tail—he stopped to laugh at his own terrible metaphor—was too tempting to pass up.

She was perfect. He could feel it. He had meant his words. If—no, *when*—she came to him, she would learn that he was not feeding her mistruths. It might take a few attempts. It might take a few pieces of bait on the line. But she would come to him.

She would also learn there were far worse things in this world than a liar.

And he was the very worst of them all.

With a flick of his wrist, his silver threads pulled aside the backstage curtain of his performance tent. He strolled in, humming and whistling a happy tune to himself. Plucking his hat off his head, he threw it like a frisbee. It landed with a skitter on the surface of his work bench. "Children! Gather 'round. Soon, we're going to make a new friend. You must all be nice to her."

"But, Father..." came the broken whisper from one of his dolls. The thing that had once been a woman lurched up from the pile. Very little of her remained inside the shell he had crafted for her. He had taken her slowly, bit by bit, and only scraps remained. How sad. Her head lolled on her shoulder. Dead eyes stared nowhere in particular. *"You could play with us instead."*

His jaw ticked. Anger rushed over him, fast and without warning.

Madness. It had upsides and downsides.

He thrust his hand out and, fingers spread, yanked his hand back toward him. The doll hurtled through the air and stopped in front of him. She was a full-scale replica of the woman she had once been. Now she was cracked, yellowed, and fading with time. Rotted scraps, just like what was left inside.

"And why would I waste my time with the likes of you, hmm?" He tightened his hand into a fist, and the doll contorted. He knew she was in pain. That was entirely the point. "Boring, broken, incomplete thing that you are. I'm surprised anything of you still burns in that shell of yours!"

"Please—Father—"

"Perhaps it's time you rest." He grinned. Crossing his hands in front of him, he arced his arms wide out to his side. The nearly invisible silver threads followed his orders. They bound around her ceramic limbs and pulled taut, then snapped.

Shattered pieces of yellow-white clay fell to the ground in a heap. He whirled to face the others standing or hanging by the walls. He snarled briefly before he forced himself to smile. "Anyone else?"

Silence.

"Good. Wilbur, get a dustpan. Clean up this mess." He pointed down at what remained of the woman. "You know how she was, always such a prima donna. She went out the way she lived, as an inconvenience."

"Yes, Father."

He pulled on the front of his waistcoat and stepped over the pile, heading toward his stage. "I have a show to prepare for. And soon, we will have to begin working on a new act. I need to start sculpting a new doll."

With the same elated humming, he shut his eyes and let himself picture her in his head. He wanted to taste her again. He wanted to make sure he never had to stop until there was nothing left of her.

"I will have the rest of you soon, Cora Glass."

3

Funnel cake was just about as gross and wonderful as Cora remembered. She hadn't had any since she was a little kid, and the memory of it wasn't tarnished by the reality. It was greasy, fluffy, squiggly, and covered in powdered sugar.

Emily had eaten a bite of it and inhaled at the wrong point, aspirating a giant pile of the dusty substance. Trent and Cora had both laughed at her as she waved her hands around, making faces from the sudden shot of powdered sugar to the lungs.

But, with lemonade and sugary-fried-slightly-deadly treats in hand, they made their way to the tent that advertised *"The Strongman! Behold, the Eighth Wonder of the World!"* She tried not to roll her eyes at the melodrama. The sign was wonderfully painted in a style she was impressed anyone could still emulate. She had figured everybody who could do old-style font by hand was long dead.

The sign looked incredibly familiar. She was certain either she or her father had taken a photo of it a long time ago, back when the paint was faded and flaked. It looked to be a painstaking restoration. She stopped to stare up at it curiously.

"What?" Trent stopped next to her.

"My dad took a photo of this, I think. I mean, the original. Not this one. But, man, I can't tell the difference in the art. It's like it was just done. It must've taken somebody days to do it."

"They're definitely all-in on this whole 'vintage carnival from the 1920s' thing, huh?" He looked around. "Not a cellphone charging station or an ATM anywhere. Can you believe we have to pay for everything in cash? Who does that? At least Emily got tipped well bartending tonight."

"Just don't forget you owe me," Emily complained.

"I never do, because you never let me." Trent shoved her shoulder playfully. "Now, come on! The show is gonna start."

And with that, he dragged both Cora and Emily into the tent. They laughed and shoved off their over-excited friend. The tent was fairly full. It looked like the performances were on a rotation, with a new one starting every hour until closing. They found a seat on a long wooden bench about halfway to the front and took their spots.

A man took the center stage. He was wearing a beige and blue striped outfit and a matching straw hat. Every inch of him looked as though he had stepped out of a vintage poster. For a second, she almost didn't recognize him because of the costume change. It was the sleazebag from the front counter.

With a grand flourish of his arms and a winning-if-entirely-false smile, he launched into a speech. "Ladies and gentlemen, boys and girls—children of all ages! Tonight, I bring to you a performance rarely seen in your *modern world,* a show of insurmountable strength and prowess! This

The Contortionist

creature you are about to see has transcended the bonds of simple manliness—"

"I hope so," Trent muttered. Cora elbowed him.

"—and into the realm of sheer godhood!"

Trent coughed into his hand with a grin. Cora elbowed him again.

The Barker was on a roll. "Hold on to your hats, and behold the magnificent magnitudinous muscle, the vigorously voluminous vitality—I give you, *Ludwig the Lion!*"

The crowd cheered as a huge—absolutely *gigantic*—man came from backstage. Cora blinked. She had never seen a pro-wrestler in real life, or a bodybuilder, but she was pretty sure that man had to be one or the other, or possibly both. The giant was covered in muscle and barely wearing any clothing. He was suitably jungle-themed for his moniker, complete with the single shoulder strap of what she assumed was supposed to be a lion pelt that looked tiny against his immense chest.

"Fuck," Trent murmured. "Yes, please."

Cora rolled her eyes.

The Strongman had short blond hair and a jaw like a chiseled block. She didn't blame Trent for finding the man attractive. He was. Well, in a freight-truck-gone-human kind of way. As the Strongman walked to the center stage, he posed, and the crowd applauded.

"Measuring seven-foot-two, and weighing in at three-hundred and eighty-seven pounds, don't worry ladies *and* gentlemen"—the Barker winked at the audience—"there is plenty of him to go around!"

"Hot. Damn." Trent stuck his fingers in his lips and let out a loud whistle.

Cora slapped him in the chest. "Stop it. He can hear you."

"I really don't care." He couldn't peel his eyes off the stage.

"You are such a size queen." She shook her head.

"Loud and proud." He laughed.

The over-oiled Strongman did all the usual things she expected he would do. He ripped a phonebook in half and folded a frying pan into a tube. He bent rebar around his neck. She wasn't sure if he was really seven-two and three hundred and eighty-seven pounds, but he was certainly impressive.

When the Barker by the edge of the stage asked for volunteers for the man's next trick, Trent was off like a rocket.

The Barker put his hands on his hips and shot her friend a look. "Eager beaver, aren't you? Typically, one raises one's hand to get picked. Although," the man in the perfectly vintage outfit smirked wryly and gave Trent the once-over, "seems like you've raised something else instead."

The crowd laughed. Trent shrugged and flashed his award-winning smile. "I know what I like, so sue me."

"No judgement here, young man." The announcer chuckled. "Well, we need five more people." After the other volunteers were selected—the proper way that time—all six went up to the stage. They were told to stand on wood platforms that connected in the center with a metal bar, three on each side.

Cora didn't miss Trent winking at the Strongman, nor did she miss the giant man's slight smile in response. *Oh, Trent.* Something told her that he'd be sticking around after the show, and it'd be her and Emily hanging out by themselves.

Again.

The Contortionist

Emily's groan from next to her told her she wasn't the only one who caught the exchange.

The strongman grabbed the metal bar once all the volunteers were in place, and with an impressive ripple of muscle, lifted all six people into the air and straight up over his head. And he did it without even looking like he was trying.

After the applause, the giant man put the platforms down gently and, once the volunteers had left the stage, he took a bow. Trent collapsed onto the bench next to Cora, comedically fanning his neck.

"Let me guess. You're going to go get his *autograph?*" Cora shot him a look. Partly teasing, partly playful, and partly annoyed. She still hadn't forgiven him for abandoning her in the middle of a football game a few years back.

"You better believe it." Trent was still smiling ear-to-ear.

Poor Emily looked heartbroken like she always did when this happened. Cora was fairly certain the girl spent every day of her life heartbroken. But like Cora's chronic pain, it was a gradient—a matter of degrees.

Trent shrugged. "You girls will get on fine without me."

"Like we always do." Cora stood and waved for Emily to follow her. "C'mon, Em, let's go find the alcohol."

"Yes, please." Emily followed, already with her hands shoved in her pockets and her shoulders caved in, as if trying to fold into a dimensional hole and disappear.

"I'll see you girls later." He didn't seem to even notice. Nor had he taken his eyes off the giant man on the stage, so they left him there.

They walked in silence through the park—Cora could actually walk again and not limp—for a few minutes before Emily finally spoke up. "I don't know how he does it. I honestly don't get it. I can't get a guy to give me a second look, and they just fall all over him."

"Guys check you out all the time, Em. You just don't let yourself see it, and you know why."

"Yeah, yeah…I don't want a lecture tonight. Not about relationships and certainly not about letting things go." Emily's voice took on a bitter edge. "Not from you."

"Wow." Cora rubbed the back of her neck. "Really? You're going to go there?"

"Sorry. Sorry. You just know how much I hate it when he…does this shit."

"Yeah. I know." Cora put her hand on the other girl's shoulder. "Let's eat some fried food on a stick and drink a beer."

The Faire was loud and impressively busy. She was shocked at how many people were there on a random Tuesday night. But excitement rarely came to this part of the state, and she wouldn't have been surprised to find out that the grand re-opening of the park had gone a bit viral. She wished she could still hop around with all her camera equipment and take photos for the local gazette.

Most of the decent food carts were all in one area, which seemed to create a bit of food court near the center of the park. It sat at the base of a giant tower that stretched high overhead. It resembled the lit-up observation tower at Coney Island's old Dreamland park. The few websites she read said that Coney Island actually got the idea from Harrow Faire, but there was some debate about whether that was true.

The sign on the door said it was still closed for renovations. That was a shame. She would have loved to climb the stairs to look down at the park and the lake from that high up.

The Contortionist

The walls of the tower were painted bright white to reflect as much of the light as possible from the hundreds of Edison bulbs that dotted its surface, all the way up to the top. But instead of a pond at the base like at Coney Island, there was a rectangular stretch of grass with picnic tables. Cora and Emily got their snacks and their thankfully alcoholic drinks and went to find a place to sit and eat.

"How was the event tonight?" Cora smiled at her friend, trying to cheer her up.

"Fine." Emily shrugged. "Just another posh business event from some mucks down in Boston. Some guy named Alistair was running it. He hit on everything with legs. I think he and Trent might have known each other from somewhere, but I don't know. I just help set up, and then I serve the drinks."

She was clearly in a mood. Cora decided not to push it and changed the subject. "I don't know how this place got fixed like this. I swear it was still a dump when I passed it yesterday."

"I know, it's weird." Emily looked around at the park and shook her head. "I didn't believe you when you texted us today. I had to drive by to see if you were joking for some dumb reason. I couldn't believe it when I saw it. You'd think somebody would have said something—put something in the news, anything."

"Yeah." Cora took in a breath, held it, and let it out in a rush. "It'll be nice to have some business around here that isn't just Castle in the Clouds and summering rich people. Maybe I'll quit the bank and work here instead." She grinned.

Emily snorted. "Yeah, right. What're you gonna do? Join the freakshow?"

"Maybe! Don't judge. I'd make a great freak."

"The Amazing Breakable Cora Glass. I can see it now." Her friend grinned.

She tossed a french fry at Emily, who squeaked and laughed, ducking her head to avoid another projectile as Cora threw a second. "Oh, like you'd do any better."

"I'd suck at it. I hate crowds. I hate being *looked* at." Emily gagged dramatically. "No, thank you. I like support jobs. I couldn't ever be on stage. Can you imagine?"

"It might be fun, having people cheering for you. Like we were for that Strongman guy." Cora found herself smiling at the idea. When she was young, she had dreamed of being a famous actress or a performer. Maybe a magician. But it never panned out—her talent had been behind a camera, not on the stage. She had seen the kind of passion and hardship it took to make it in that kind of world and decided it wasn't worth it to her. "C'mon. It's late. We didn't get to see much. Maybe we can come back tomorrow? I know I don't have anything better to do."

"That'd be nice. I really do want to see the freakshow. Maybe they're hiring, and you can get your wish." Emily pushed up from the table, and the two of them walked through the park toward the exit, taking a different path from the way they had come.

The circus was an array of beautiful lights and strange flashing signs. It was an overwhelming array of movement and life. The tilt-a-whirl rides and haunted houses with their loud mechanical laughs were somehow both insultingly campy and wonderfully enticing at the same time.

Tomorrow, she'd have to dust off her Nikon and come back to take some photos. The lighting was just incredible, and even with a pretty fast exposure speed, she was sure she could catch some great shots of the spinning lights in action.

The whooshing sound of the carts rushing by on metal

The Contortionist

tracks, of the machinery, and the grind of the hurdy-gurdy made for a heady mix. Coupled with the smell of grease and sugar, it made her all at once a little uneasy but also brought a smile to her face. Places like this were just...fun. That was the only thing they were about. Well, okay, and making a buck. But that was American entertainment, wasn't it?

Do a dance, get a dollar.

Nothing quite captured that as purely and simply as a carnival, circus, or fair. And this place was all three rolled into one. Not that she could really tell anybody the difference between the designations if she tried.

When they passed one tent, an old woman was standing outside it. The tent was smaller and looked only fifteen or twenty feet in diameter, and much shorter than all the others. It was painted in purple, accented in gold metallic polka dots. The woman was dressed head to toe like a cartoon fortune teller. Resplendent in colored scarves that dangled shining gold coins, they hid her stringy, pale hair. The sign next to her read *"Heed the Soothsayer's Words!"*

"Miss, can I interest you in a fortune?" the old woman called to her. She had a thick Eastern European accent. Of course she did. She looked like a walking cliché just like everything else in the park, so she might as well sound like one too.

"I'm all set," Cora answered with a polite smile. "Thanks, though."

"I think you might be interested in what I have to say, Cora Glass."

She froze. *Not this shit again.* It gave her chills, even though she knew it was entirely bunk. They probably all had headsets, and somebody was tracking her through the park.

Emily's eyes went wide and looked between her and the fortune teller in horror. "How does she know your name?"

"Old Maggie knows many things, Emily Dennis," the old woman said with a warm smile.

Emily took a step behind Cora and hid from the woman. "What the fuck?"

"I think they IDed me on the way in. Probably found you through Facebook friends or whatever."

Emily groaned. "This is an invasion of privacy. I don't like this. This isn't legal!"

"Laws." The woman chuckled. "Come in, Cora. I have much to tell you." Maggie waved her over with a grizzled hand.

"I'm not interested in whatever racket you have going." Cora tried to sound as firm as she could. She didn't know why she felt the need to protect Emily, but she did on an instinctual level. Whatever happened to her in that dark tunnel *thing* shouldn't happen to her friend.

Not that she really believed what happened in there.

It was all rather conflicted in her head.

Maggie smiled sadly. "We don't have any interest in her. And if we wanted to pick your pockets, we would have already. Come, my reading for you tonight is free."

"You're not going to make me run around in darkness screaming my head off, are you?" Cora narrowed an eye. "Already did that once tonight. Don't feel like doing it again."

Maggie laughed. "No, no...I haven't run in a long, long time. I'm hardly in any condition to chase you." She turned and walked into her tent, waving for Cora to follow. "Leave your friend outside. These words aren't for her."

Cora looked at Emily and shrugged.

The Contortionist

Emily frowned. She clearly didn't like the idea of being left behind. "How the fuck does she know our names?"

"I don't know. The guy from the ticket booth knew mine, too. I think they must be doing some weird facial recognition software thing and looking us up online."

"Are you seriously going in there?" Her friend was clinging to Cora's arm like she was a life raft. "You really shouldn't."

"I know." Cora paused. She knew she shouldn't. She knew it was insanely stupid. She knew this was the wrong thing to do. But, man, she was *incredibly* curious. "I guess I want to know what the big deal is. If they're setting me up for some stupid game by looking me up, I want to know what they want." She zipped up her coat pockets to make sure nobody could lift her phone or her wallet without her noticing.

Although they already had gotten hold of her phone once and opted to return it. Maybe they hacked it, and that was how they knew so much about her.

Emily frowned. "What'm I supposed to do? Just stand here and wait?" She crossed her arms over her chest. "Why am I always getting ditched by you people?"

"This is exactly the first time I've ever ditched you, Em. I'll be right out in a second, anyway. I promise. It's probably just a sham, and they want to sell me on some kind of freaky circus timeshare." She grinned and walked toward the tent. "I'll be right back. If I'm not out in half an hour, call the cops."

"Oookaaaay," Emily said in a long, drawn-out sigh. "My friends are all idiots."

Cora laughed at the comment. Emily wasn't entirely wrong.

The smell of incense just about smacked her in the face

as she walked into the dark tent. She coughed. There were candles burning around the room, sitting in large bowls of wax made of hundreds of previously spent tapers, their colors all mixed together into muddy messes. Banners and large sections of fabric draped up from the walls to the center of the tent, giving the whole place a slightly claustrophobic feeling.

"This place looks flammable," Cora commented dryly. "Does OSHA know about this?"

"What's OSHA?"

Man, they knew how to stay in character. "Never mind. It's just that the candles aren't probably a great idea."

The old woman was already seated at a circular table covered in a midnight-blue fabric and gold painted stars. A crystal ball—a legit crystal ball—sat in the center of the table next to a deck of weathered old cards. They were too big to be regular playing cards, but what they were, Cora wasn't quite sure.

Maggie laughed. "I suppose not. Come, Cora. Sit. Listen to what Old Maggie has to tell you."

Cora moved to stand by the table for a moment. She hesitated then, with a groan, sat in the chair across from the old lady. "Why do I get the feeling it was an exceptionally bad idea to come here?"

"Oh, my dear, sweet, wonderful child." Maggie reached out and picked up the old and battered deck of cards. Her fingers shook a little with age. The woman's eyes were warm, and almost sympathetic. "That's because...it was."

4

Cora sat back in her chair and watched the old woman warily. "Are you threatening me?"

"No, no...I'm no danger to you. Old Maggie is no danger to anybody." The woman began shuffling the cards. "Everyone thinks I'm to blame for the bad things that happen to them. That I'm the lightning that struck their house and burned it down. I'm not. I'm only the person telling you that it's about to happen."

"So...you're saying my house is going to burn down?" Cora narrowed an eye.

Maggie laughed. "No, no. It's a figure of speech. Metaphorically, your house is about to burn down." She smiled warmly like that made it so much better. It didn't. "Metaphorically, your life is about to end."

"You're saying something terrible is about to happen to me?"

"It already has. The clock has already begun ticking. It'll strike midnight soon enough, then all your world will disappear. But a new one will take its place." Maggie began cutting the cards into several piles. "Tell me, Cora, what's your favorite color?"

"Not this bunch of bull again." She sighed and leaned back, folding her arms over her chest. This woman was clearly on the same radio system as everyone else. They were all working together to mess with her. "What're you guys trying to get out of screwing with my head? Hoping I'll go back and tell everybody on social media how they have to come and see this insane circus? I hate to disappoint. I don't have that many friends."

Maggie only kept a faint, knowing smile on her face. "You can't tell me your favorite color because it's gone now. But you can remember having one, can't you? Think about being a child and being asked that by your teachers. You know you had one."

Cora tried to fight off the memory, but it was like when somebody told her not to look down. Of course she was going to look down. Nobody said "don't look down" without then fully expecting that person to do precisely what they were told not to do.

She could remember being asked. She could remember having a favorite color.

She just couldn't remember what it *was*.

"This is a lie." Cora rubbed the back of her neck. "It's a trick."

"It's a trick, all right." Maggie began to place the piles of cards in front of her. Five in all. "But it isn't 'a bunch of bull.' This isn't a lie. Now. Listen carefully to what I have to say, Cora Glass. I don't give out free readings twice."

She flipped the first card over. It was painted to look like a tarot card, but she didn't recognize the figure. To be fair, she knew jack shit about tarot cards. Only what she'd seen in movies or on TV. The figure was a woman with long dark

The Contortionist

hair, bent backward at an alarming angle. The text on the bottom read *"0. The Contortionist."*

"You are on the beginning of a journey. A chapter of your life has ended, and a new one is about to begin," Maggie explained. "The Contortionist is full of hope and wonder." She tapped the card. "But the road you will walk will not be an easy one."

Maggie turned over the card on the top of the next pile. It was reds and blacks, with a man standing there, a fiendish and sinister grin painted on his face. He wore sunglasses, one lens tinted red and the other black. His shadow seemed to be alive—in so much as it had features—and its face was twisted in a deranged and inhuman smile. Like the Cheshire Cat, if it had done drugs. More drugs, anyway.

The bottom read *"15. The Puppeteer."*

"Many will seek to manipulate you. They will see your youth, your energy, and will want to twist it to their own needs and desires." Maggie wrinkled her nose, her already creased face bunching up in more lines and crags. It was clear that she was disgusted by that card. "They will tempt you with things you *think* you want. They come with terrible costs."

"Great. Sounds like a blast." Cora shook her head. This was all nonsense. But hey, whatever. It was free.

Maggie rolled her eyes. She flipped the next card. *"13. The Clown."*

Cora made a face. "What's with Baron Samedi in the clown wig?"

"Oh? You know your voodoo loa, do you?" Maggie chuckled.

"I know my classic James Bond movies." Cora peered down at the card. The figure wore a baggy outfit that was entirely black and white, with puffy white buttons running down the front. He held a bug-eyed rubber chicken in one hand, and a bloody knife in the other. But what had struck her was that the paint on the man's face wasn't like that of a normal clown. It was painted like a skull, in black and white. His eyes were just a black void where the sockets would be. "And this one is supposed to mean...what...death?" Cora shot the old woman a raised eyebrow.

"Indeed." The old woman picked up the card and looked at it with a fond smile. "But not in the way that you think. All things die. But it is not tragedy. It is only that way if we cannot accept that things end." She placed the card back on the pile. "You will suffer a great loss. An enormous loss. But if you do not see it for what it is—as a new beginning—it will destroy you."

Cora watched the woman oddly. She was certain that was the kind of warning that could be attributed to the loss of a loved one or a flat tire. Fortunes were always super vague so anything could be what they were referencing. "I promise I won't forget to feed my fish."

The woman chuckled. "Cynical. Sarcastic. You'll do well." She flipped over the fourth card. It was a huge, smiling man, a long whip coiled in the air around him, as if ready to strike. His clothing was all black, greens, golds, and creams, and offset the darker tone of his skin. A top hat made him look towering. He was thickly built, but not fat.

"4. The Ringmaster."

Like she couldn't have guessed.

But it was upside down from the other ones. "What's that mean? It being upside down?"

"Aaah, it means it's inverted, dear Cora. It allows us to see the darker side of the cards. Here, what should be a magnanimous leader is a tyrant. He is the rusted shackles of power that have long since ceased to be useful. They must

The Contortionist

be shattered. A new power must come to bear. But in all coups, whenever power is first overthrown, there is chaos."

For once, Cora had no smartass comment. She just shrugged uselessly. Maggie turned over the fifth and last card.

It was a painting of the huge tower in the center of Harrow Faire. It stretched up with its white painted walls and array of lightbulbs. It glowed against a night sky. Around its base were the tents she recognized from outside, and a Ferris wheel in the background. *"21. The Faire."*

Maggie let out a rush of air. "The end. The cycle finishes. The story that begins with the Contortionist ends with the Faire, only to begin again. And to begin anew. All things are reborn. And you must be ready for when it happens. It will be your choice whether you look to the horizon, or if you let yourself wallow in failure and stagnation."

"Lady, all I am is failure and stagnation." Cora snickered. "My life is already a disappointment. You're not warning me against much."

Maggie hummed thoughtfully. "So you think. But listen to my words, Ms. Cora Glass, and remember them. They'll make sense later when you start believing what is happening to you."

"What's happening to me is that you guys have a very clever system of using facial recognition and Google to figure out who I am, and to play weird games with me for... reasons, I don't know." She reached into her bag, and pulling out her small money clip, pulled out a twenty and put it on the table. "Here."

"The reading was free." That didn't stop Maggie from reaching over the table to take the money, however.

"It's a tip. I don't know. Thanks. I guess." Cora pushed up

from the chair and headed for the exit. "Good luck with your next patrons. Good night."

"Sleep well, Cora. I'll see you soon. May your dreams be quiet."

What an odd-ass thing to say to someone.

What an odd-ass night.

What an odd-ass carnival in general.

Cora shook her head and left without another word. Emily was waiting for her, leaning against a railing, munching on some cotton candy they had gotten from a stall about an hour earlier.

It really was better stale. But Emily must be bored to tears, so she wouldn't judge her for opening the package. Cora tucked her hands in her pockets, glad to find she still had everything she came with. "Sorry about that."

"Anything interesting?" Emily asked as they resumed walking toward the exit.

"Just vague mumbo-jumbo. But I still have all my belongings, so I'll call it a win." Cora shrugged and reached for the bag of cotton candy. She pulled off a handful and handed it back to Emily. At least it was "blue" flavored, which was her preference. Red was supposed to be cherry, green was sour apple—which was just awful—and blue was...she could never quite figure it out. It just tasted like "blue." Raspberry, maybe?

But blue was tasty. She didn't even mind how it stuck to her fingers. It was cotton candy. That was the point. Nobody bought it to look dignified.

"Any texts from Trent?" Emily asked.

Cora checked her phone. Nothing. She shook her head and slipped it back into her pocket. "We should probably just head out. He took his own car, yeah?"

"Yeah." Emily sounded deflated. Cora slung an arm

The Contortionist

around her friend and hugged her as they walked, trying to cheer her up. It worked, insomuch as it put a smile on the girl's face. "I don't think I've eaten this much sugar in years."

"Eh, fuck it. Life's short, right?" Cora pulled off another section of the spun-sugar substance. The shit really was a disaster, but it was a tasty, amazing disaster. "It's not like we're eating this every day."

"That's good enough of an excuse for me." Emily laughed. "I think if I ate this every day, my life would be much shorter than it should be."

They made their way toward the exit gate and the turnstiles that counted people in reverse. Mostly to stop people going in the exit and not paying their fee. Which was silly because it wasn't like they weren't super easy to jump over. But the two creepy clowns in full face masks standing at each side of the exit gate would have been enough to scare her off as a teenager.

They stood there like statues, and for the longest time, Cora assumed they were just that. That they were props set up to scare off people looking to sneak inside. But when they both turned to look at her—and *only* her—she froze.

"Ooh, I hate clowns!" Emily hugged Cora's arm and hid half behind her. "I don't like them. Why're they looking at us?"

I don't think they're looking at us, Em. I think they're only looking at me. She didn't know how she knew. She could just sense it. Like she could sense that something had been taken from her in that dark place.

"This is stupid. This is all just a bunch of cheap scare tactics. C'mon. They can't do anything." She walked through the turnstile and dragged Emily behind her. Pretty soon, they were in the parking lot, and the scary clowns were around a corner and out of the line of sight. After that, Emily calmed down significantly.

"I didn't know you were afraid of clowns."

"It's never come up. It's not something that's ever a problem." Emily folded her arms over her chest. "Afraid of bees, fine, that happens. You meet bees in the wild. I'm never in a field and then just—suddenly *clowns*. They're not, like, roving scourges or whatever."

"Now I want to pay one to come to your work and just follow you around." She mimed holding up an invisible horn and squeezed the bag at the end. "Ha-honk!"

"Stop it! You wouldn't."

Cora laughed. "Ha-honk!"

Emily shoved her. "Not funny."

"It's super funny." Cora cackled. "Ha-honk!"

"Yeah, yeah." Emily was laughing, though, and the good-natured teasing was at least cheering her up. And distracting from the fact that they both knew where Trent was, and exactly what he was doing. Or who was doing him.

Whatever.

Details.

"Talk to you tomorrow, Em."

"You too, Cora."

As she drove away from the Faire, the Soothsayer's words stuck in her head. *"May your dreams be quiet."*

What the hell kind of warning was that?

5

It wasn't long before Cora understood the warning.

She hadn't ever been one for lucid dreams. They had only happened a few times in her life, and mostly when she was a kid. The last time she had one was after a surgery on her elbow, and she figured that was probably just a result of the pain medication. Hydrocodone was a hell of a drug.

So, when she found herself standing in a field, the long blades of grass brushing against her fingertips, she could have sworn she was really there. But the world felt a little out of focus at the edges—a little too surreal—and she knew she was dreaming. The scene in front of her was a beautiful landscape. Rolling fields, a soft breeze, and she could see a farmhouse down at the bottom of the hill. Sheep, white dots against a rich green background, were wandering around aimlessly.

Clouds overhead dappled a stunning blue sky. It was the definition of picturesque. She looked down at the grass that surrounded her and brushed her hand over the blades. They had grown so long that they had seeds at the top in little bunches, and the feeling of them against her fingers brought back memories of childhood.

The wind blew through the field, folding the long stems in waves. It was rare that a person could see the wind. There was something serene about watching it flow like the ocean over the fields.

It wasn't anywhere she'd ever been before. Something told her this wasn't even in America. There was a thin dirt road down below, and there were no power lines running along it. She'd never seen a sheep farm before—and the cottage next to it didn't look like anywhere she'd seen in New England.

But where?

And why?

Not that she'd complain. It really was lovely. She could feel the wind blowing through her hair. The sun was warm on her face. If this was what lucid dreaming was like, she really was missing out. This was almost as good as reality.

She turned to see if she could glean any more information about where she was and jumped in surprise. She wasn't alone.

There was a man standing there, although he didn't seem to notice her. He was far more interested in a canvas on a large easel in front of him. She couldn't see what he was painting. He was facing her, so the canvas wasn't. She assumed it was the landscape she had just taken in.

He was humming to himself, some classical-sounding tune, and dabbing at a palette in his hand with a brush, then working on a spot on the canvas.

He was beautiful. And *tall*. Easily over six feet, if not close to six and a half. It made him look thinner than she assumed he was. His features were sharp, and he had dark

The Contortionist

hair that framed his face in messy curls. A bit of paint smudged his forehead near his hairline. A smock over his clothing was stained with a myriad of blues, greens, and white smears.

There was something about him. Maybe it was how handsome he was. Maybe it was how he trapped the tip of his tongue between his teeth and leaned into the canvas to focus on a particularly small detail. He was captivating.

She hadn't found herself attracted to anyone in a long, long time. It was for a good reason. She had decided that between her history and her illness, dating just wasn't in the cards for her. She turned that part of herself off. Oh, she got lonely. She just stopped bothering to look.

But if this guy were real and not just in her dream? Maybe she'd be forced to change her mind.

"Drat!" He growled in frustration and picked up a little scraper out of his smock and scratched at something on the canvas. "Blast it all. Bad sheep. Do as you're told," he muttered to himself. She could barely catch the words. He dropped the scraper back into his pocket and wiped his hand across his chest, leaving a smudge of white and green paint on the canvas fabric of his smock.

She smiled.

His clothing was strange. It didn't look...modern. It was hard to tell, as he wasn't wearing a coat or anything. He was wearing a white shirt with the sleeves rolled up and black trousers, but something about him seemed dated. The cut of his slacks wasn't modern. *Who wears slacks and not jeans in a field, anyway?*

"Hello?"

He didn't answer. Didn't even glance at her. It was like he couldn't hear her. It was a dream, after all. Maybe he couldn't. She walked up to him slowly, fascinated. He truly was gorgeous. At least if she was going to dream up a stranger, it was this one. She smiled and tried again. "Hey, tall and sexy. How's it going?"

Still no answer. Not even a twitch of a smile or any inkling he could hear her. With the tip of a finger, he touched the painting, as if trying to use his fingernail to get something just right. When he did, he caught the tip of his tongue between his teeth again, clearly focusing on what he was doing.

Sexy and cute. There were definitely worse people to dream up. She shrugged. She could see that his eyes were a bright blue, almost cyan like the overhead sky. Curious to see his painting, she walked around to look at the canvas.

And felt her heart drop into her stomach.

She didn't even know that could happen in a dream.

She had expected an oil-painted landscape. Wistful clouds over a sea of green and white-dotted sheep. An adorable cottage, perhaps.

None of that was there.

There wasn't even paint.

There was only blood.

She jumped back, her eyes wide, and gaped at what she saw. The canvas was covered in gore. It dripped from the edge of the surface into the grass around his feet. It hadn't been like that a second before. Crimson coated his brush, his pallet, and his hands.

His face split in a grin. An unkind, sadistic, cruel grin. It seemed like such a far cry from what he had been a second prior. Then...he looked at her. "Hello, Cora dear."

His eyes weren't sky blue anymore. They weren't right. They weren't right at *all.* The pupils weren't black like they should be—they were white. The irises were *bright red,* and

The Contortionist

the sclera—the part of the eye that should be white, were jet black.

Like someone had inverted the color of his eyes.

He reached out his hand to her, stained red with the oozing ichor. "Your favorite color was red. Mine, too, cupcake."

She screamed and jumped back from him. She tripped and landed in the grass, hitting it hard with a pained *unf*.

Something underneath her squished. The ground hadn't been wet a moment ago. But now it felt like she was in the grass next to a pond. It was saturated and thick with mud and packed strands.

She didn't want to look.

She knew what it was.

She knew what she had landed in.

It was warm.

But, like being told not to look down, she did it anyway.

Blood. Inches of it. Thick and old, like mud. But it was unmistakable. She wailed.

He laughed.

He cackled like a madman, and his strange, bizarre, and horrifying eyes lit up in joy. He was standing at her feet and held his hand down to her again, as if to help her up. But it was still covered in the same mess she had landed in.

"I can make all this go away," he cooed. "Take my hand."

It was him. She recognized the voice now. More than that, she recognized the laugh. It was the man from the darkness of that weird labyrinth she had gone through at the Faire. The man from "the Dark Path."

She screamed.

And the dream shattered.

She was sitting up in bed before she realized she was even awake. She was shaking, and the sheets were sticking to her from the sweat that was beading on her skin. "Oh, fuck." She put her head in her hands and tried to take a deep breath.

Now she really understood what the fortune teller had meant. Damn it! It was that old woman's fault. She'd only had the nightmare because the stupid old lady had put the thought into her head. Pushing out of bed, she decided she needed to take a shower. Glancing at the clock, she discovered that it was four in the morning. She grunted. Late enough that it probably wasn't worth trying to get to sleep, but early enough that it was going to ruin her day.

It usually took her a few hours to fall asleep. She'd lie there, tossing and turning, trying to find the right position that didn't hurt badly enough to keep her awake. Then she'd try that for a bit, only to have it ache after twenty minutes, and have to try to find another.

Shitty sleep was a *super fun* side effect to chronic pain. It was like insult to injury. It wasn't bad enough that she went through every day in pain, she had to be groggy and exhausted on top of it.

Resigning herself to the fact that she was just going to be awake now, she took a shower and changed, rubbing a towel through her hair. Then she checked her phone. She had a few spam emails and a new text notification. Checking her text, she rolled her eyes.

Trent had launched off a text to her, Lisa, and Emily at two in the morning. *"We're so going back tonight!"* It was followed by a bunch of hearts in a string, then the emoji of an arm flexing.

He really was an idiot. An adorable idiot, but an idiot nonetheless. He still made her smile. He always did. Trent was her best friend. They had been inseparable as children, and although they didn't hang out as much as they used to

The Contortionist

now that they were adults, he was still the person she considered herself closest to in the world. Especially since the issue with Duncan.

That made her sadder than it should.

Once she made it to work, she sat at her spot at the counter and tapped her pencil on the pad of stationery she kept in front of her. She was doodling her coffee mug. It read *"Another Day, Another Dollar."*

Her boss let her keep it at her desk because he thought it was a reference to her job at the bank. It was, but he entirely and utterly missed the sarcastic statement behind it. Oh, well. She kept doodling. She was a terrible artist. But it never stopped her from trying.

The perspective was all wrong. The handle was dinky, and the font didn't wrap right. *Stick to photography, loser.* Not like she could even do much of that anymore. Before heading to work, she had dug out her Nikon and some of her smaller gear out of her closet to take to Harrow Faire tonight. Trent and Emily didn't have an event to run, so they could all meet up as soon as Cora got out of work just after five.

And it seemed Lisa was actually coming for a change! She was bringing Robert, her husband, and her two kids, Jane and Tom. Trent sent her a private text complaining about the presence of the kids, but she reminded him that carnivals were pretty much designed for children, so he could deal. Besides, he wasn't going to be hanging out with them for long. He was going with one thing in mind. Ludwig the Strongman.

Trent's snarky reply had simply been *"Yeah, and?"*

She shook her head with a laugh. Whatever. The day came and went like all her days at the bank came and went. Boring. She cashed some checks, counted some coins, validated a few bills that somebody had thought were counterfeit, then balanced her drawer at the end of the day.

As creepy as last night had been at the Faire, she was honestly a little excited to go back. It was something unique and interesting. A blip in the stream of events of her life that all seemed to blur together into one endless stream of *meh*.

When she got to the packed parking lot, she slung her camera over her shoulder and tucked a few lenses into her bag. She figured that once Trent ditched them all to go hang out with his latest fling, they'd take Lisa's kids around to see all the sights. She could take photos while they were on the kiddie rides.

Checking her phone, the rest of them were already inside. Walking up to the counter to buy her ticket, she reached the ticket booth. And groaned.

"Well, hello!" The sleazebag. The carnival Barker, or whoever he was, was sitting across from her, leaning his elbow on the counter, his chin in his palm, smiling at her. "Welcome back."

She hated his mustache. Nobody should wear a pencil mustache anymore. She wondered if it was glued on. She wanted to yank on it to find out. She shot him a dry expression. "Hi." She wasn't sure she liked him very much. She reached for her money clip to pull out a twenty to pay for her admission.

"Want to go back through the Dark Path instead?" He jerked a thumb in the direction of the skull-faced interior. "You still have so much more seity we could steal."

"No, thanks."

"I thought you didn't believe in my silly nonsense?" He smiled.

"I don't like getting chased around in the darkness, manhandled by some tall-ass laughing weirdo, and end up

The Contortionist

limping the rest of the night because of it." She put the money on the counter. "But thanks anyway."

He shrugged and took the twenty and started getting her change. "Suit yourself."

The ticket entrance fee was only ten dollars. The rides and the tent shows were all free, but the food and the games weren't. She figured that was where they made most of their money. And the food, while it was definitely from a carnival, hadn't been that bad. "Quality carnival food" wasn't really a thing, but they were trying.

"My name's Aaron, by the way," he said to her as he passed a ten-dollar bill back to her. It was an old one. Looking down at it, the date was from the forties. Huh. They were usually taken out of circulation. She'd have to change it out for a new one at the bank if she didn't spend it at the Faire tonight.

"I'd tell you my name, but you already know it. Which is creepy. And makes you, *ipso facto*, a creep." She smiled sweetly at him. Her sarcasm was about as subtle as a truck.

He shrugged again and smiled back at her. "Nothing to be done about it, I suppose. Well, here's your ticket. Now go on in, Cora." As she began to walk away, he called after her. "Oh! One last thing." When she turned, his expression was unusually serious. "Stay away from Simon. I'm not kidding. Stay the *hell* away from Simon, whatever you do."

"Who's Simon?" She raised an eyebrow.

"You've already met." He turned back to the line of people in front of him.

She supposed that meant she was dismissed. She shook her head. Weird man. Weird Faire. Weird everything.

Taking her ticket to the turnstile, she gave it to the creepy clown who was ripping them in half. She stepped through, thanked the man—or woman, it was hard to tell with the baggy clothing and their masks—and headed inside the Faire. *Clowns are a little creepy, Emily. I'll give you that. At least these ones are, anyway.*

Swiveling her camera around, she flicked the switch to turn it on, took the cap off the lens, and lifted it. The old-fashioned merry-go-round by the entrance was beautiful, and it looked great against the backdrop of the white observation tower and the brightly colored tents and food stalls.

She was excited to snap some shots at sundown. It felt good to take photos of something interesting. It just felt good to brush off her equipment and remember what it was like to do it for a living, period. But what followed was the bittersweet reminder that those days were gone.

Texting her friends, she let them know she was here and inside the park.

Trent responded again in a private message. *"Wanted to see the freaks. Lisa pitched a fit. Heading to the lame puppet show instead. Fuck me."*

"That's Ludwig's job," she texted back.

"LOL yeaaaah."

She shook her head and sighed. Trent liked Lisa well enough, but resented Robert and her children for always "ruining things" when they were around. He never felt bad when Lisa couldn't come out anymore. It was a shame, but that was what happened when people had kids, she supposed.

Kids. She wasn't interested. Never had been. And now, it wasn't like she could. Oh, she was biologically capable, she was sure—but raising kids with her illness was a recipe for a nightmare. She had a hard time picking things up without pulling her joints out of place as it was. Not to mention, she'd probably pass her syndrome on, and that wasn't some-

The Contortionist

thing she'd wish on her worst enemy. Well, maybe the jerk in the tunnel, now that she thought about it.

And after her relationship with her ex had ended so horribly, she didn't even have anybody in her life she wanted to be with, let alone have kids with. It just wasn't for her. Not that it kept her mom from asking. Mom had moved to Florida a few years prior to be with her sister after Dad died. Cora never realized how much her dad must have kept her mother from pestering her about getting married and having kids. Now that he was gone, there was nobody to tell her not to. The emails and calls were bi-weekly.

She shrugged it off, as she did everybody else's comments about her being alone. She just wasn't ready. And she didn't care if people understood that or not.

It took her a while to find the right tent—after asking directions—but she finally got there. It was about a hundred feet in diameter and maybe thirty tall. It was a big structure, composed entirely of bold black and red stripes. A wood façade around the entrance advertised the show as *"Wonders Beyond Imagining! Watch The Puppeteer Bring Your Wildest Dreams To Life!"*

Great. Creepy puppets. That sounded "fun." She saw her friends gathered in a small clump outside the entrance. Walking up, she smiled. "Hey, guys!"

"Cor-Cor!" Jane ran from Lisa and hug-tackled Cora's legs. Lisa's little girl loved Cora, and vice versa. While Cora didn't want kids, she liked them. Especially when she could give them back. She always looked forward to babysitting for Lisa.

Tom, Lisa's son, was more reserved, and just shyly waved from where he was standing by his father, holding his dad's hand. Jane was five, and Tom was three, and it was fun to see them growing up and developing personalities. Jane clearly took after Lisa, and Tom after his father.

"Hey there, Janey!" She ruffled the little girl's hair and smiled. "Are you enjoying the carnival so far?"

"Uh-huh. I wanna go on the big rides, but Momma said no." Jane pouted. "Said I wasn't old enough."

"She's right. You'd fall out. We can't have that." Cora chuckled and smiled at Lisa, who smiled back at her. "We can take you on the rides made for people your size, though. After the puppet show, maybe."

Jane clapped her hands and smiled up at her mother. "Can we? Please? Please?"

"They have kiddie rides here?" Lisa asked.

"Yeah. I saw a few farther into the park yesterday."

Trent was standing there, clearly fidgety. "I'll stick around to see the puppets, but then I'm going to meet up with my friend. He said his last show ends at eight."

Robert rolled his eyes. He knew what the word "friend" meant. Luckily, it didn't seem like anyone else caught it. Emily was too busy surfing around on her phone, and Lisa was distracted with Jane's exuberance.

"Can we? Can we please?" Jane wasn't going to give up the idea of climbing into a metal death trap on rails. "Momma, please?"

"Okay, sweetheart." Lisa conceded a battle that hadn't ever really started. But that didn't stop her daughter from screeching happily in victory—a sound that made Trent wince—and hug Cora's leg again.

"Let's go in and get a seat. The show's going to start soon," Robert said as he walked into the tent, pulling his son along gently by the hand. Jane let go of her leg to chase after them, not wanting to be second in line to anything.

The Contortionist

Cora shook her head with a smile and walked in after them. She fell into step with Trent. "Be nice, T-bag."

"What? I'm being perfectly nice." He scoffed and muttered to her so nobody else could hear. "It's not my fault they get in the way."

"If there's one thing I know, it's that nothing gets in your way." She nudged him in the arm with her elbow.

He smiled broadly. "Sing it, sister."

As they entered the tent, she could hear the murmur of people. For a puppet show, there was a big crowd. She hoped they could get seats where the kids could see.

And there, just standing on the inside of the flap, was a man. He was tall, wearing an elaborate suit. It was bright red with black pinstripes and screamed of an age that was long since gone, mixed with an eccentric design she knew had never been in fashion. It cut his already imposing figure into sharp angles and drastic lines.

Before she could get a good look at him in the dim light of the tent, he bowed gracefully and gestured his hand wide.

It was his voice that gave her the first hint of danger.

"Welcome to my show. Please, take a seat wherever you like. We're about to begin. I do *hope* you enjoy…"

She froze. Her friends didn't notice. They all walked past him, thanking him, and went to find a place where their group could sit in the relatively packed tent. It left her standing there, gaping at the man in shock. It left her alone.

With *him*.

He straightened, and the next thing she recognized was the sadistic and insane grin on sharp, handsome features. She was shocked his teeth weren't pointed like a shark's. His dark hair was swept back from his face in curls and waves. It would be chin-length if it were wet.

Sunglasses hid the eyes she knew would be inverted and

wrong. Those terrifying eyes from her dreams that were black where they should be white, white where they should be black, and crimson instead of blue. The sunglasses were equally as bizarre as the rest of him. One lens was red. The other was black.

He tilted his head to one side, as if pondering her. "Hello, Cora dear." His grin twisted into a smile that looked predatory and hungry. "So wonderful to see you again."

6

Cora took a step back.

It was him. She knew his face. She had seen him in her dream. But that was *impossible*. Dreams weren't real. But then, how was he here? Or rather, how had he been there, in her mind? She would have remembered seeing him in a crowd. He stood out. Literally and figuratively. There was no missing this man in a sea of people. None at all.

So, *how?*

She hadn't seen him in the darkness of that stupid labyrinth thing. She hadn't been able to see anything at all.

It didn't make any sense.

He took a small step toward her. "Cat got your tongue?" The way the words rolled out of him was sultry and dangerous in equal measures. He had a British accent, but it seemed weathered by time in America.

She took a large step back. She was shaking like a leaf, and when she tried to speak, nothing came out. Namely, because she didn't know what to say. She stammered uselessly for a moment. Finally, she managed to spit out a single word. "How?"

"Hm? How what?"

"How—you—" *You were in my dream. But you couldn't have been.* She could say it out loud, but she'd sound like a complete lunatic. And while this man looked to be a few cards short of a full deck, judging by the demented smile on his face, she wasn't about to commit to joining him just yet. "No."

He raised a dark, thin eyebrow. "Are you feeling quite well? Or do you generally speak in single-syllable words?" Everything about him seemed too smooth, even as everything about him also seemed too sharp. He took a slow step toward her. And she took a matching one back. She hit the edge of a long wooden bench and ended up sitting on it rather unexpectedly. She let out a startled noise. He moved closer until his legs brushed against hers and he towered over her.

"Leave me alone," she squeaked. She tried to sound strong. But he was terrifying. The light in the tent caught the lenses of his sunglasses, making them flash eerily in the dim environment. But in just the right moments, she could catch a glimpse of his eyes.

Ones that were black, red, and white. In all the wrong ways. They almost seemed to glow in the amber light.

"Why are you afraid? I thought I was tall and sexy." He smiled again, white teeth flashing like a shark. The comparison came back to her again.

Fresh panic flooded her. *I called him that in my dream, but he—no, this isn't—* "No—please—this can't be real. It can't—"

"Hm? I'm not? How troublesome." He poked himself in the chest a few times. "I feel quite real. Ah! I know what the problem is. You're referring to your dream, yes? Well, I hate to say, but we're a bit linked now, you see. I have a piece of

The Contortionist

you within me. It was quite delicious, too, if I may say so. I could go for a spot more, Cora, my little cupcake."

His rambling gave her a few seconds to process. "This is —this can't be happening. How is this possible?"

"I ate the little piece of your seity that you gave up yesterday. The Barker picks his marks, and you took the bait. You were my snack for the evening." The man gestured dismissively. "More or less."

"You *ate* a piece of my personality?" This wasn't okay. None of this was okay. "You're all fucking insane. I'm leaving." She went to stand, but he stepped in front of her, blocking her. She sat back down to keep from bumping into him. She'd already done that once; she wasn't interested in doing it twice.

"Guilty as charged! But it isn't insanity that I speak. You knew the cost. He told you. He tells everyone. It's your fault if *yooooou* didn't believe it." He leaned down closer, using his height to his advantage. It was clear he liked to do that. He also drew out his words in strange ways. "Do you believe him now?"

"Stop it."

"It's not *my* fault." He placed his palm to his chest. "I was just chosen to be the recipient. Each of us who lives here eats in turn. I wasn't the first to feed last night, nor was I the last. I just got a piece of you. And I fear it's made me hungry for more." He reached out to touch her.

She recoiled, leaning back on her hand. "Don't touch me. Leave me alone!" She knew people were staring. She barely registered the audience around them watching, probably wondering if this was part of the show. She was too distracted by the freak in the sharply cut red suit that was looming over her and grinning like the devil himself.

He smiled as if he were speaking to a child. "You came

here. I'm not stopping you from leaving, am I? I am merely saying hello. And you, my dear, look as though you've seen a ghost. I can't *imagine* why."

"Who are you...?"

"Who am I?" With a broad flourish, he took a step back and bowed, folding one arm in front of him and the other at his back. "I am Simon Waite. I am the Puppeteer." He snapped back up to vertical with alarming speed, making her jump. "I am *very* delighted to meet you, Cora." He snapped his fingers. "Oh! I must commend you on your comment about the pogo stick yesterday, by the by. I used to own one, you know, and I sat there and thought about it for quite a while before I realized how wonderfully visceral your suggestion really was when you insisted I go pursue relations with it. I'm impressed."

She didn't know how to respond to that. Luckily, she didn't have to try for long.

"Cora?" It was Emily. She was standing next to Simon. "You okay?"

"Hm? Oh. Hello." Simon took a graceful step back, giving Emily some room. "I think your friend here might not be feeling well," he responded to Emily with a gentle smile, stepping back again from the bench to allow Emily to step closer. "She seemed faint and had to sit down. I was worried she might hit her head, so I was watching over her."

I'm going insane. I'm absolutely going insane. This is not possible. Not at all. She was shivering again and pulled her coat tighter around herself. "I'm okay, Em." *No, I'm not. I'm really not. There's no explanation for this. None. I have to be making it up.* "Probably didn't eat enough today, and I didn't sleep well last night."

Simon's grin widened at her last comment. Emily didn't see it. But Cora knew it for what it was. He bowed again.

"Well, if you'll excuse me, I must start the show. I do hope you feel better, Cora dear. Perhaps go get a glass of water and take a breath of fresh air." He left then, strolling up the aisle, whistling loudly.

"This place is staffed by weirdos and creeps," Emily muttered as she watched Simon walk away. It was the understatement of the year.

Cora stood and checked her gear. Good. She didn't crack her camera when she fell. "He's right, though. I should probably go get some fresh air." *I can't stay in here with him. I can't.* He gave her the willies. He was absolutely terrifying.

And he had been inside her goddamn dreams.

No. That wasn't possible. But then...what had happened? If not the impossible...then what?

"Do you need me to come with you?" Emily put her hand on Cora's arm.

"No, it's fine. I'll be fine." *I can't explain this. To you, myself, or anybody else. I need to sit down, have some water, follow it with some vodka, and think it through.* She couldn't say that, though, so she just smiled gently at her friend and walked away.

There wasn't any understanding what was happening, but she had one way to find out. One person knew what the fuck was happening. Aaron the carnival Barker had told her to stay away from Simon...and now she knew what he had meant. And he was right.

I bet Aaron has answers. They might be bullshit answers, but they're something. I'll take anything at this point.

She struck out of the tent and headed back toward the entrance to find him. When she went to the ticket booth, he was gone.

"If you're looking for Aaron," one attendant said, "he's off by the Freaks, getting ready for the show." The woman smiled at her sweetly, but her eyes seemed empty. Like all the lights weren't fully on upstairs. Something about her seemed robotic and flat.

More weird people. More weird things. *Add it to the list.* "Thanks..." Cora turned and left, showing her ripped ticket to the weird clowns. They checked the date but let her through.

Walking through the Faire by herself gave her a chance to try to clear her head. The chill air was helping. It was still early spring, and as the sun went down, so did the temperature. But she couldn't stop poring over what had just happened.

And every time she thought about it, she began to panic.

And every time she panicked, she forced herself not to think about it.

And every time she forced herself not to think about it, she thought about it.

And around and around she went.

When she got to the tent for the Freakshow, people were looking at her with the kind of curiosity a person gets when they see someone having a breakdown. She must look as though she were about to throw up, panic, or pass out. She kinda was.

There was a man in my nightmare I didn't know.
Then he showed up.

Just outside the tent was a box, some three feet square. Standing on it was Aaron, in his blue and cream suit and his matching straw hat. He was talking to a larger woman who was covered in tattoos and had a beard that stretched down to her copious cleavage. Both beard and boobs were proudly on display. The two were chatting idly, and both went quiet as Cora walked up.

"Are you all right, Cora?" Aaron's brow furrowed in

The Contortionist

concern. As though he cared. He hopped down from the box and reached out to put a hand on her shoulder. She stepped away from him, shaking her head. They weren't friends. He put his hand down. "What's wrong?"

"How? How is this happening?" She felt like she was on the verge of a breakdown. "It's not possible. That freak shouldn't be real, but he—" She broke off and glanced to the woman, feeling her cheeks go warm. "I'm sorry."

"None taken, sweetheart." The bearded woman smiled. "We're all freaks here. I just wear mine on the outside."

Aaron sniffed and looked off. "You saw Simon, huh?"

"He was—" Cora paused and cringed. "I'm going to sound insane. But all of this is insane, and all of it's your fault."

"Whoa!" Aaron looked back at her and put his hands up. "I didn't do shit."

"You told me to go through that stupid dark path thing—"

"I said you *could*. I gave you the option. I told you exactly what was going to happen." He pointed a finger at her. "I warned you, and now you're mad that you didn't listen. You didn't believe a word I said, and thought it was all bullshit. That's not my fault."

"It *is* bullshit." She was shaking again. She fidgeted with the strap of her camera, trying to focus on something—anything—that wasn't the reality she was in. Tears welled in her eyes. "It has to be."

"Or what?"

Cora looked up at Aaron. "Huh?"

"It has to be bullshit, or what? What if it isn't?" His defensive anger faded. "Oh, poor thing. You look like you're about to snap. Bertha, baby, can she go in and take a sit?"

"Of course." Bertha gestured for Cora to follow her.

"Come with me, sweetheart. I'll get you a glass of water and something stronger to chase it with. If you had a run-in with the Puppeteer, you need it."

That was exactly what she needed. She nodded weakly and followed the tattooed woman. She didn't know them. She didn't trust them. But she didn't know what else to do. She followed Bertha into the tent, with Aaron following them. There was a narrow hallway inside with a large painted finger pointing to the left. Instead, Bertha lifted a flap of the fabric hallway and ushered her in to the right.

It looked like backstage. Boxes of props, cages containing a few random animals, and a few other people walking around. She noticed a man who was about two feet tall but who looked fully grown. Another man was covered in hair over every inch of his body. There was a woman with three boobs. She tried not to stare and instead looked down at her feet.

"It's fine, Cora." Bertha laughed. "Staring is expected. You're not going to throw things or call us names, are you? You don't think we're monsters, right?"

"Of course not." She looked back up at the woman, shocked she would think that. "Can't help how you were born."

Bertha smiled warmly and patted a hand on Cora's shoulder. The woman felt incredibly strong. "Then stare all you want. We're weird-looking. There's no helping it, and we've decided to use it to our advantage. It's our choice. It's how we make a living. Now, come on." She walked away, and Cora could do nothing but follow. Bertha led her farther backstage, until she got to something that looked like a dressing room. She gestured for Cora to sit on a bench by the wall.

She hadn't realized how shaky she really was until she

The Contortionist

sat. Her legs almost gave out the moment she started to bend them. She felt woozy. Aaron sat next to her but kept a respectful distance.

Bertha returned a moment later with two bottles—one of water, and another of gin. She handed Cora the bottle of water. It was glass, with one of those flip-top seals on the top. Weird. Maybe they were trying to be environmentally friendly and not use plastic.

"Thanks..." She flipped the top and took a sip. God, it tasted good. Underrated thing, water.

"Anytime." Bertha pulled over a chair across from them and sat with a grunt. "Barker, no hats inside." Bertha leaned forward and flicked the brim of his hat. Aaron took it off but grumbled about it quietly. "So," the bearded and tattooed woman began again, "what happened, sweetheart? Start from the beginning. Or, well, after Barker here talked you into going through the Dark Path."

"Last night I...had a dream. There was a man in it. Tall, with sky-blue eyes. He was painting a landscape. When I walked around to see what he was painting, his canvas was covered in blood. Then his eyes...changed. They were all wrong." She swallowed thickly, tasted bile, and took another gulp of the water.

"Let me guess. Black where there should be white, white where there should be black, and red instead of blue?" Aaron sighed heavily, as if he already knew the answer. "I knew this was going to mean trouble. When he went after her in the Dark Path, I knew this was going to happen."

Bertha stroked her hand over her beard thoughtfully. "You don't think he's going after her, do you?"

"He hasn't done that in years. He's not allowed to, what with Hernandez and all." Aaron shook his head. "But he might try anyway." He looked over at her, concerned. "What has he said to you?"

"Creepy shit." Cora took another swig of the water.

Bertha snorted. "That doesn't narrow it down. Not even a little."

Cora smiled. She liked the big woman. She wasn't sure why, or if she should, but something about her seemed genuine, if nothing else. "He..." She gritted her teeth and shook her head. "This is nonsense."

"Nothing is nonsense. Nothing you can say is going to make us think you're crazy." Aaron leaned in toward her a little. "Trust me. What has he said to you?"

"He asked me what I would be willing to give in order to make my pain go away." She paused. "I have a chronic—"

Aaron swore. Loudly and suddenly. The noise made her jump. He looked at her sheepishly. "Sorry." He stood from the bench and ran a hand over his heavily gelled, slicked-back hair. "I need to go. I need to go warn Ringmaster. Cora. Stay away from Simon. Whatever you do."

Before she could respond, Aaron was gone. He had half-run out of the room.

Bertha put her hand on Cora's, pulling her attention back to her. "Simon is dangerous. Very dangerous."

"I wasn't trying to go near him. I didn't know..." Cora chewed on her lower lip. "What's happening?"

"You won't believe me if I tell you. My recommendation is...enjoy the Faire. Ride the rides, watch the shows, eat the food. But stay away from Simon."

"But—I don't care if I won't believe you—I probably won't. But I want to know what you think is going on. How... how was he in my dream?"

Bertha sighed and stroked her hand over her beard again. "All right. He has a piece of you. The Faire took some

The Contortionist

of you away, and it grew a little stronger when it did. It then passed what was left to Simon, to help keep him going. Because of that, you're linked. He's using that to try to manipulate you. Because he wants the rest of you."

Cora stared at her blankly.

Yup. She barely understood any of that, let alone believe it. She shook her head dumbly. "Sorry. I don't...I don't follow."

"Here's the short of it, sweetheart." Taking the mostly empty bottle of water back from Cora, she dumped the remainder out on the packed dirt of the tent. "Simon is a dangerous, murderous piece of shit." Bertha unscrewed the cap off the bottle of gin and started to pour gin into the smaller bottle. "No matter how tempting his offer is, don't listen to a single thing that comes out of his mouth. Stay away from him like your life depends on it. Because it does." When the smaller bottle was a quarter full of gin, she handed it back to Cora, then promptly took a heavy swig from the bigger one.

Cora sipped the gin. It was good. She didn't recognize the brand. The label was designed to look old and vintage and was probably from some hipster distillery. "I'll do what I can. I don't think I want to go anywhere near him, so don't worry about it."

"Good. He's trash. And he's very good at tricking people into giving him what he wants."

Cora nodded weakly. She sipped the gin again. It was going to help her feel better, one way or the other. "Thank you. I should go find my friends before they get too worried."

"That's for the best." Bertha smiled and stood, putting her chair off to the side. "If you ever need anything, or need somewhere to hide, come right on back to Bertha, you hear?"

They were all talking as though she lived in the park. "I don't know if I'm going to come back to the Faire after tonight, but thank you anyway."

There was an odd, knowing, and sad smile on Bertha's bearded face. "I hope you're right." She showed Cora out of the tent and placed a heavy hand on her shoulder before she walked away. "I didn't believe either, when I came here."

"I really wish you could comprehend how little sense any of this makes." Cora sipped the gin. "But the booze is appreciated."

"Well, if I can't give you the answers you want to hear, I can at least give you some hard alcohol." Bertha laughed and walked back into her tent. "Have a good night, Cora. I'll see you soon."

Nope. You won't. Because I'm gonna put this place in my rear-view mirror and never come back. I might even start taking a different road to work. "Yeah. You, too." She walked away and chewed her lip. She made it back to the Puppeteer's tent, just in time to watch people streaming out of it. The show was over. And there, by the entrance, was Simon. He was thanking people and accepting what looked like gushing praise from everyone who came out.

Many of the patrons looked wide-eyed and amazed, as though they were people walking out of a movie theatre for the first time in their lives without ever having known one existed. People were talking to each other excitedly about what they had seen. Whatever it was.

It was a puppet show. She couldn't imagine it was that spectacular. But everybody else seemed to disagree.

She kept her distance, some fifty feet away.

But it didn't stop Simon from finding her in the crowd.

The Contortionist

He smiled at her and, raising his hand, wiggled his fingers at her in a greeting. She blenched and looked away briefly. When she managed to turn back, he wasn't focused on her anymore.

He was focused on Jane. He had Lisa's daughter scooped up in his arms, and she was hugging him around the neck. Whatever the girl was saying, Cora couldn't make out from where she was. But by the pitch, it was excited and thrilled. Simon was laughing.

Cora fought the urge to rush over to him and snatch the girl out of his arms. The instinct to protect the child from the man who was clearly a psychopath on a good day and—if Aaron and Bertha were to be believed, which was a stretch—a murderer on a bad one.

You're falling for their plot. This is just some interactive theatre nonsense. They've got you hooked into their stupid story. She made it two steps before she stopped herself. *Lisa and Robert are right there. It's fine.*

This is all just a stupid game. You must have seen him in the darkness well enough to make out his face, and you didn't realize it. That's why you dreamed of him.

Then...how did he know I called him sexy?

Hot and cold, fiction and reality, fear and anger, they warred in equal parts like zeros and ones. Half of her wanted to believe the nonsense. Half of her knew it was all a lie. Both parts of her wanted to go home.

She saw Trent walking away from the rest of the group, and Cora rushed up to meet him. "Trent!"

"There you are! Em said you weren't feeling good. Are you okay?" Trent put his hands on her shoulders. "You look fine. And you smell like alcohol." He cracked a grin. "If you wanted to go get drunk and skip the puppet show, why didn't you say something? I would've joined you." He stole the glass bottle from her hand and sniffed it. "Woof." He took a sip and coughed. "You always liked the strong shit. Is that straight gin?"

"I—there's some weird shit going on. I don't know how to explain. I think I need to leave."

"That's fine. I'm surprised you've been up and walking around as much as you have been, what with your Raggedy Ann joints and all. You must be a wreck." Trent took another sip of the gin, wheezed, and handed it back to her. "I prefer margaritas."

"I—"

Trent wasn't listening. "I'm gonna go meet Ludwig. He's such a teddy bear. Maybe tomorrow I can introduce you two." He pulled out his phone, turned on the front-facing camera, and started fixing his hair. Because it was apparently the wrong kind of messy. Cora never understood and had stopped trying.

"Trent, I think this place is dangerous."

"M'kay." Trent was seriously not listening. There wouldn't be any getting through to him. "I'll talk to you tomorrow, okay?" He leaned forward and kissed her on the forehead. "I have a date, after all. Ta!"

Cora reached out to grab his arm and shake him and scream *I think this Faire is murdering people,* but stopped. She had no proof. What, because she had some weird-ass dream with some weird-ass guy in it? And some bizarre conversations with a sideshow freak and the carnival Barker?

None of this made sense.

She found Emily, Lisa, and Robert when they finally were far enough away from the tent that she felt comfortable going up to them. Numbly, she told them all she didn't feel well, and that her pain was flaring up. It wasn't true—

The Contortionist

not really—but it was so common that nobody questioned it.

She hugged Jane and Tom and waved goodbye to them. As she walked past the entrance of the tent, she saw Simon standing there, leaning against the wood frame of the painted façade, watching her with a faint smile.

He blew her a kiss.

Stomach churning, she rushed to her car and went home. Somewhere she felt safe. Somewhere she felt like he couldn't find her. Too bad it wasn't quite true.

As she crawled into bed, sleep found her.

And so did Simon.

7

It was such a strange thing. Nightmares were supposed to be set against terrifying backdrops. Spooky castles, hellscapes, graveyards, or, more recently appropriate, a freaky circus. Monsters should appear in places suited to them.

Not inside her condo.

It was a mundane, if incredibly vivid and lucid, dream. Something so utterly boring, she didn't quite understand why her mind had summoned it. Instead of running away from monsters, or pulling from her stress from the day, it was—at least on the surface—utterly benign.

She was standing in the kitchen of her condo, cooking pasta sauce. Just standing and stirring the red liquid, watching it simmer. Steam curled up from the ingredients in delicate curls only to vanish quickly in the warm air.

Everything seemed fine.

She should have known better.

Not all monsters needed a scary backdrop to be terrifying. In fact, some were more frightening without one.

A shadow crept up the wall next to her. She looked up in

The Contortionist

confusion, her brow furrowed, and instantly recoiled in fear as though a giant spider had appeared on cabinet doors. It wasn't a spider. It was worse.

The shadow had a face. Misshapen and mismatched eyes that were spirals of light cut through the darkness of whatever cast it. And a large, toothy, fiendish grin that would have made the Cheshire Cat ask him to tone it down. She recognized him—she had seen something like this before. It took her a second in the fuzziness of the dream to remember.

The Soothsayer's tarot card. The one with the Puppeteer on it.

The shadow was also *alive*. He grinned wider, opening its jaws, and silently cackled. Long, dangerously clawed, shadowy hands reached for her, like they were projected along the surface of the cabinets.

She staggered backward, bumping into her kitchen island, and gaped at the silently laughing thing. He waved at her. He was only vaguely recognizable as the outline of a human.

"Nice place."

She screamed. Whirling, she realized that in order to see who had spoken, she had to expose her back to the shadow. She quickly retreated to somewhere she could see both, running around to the end of the island. She grabbed a knife from the block on the way and held it aloft, pressing her back to her kitchen wall.

Somebody laughed.

Simon. The Puppeteer. He was standing in the middle of her living room, looking freakishly out of place in his bright cardinal suit with black pinstripes and bizarre mismatched sunglasses.

"Really? A knife? For me? Aw, I'm touched." He smiled,

as if it were the most adorable thing in the world to him. As if she were a child who came up to him with a drawing that was ostensibly trash, but that was to be highly valued because of her innocence. "One, we're dreaming. Two, it wouldn't work." He pulled in a breath and, on the exhale, let all his words out in a fast rush, everything streaming together. "Trust-me-better-people-than-you-have-given-it-a-go." His grin twisted into that toothy, overly hungry smile that reeked of insanity and malice. He was a lunatic. And he was in her dreams. Again.

"Go away. Leave me alone!"

"No-*pe.*" He let out the last half of the word as an audible pop. And with that...he made himself at home. He began to stroll around her living room. He picked up her lamp and turned it over thoughtfully, flicking the switch on and off a few times. "Huh. What's that?"

"A—a lamp..." Weren't monsters supposed to be chasing her around? He wasn't torturing her. He didn't even walk up to her. He was messing with her stuff.

"I know *that.*" He shot her a glare over the top of his glasses. She could see his bizarre and unsettling colored eyes over the top silver rim. "I'm not stupid. I mean the bulb. It doesn't have a filament."

"It...it's an LED bulb." She still kept the knife pointed at him, even if she was extremely confused.

"What's that?"

"I think—I think it stands for light-emitting...diode? It's electronic!" She glanced at the shadow, who was still looming up against the wall near her, grinning. Not doing anything terrible, at least. Just blinking occasionally. Watching her.

Shadows shouldn't blink.

The Contortionist

Shadows should also be *cast* by something. Not just... free-range.

"Well, of course, it is." He wiggled the wire. "What else would it be?" He put the lamp back down and continued his exploration of the apartment. "Are you a little slow in the head, Cora dear?"

"Get out of my home! Or my dream. Or both. Or whatever the *fuck* is going on." She tried to sound firm. But it was hard to do anything of the sort when she was pressed against the wall and brandishing a knife with both shaking hands.

"Mmh, we went through this." He picked up her TV remote and, turning it over a few times, began pushing the little rubber buttons. When the electronic clicked to life and lit up, he cackled in joy. "Oh! Glorious!"

"What the hell are you doing?"

"Exploring. Learning. You could say I don't get out much." He jammed a few more buttons, and after a long moment of staring, seemed to master what the little symbols meant and turned the TV back off. He put the remote down and kept rifling through her things. Charge cables, her headphones, anything that resembled technology seemed to attract him like a moth to a flame. He even picked up her TV, snickered, and muttered something about them not weighing nearly as much as they used to before setting it back down.

"Who are you?"

"We've been through this. Simon, the Puppeteer." He glanced over at her with an eyebrow raised. "Are you challenged, Ms. Glass? I'm not judging. I'd simply like to know so I can show extra patience with you."

"I'm not stupid! Don't come in here, invading my—whatever this is—and insult me!"

The shadow on the wall near her silently laughed. He reached out for her, the pointed talons of his hand sliding against the surfaces and onto the wall near her. She ducked away from him, moving away from the wall to keep the shadow from reaching her.

"Get away from me!" She dropped one hand from the handle of the knife to steady herself on a piece of furniture, pointing the blade at the shadow with the other.

"Oh, don't mind him. He's harmless," Simon said from very close to her.

She jolted. She whirled and slashed at him with the knife.

Or tried, anyway.

Her hand froze in midair.

Something had caught it, but she had no idea what. At first, it looked like there wasn't anything there. But now and then, light seemed to catch a thread that ran from somewhere in space to her wrist. It shone like silver, like sunlight on a spiderweb. Sometimes there, sometimes not. A dozen or more, running at bizarre and nonsensical angles, had her wrist and hand caught firmly in its grasp.

Simon was standing there, only a foot away, smiling like the cat who ate the canary. His left hand hovered in space near hers, his fingers crooked at odd angles. Like he was holding a puppet that was not there.

No, he was holding a puppet.

He was holding *her*.

"Let go of the knife, Cora dear." He had the patient tone of a teacher. Or someone trying to coax a jumper off a bridge. Calm and soothing. "There's no reason to frighten yourself any further."

"This is just a dream...this isn't real."

"Who are you trying to convince, you or me?" He took a

The Contortionist

step toward her, halving the distance between them. He was so close now, nearly touching her hand. He carefully took the knife from her fingers with his free hand. She let him. She was shaking too hard to fight him. "Good girl. Now...yes, this is a dream. But I'm afraid to tell you that this particular gift of mine, my strings, are *very* real. Perhaps when you come to see me tonight, I will show you." He grinned. "What fun that will be!"

"I'm not going anywhere near you. There's no way in *fuck* I'm setting foot in that carnival ever again."

His expression fell. Deflated like a popped balloon. He looked almost comically disappointed. It was one of the few times she'd seen him without a smile of some kind. "What? Why?"

"You!"

He glanced over his shoulder as if she were accusing someone who wasn't there. When he looked back to her, he pointed at his chest. "Me?"

"Yes, you." Christ, he was a lunatic.

"What on Earth did I do to you?"

"This, for starters." She yanked on her wrist, and nothing happened. The strings, whatever they were, might as well have been aircraft cable. She couldn't budge them and, because of how tiny they were, only succeeded in digging the threads into her skin. It hurt. She hissed in pain.

"Ah, I wouldn't recommend that. You'll rip your own arm off before you manage to break my strings."

"Let me go."

"M'kay." He flicked his fingers, and she felt the threads release. She shook her wrist and took a step away from him, rubbing her hand with her free one. "I would like to remind you—" He pointed the knife at her, waggling it in the air like a pencil as he talked. As she took another staggering step back from him, he looked down at the blade. "Hm. Yes. Sorry." He walked over to the kitchen block and slipped the knife into the empty slot. When his back was turned to her, she dashed to put the coffee table between them.

When he turned back to where she had been, he opened his mouth to keep talking. He paused upon seeing her missing then quickly found her again. He smiled. "Jumpy thing, aren't we?"

"Go the fuck away!"

"I want to know what you think I've done to you that's so terrible." Simon strolled into her kitchen as he talked. "If anything, the gremlin at the front gate is to blame for all this, not me." He opened the fridge and began poking around. Picking up each container of everything and reading the labels. "Barker talked you into going through the Dark Path. I was merely the lucky winner to whom the Faire gifted your seity. Why am I to be blamed for that?"

"The Faire doesn't eat people."

"Oh, yes." He grinned at her, sadistic and cruel. His voice dropped to a low, husky sound that sent a shiver up her spine. "It does. It *very much does.*"

"None of this is happening. None of this is real." She was shaking, and she wanted to sit down. She felt like her legs were going to give out. But she didn't dare put herself in a position where she couldn't run. Even if the freak in her kitchen had gone back to rifling through her apartment. His new target was her fridge.

His shadow was still up on the wall near her, smiling. The ends of his cartoonish, drawn-on smile were curled into tight spirals that would be comical if they weren't just a bit too pointy.

"Poor thing. Well. Let me explain it to you slowly, hum?" He pulled out a container of limeade, and after reading the

The Contortionist

label, began rooting through her cabinets for something. A glass, she assumed.

"I just want you to leave me alone. Please."

"Afraid not. Besides," he smiled at her slyly, "I thought you found me tall and sexy." He located the glassware and poured out a glass of limeade. He put the bottle back in the fridge. Walking up to her, he offered her the glass. "Drink something and sit down. You look as if you might be sick. And in a dream, that is quite a trick, I promise you."

A monster. A literal, likely murderous *monster* with a freaky, disembodied shadow...was offering her a glass of juice. With a trembling hand, she took it, not knowing what else to do. She had expected him to tear her to pieces. Not... be nice to her.

He gestured to her sofa. "Sit."

Glancing nervously at him, then to his shadow, she shook her head.

He sighed. "He won't hurt you. He can't. He can't even *touch* you, let alone harm you. Not even here."

"What is he?"

"My shadow, of course."

"I know that, but..."

"Why is he like that?" He glanced over at the creature on the wall, whose grin split like a jack o' lantern. It was as though the shadow liked being talked about. "It's complicated. Short version, he is my subconscious." The shadow stuck his tongue out at Simon. The Puppeteer rolled his eyes. "Now, sit, please. We have a lot to discuss, and you should calm down before we begin." He gestured at her sofa again.

This was all madness. Utter madness. But this didn't feel like a dream—it felt *real*. The glass in her hands was cold. She could smell the lime. Nothing felt fuzzy or strange. She slowly sat on the sofa and wedged herself into the far corner, trying to make herself as small as possible.

Simon smiled at his victory. "Good. Now. Take a breath." He reached down and patted her knee. She jolted at the contact, but it didn't seem to register with him. He walked away from her, clearly too curious about her home to give up prowling around. He returned to the kitchen and flicked off the stove that was still-simmering pasta sauce.

He dipped his finger into the sauce and tasted it, let out a thoughtful noise, and began digging through her spice rack by the stove to find something. "Not bad. Needs a little oregano. But that isn't bad at all."

"I don't like this dream."

He laughed hard as he put a few dashes of the seasoning into the mix and began stirring it. "Dream or not, seems a shame to mess this up. Do you like to cook?"

"Yeah…"

"Have you any skill at it?"

"I think so?" What the fuck was happening? Seriously? Cora sipped the limeade and tried to calm down. But everything was so confusing, so unexpected, she didn't know what to do.

"Good. I haven't had anyone who can cook in a long time." He finished tinkering with her sauce and discovered her microwave a moment later. He opened the door with the button and jumped in surprise as the door ejected toward him. "Oh. Hah. Yes. Firebreather has one of these, but it's much older and…not nearly so fancy." He poked at the buttons, making it loudly beep a few times. He cackled in amusement and poked a few more, resetting the clock in the process.

"What's wrong with you?"

He grinned at her toothily again. "That, my dear, is a

The Contortionist

very large question with a very lengthy answer, best left for a day where you are not on the verge of weeping in terror." He sniffed. "But the heart of the question I think you're asking is in regard to my fascination with all your shiny toys."

No, I'm asking why you're a fucking lunatic, but that's a good start, I guess. "Sure." Best not to provoke the crazy ones. Especially the crazy ones who had weird super-powers that could probably rip her to pieces and a disembodied shadow that was still *staring at her.*

"I can't leave the Faire. None of us can. This is as close as I've been to 'out' in a very, very long time." He was now examining one of her pieces of artwork on the wall. It was a photo she had taken of a lighthouse on the coast five or six years ago. It was one of her favorites, and it had won a few awards. He tilted his head thoughtfully. "I saw your camera. Is this one of yours?"

"Yes."

"It's beautiful." He reached out and laid his fingers on the glass, tracing the light and dark. "Lovely use of contrast and form."

She paused. He was complimenting her. "Thanks…"

"You take photographs for a living. Or at least…you used to." He looked to her, his expression sympathetic. "Until your illness took that away from you. Tragic, to have the world denied this beauty because of your bad luck. Worse, to add the pain of losing your passion to the pain of your body."

She cringed and looked away, taking her eyes off him and the monstrous shadow for a moment. His comment was too on point. It stabbed at her. She coped with her issues by not facing them, most days. Being reminded of it like that was too much. Especially from him. She looked down into her limeade and didn't know how to answer.

"You are in such pain, such constant agony. Look at you. You're strong to not fall apart. You're struggling to keep yourself together—literally—aren't you? What is it that you suffer from?"

"Ehlers-Danlos Syndrome." She felt her jaw tick, and she glanced away from Simon for a moment. The sunglasses were eerie. Everything about him was eerie. It was like he wasn't quite possible. This was a dream, after all. But she knew that wasn't a real excuse. "It means my tendons and ligaments are too loose. My joints are hypermobile. It's not as fun as it sounds. At least I don't have the version where my organs fall out of place or rip open. I can walk. Some people with my disease can't."

"Fascinating…I've never heard the name of it before. Poor, pretty thing like you. You shouldn't be this way. I can make it so you never feel pain again."

"What's happening to me?"

"We've been through this." His voice was right there near her, and she jerked up. She nearly spilled her drink, and would have, if he hadn't caught it. He sat on her coffee table across from her and handed the drink back to her. "The Faire took a piece of you. This much you know."

"It's a lie."

"It isn't. You can keep hoping it is—but everything you have seen, and felt, and *know*—" He reached out and poked her in the chest between her collarbones. She shrank away from him. "Tells you otherwise."

She swallowed thickly. She didn't like how close he was. His knees were on either side of her right leg, toothed together with hers. If she wanted to run, he'd catch her easily. But she was already trapped, wasn't she? Those strings of his…there was no telling what they were capable of, but she figured she had only seen the beginning of it.

The Contortionist

For the moment, he seemed content not to hurt her. She sipped the limeade to try to settle her stomach and her pounding heart. He took the glass on the way down and sipped it himself, humming. "That's good. Better than lemonade, I dare say." He handed it back to her. "Now. Can I begin? Or are you going to have a panic attack?"

"Begin...what?"

"Convincing you."

"Of what?"

He grinned. Or maybe he never stopped. She wasn't quite sure. Leaning forward to rest his arms on his knees, he hovered close to her. She recoiled, suddenly worried he was going to kiss her.

His words felt like they came from the pits of Hell, even if she knew he meant them to sound like a trumpet of the Heavens.

"That I am the end to all your problems."

8

"But...why?"

Simon blinked in confusion. He sat back a little bit and pondered her. "What do you mean?"

"Why me?"

"Ah. Yes. Well, you see, I get something out of this, too, of course." He shrugged. "Can't get something for nothing, after all. As I said, the Faire sustains itself on taking from those who enter it as you did—foolishly not heeding Barker's warning. But it isn't in the content that it survives—it's in the act of the taking. Like a fisherman who throws his catches back into the sea might still find satisfaction in the deed."

She stared blankly at him. He probably thought that meant she was listening to him. She was. It just didn't make any damn sense.

"But the Faire doesn't toss the fish back to where it came. It gives the prey to us." He placed his palm on his chest. "Its chosen children. Myself, Barker, Rigger, Bearded Lady, Soothsayer. The others who you've met. There are twenty-one of us in all." He sniffed dismissively, his expression

The Contortionist

flashing dark for a moment. "Twenty who matter." He smiled, the instant of rage vanishing like it had never been there.

The man rocketed from zero to sixty and back again like a hummingbird. It made him dangerous. It meant that at any moment he could just snap for no reason. She wished she could vanish into the cushions of the sofa.

He was waiting for her to say something.

"Okay?"

He arched an eyebrow. "Are you following me?"

"I understand what you're saying. But it doesn't mean I believe you."

He sighed. "Skeptics. So frustrating sometimes." Shrugging, he continued. "No matter. Now, listen to me, Cora. Each of us at the Faire have particular talents. I, as you have seen, command strings to manipulate the world to do my bidding. But that is not all. I, like some of the others, can control other aspects of the world as well. Such as you, and your terrible ailment. I wish to take it from you."

"Take it…like you took my favorite color?"

"In a manner of speaking." He smiled. "It's all very complicated."

"What's the catch?"

He leaned in toward her again. He gently picked her hand up from where it rested on her lap and laced his fingers into hers. She froze and was unable to do anything but watch as he pulled her hand toward his face and placed a gentle kiss to the backs of her knuckles. "What would you give to make the pain stop? What would you trade…to never have to wake up in agony ever again?"

She shivered. Partially at the dark purr of his words, but mostly due to his touch. It was too sensual. Too personal. She pulled her hand from his and grasped her nearly empty glass with both hands. "I'm not going to fuck you, if that's what you're after."

He leaned back and dramatically snapped his fingers in disappointment. "Fie! My plan is foiled once again." He shook his fist in the air. "Curse you, and your modern ways, for seeing so easily through my dastardly ploy!" The melodrama increased. "How will I succeed in my nefarious plot when you can decipher me so easily?" He plastered the back of his hand to his forehead and fell back on her coffee table, draping over it like the heroine of some silent movie. "Woe! Woe is me."

She couldn't help but laugh. It was too ridiculous not to. His overacting was both bizarre and...disarming. She wouldn't go so far as to call it charming—but she wasn't gripping her glass like she wanted to smash it in her hands anymore. "So, that's not what this is about?"

"No." He lifted his head and shot her a smirk. "I wouldn't say no if you offered, mind you."

She glared.

"That is a negatory reply, I take it. Drat." He huffed back up to sitting. "Come see me in my tent when you want to discuss the terms of our arrangement. We can negotiate, but I will not do it here in your dreams."

"I don't want to go back into the Faire. I'm not going to go anywhere near you."

"Meh. We'll see." He reached out, and she froze as he stroked a hand over her hair. He caught one of her long, wavy strands and curled it around his finger, releasing it to let it dangle down along her cheek. "Just remember when you wake up...and find yourself contorted in suffering from what ails you—that I am not lying, cupcake. I can take it all away. Come see me, and we'll talk."

The Contortionist

She raised an eyebrow. "Just talk?" *No. I'm not considering this. I'm not!*

His ever-present grin widened, and he leaned forward. Suddenly, he was caging her against the back of the sofa. His knee was on the cushion between her legs, and his hands were on either side of her as he moved, lithe as a panther, and trapped her.

He placed one hand to her cheek, and she jolted at the touch. He shushed her quietly and leaned in just a few more inches. He smelled faintly like an antique shop and cologne. A little bit like that pleasant and warm smell a place gets when it's filled with old things. And *shit,* he was tall. She thought it was just a trick of his pinstripe suit and the way it was tailored to show off his trim frame. No. He really was easily three-quarters of a foot taller than she was.

She felt like a fly caught in a spider's web.

His voice was a low hum as he talked. Smooth and *sultry.* God help her, but no one had ever talked to her like that before. Like nothing else in the world existed for the span of this moment—just the two of them. "Just think of it...waking up in the morning and not feeling the pain. Not feeling so tired from the way it breaks you down. I see it in your eyes—the weariness. Every day greeting you with nothing but the promise of more *suffering.* What would you give to make it all go away? What would you sacrifice to never feel that way again?"

To never wake up with her shoulder or elbows out of place? To not feel her muscles screaming in her back as they tried to hold everything together? To not always feel so *tired* all the fucking time?

What would she give away to make it all stop?

The answer scared her.

Everything.

She pressed back against the cushions as hard as she could, trying to put as much space between them as possible. She tilted her head to the side as he leaned his in closer to her. He grazed his lips against her ear. He smelled like the past, and it was calling to her.

The glass of limeade fell to the carpet, quickly abandoned as she pressed her hands to his chest and pushed. But he wouldn't budge. She might as well have been shoving on a wall. "Stop—"

"Shh…" His breath was warm against her, and she felt goosebumps explode over her as he whispered. "Come to me, Cora dear. I can make all your troubles melt away."

He pressed a kiss to her cheek, soft and slow, and her dream shattered.

―――

SHE WOKE up just as Simon had predicted. Her shoulder was out of place. She whined in pain and pushed herself out of bed. It was easier said than done. Going up to the doorjamb, she placed her shoulder against the ridge and pressed until she felt it *crunch-slide* back into place.

She winced. It had gone numb, and now it was all pins and needles, and she hated that sensation. But leaving it out wasn't going to be workable either. She just shook it out and tried to regain the feeling in her fingers. It would ache later.

"I can make all your troubles melt away." The psychopath in her dreams said he could fix it. But how? And more importantly…at what cost?

No. It was just a stupid dream. A stupid, very creative dream. Her fingers were tingly, and she shook her hand to try to get it to stop. She needed a shower. She needed some coffee. She needed to think.

The Contortionist

She sat at her table and drank her coffee, thumbing through her phone. She hit Google and started trying to dig up anything she could on Harrow Faire. Anything that might reveal the trick or the scam they had going. The place had to have a reputation—anything at all.

All she got were historical pages and old photos. The Faire had first opened officially in the middle of the nineteenth century, but it opened in a field that had unofficially hosted carnivals and celebrations for a long time before that. No one was quite sure what year it really opened.

But no mentions of missing people. No mentions of murder, or the Faire being plagued with violence. Nothing about missing *seity* or any creepiness. And very few references to Mr. Harrow, the Faire's creator. There were no photos of him, and only vague references to the man who was the mastermind behind the whole creation and its rides that had been groundbreaking for their day.

In fact, there weren't any pictures of any of the Faire's employees. Shots with people in them, but only patrons. Weird.

Clicking through to another page, she wound up on a library's website. They had newspaper articles that were catalogued on microfiche but hadn't been scanned in yet. That wasn't shocking. It wasn't like she lived in a rip-roaring metropolis on the cutting edge of technology.

Sighing, she ran her hand over her face. Going back to her phone, she flicked over to email and wrote to her boss telling him that she would be out sick today. It was too early to call. Besides, Gary always checked his email. She rarely called out, and the man knew she had a chronic illness, so it was a viable excuse.

She hated doing it. But she needed to know more about what was happening. She needed to pull back the curtain and find out that the Great and Terrible Oz was just some doddering old asshole yanking on levers.

The library opened at nine. It was at Laconia, which was a few towns over. It was only eight, but she'd find a coffee shop and stop for a second cup on the way there. Picking up her camera, she slung it over her shoulder. Almost forgetting to feed her fish, she said good morning to them, apologized for her near neglect—not that they cared—and headed out.

The drive took her past the Faire. She slowed down as she did, and half expected it to be abandoned again. But there it was. The gate to the parking lot was closed, advertising that it was open for business at eleven. She kept driving. There had to be answers. Rumors of murder. Anything.

There had to be some explanation of what was going on. *The Faire can't be eating people. Simon wasn't really in my dreams twice.* But she had no explanation for how he was in her dreams the first time, let alone the second. And his comment in his tent yesterday had proven that he remembered it. *That's what I get for calling someone sexy. See, Cora? Don't flirt with people. It nearly gets you maimed.*

She laughed sadly. *That really shouldn't be true, but it is.*

And that didn't count the fact that she had felt something terrible happen to her when she walked through the Dark Path.

"Okay, cool," she said to herself as she drove, tapping her fingers on the steering wheel. Her music was playing loudly, but it didn't bother her. "Okay, let's play a game. Let's say it's real. Let's say that it's not a trick, and everything they're saying isn't a lie. What then?"

It means that place really did take a piece of my personality for a snack and gave it to Simon. And now, he...is offering to help me, for a price. And if magic is real—if that Faire is alive—then there's no telling what that fee is.

"This is stupid." She sighed. The rest of the trip to the library went exactly the same way. Her thoughts kept going around in circles between *this is a lie* and *it can't be a lie*.

Around and around she went.

She had proof that the supernatural was real. But was it enough? Or was she just making excuses? Or losing her mind?

Walking into the library, she couldn't help a small smile. She loved big, old places like this. They were just more pleasant than more modern places. They made her want to choose some well-loved piece of fiction with its dogeared corners, find a corner somewhere, and lose herself in another world. Places like this felt dignified. They smelled a little like dust. Like antiques. *Like Simon.*

She shivered at the memory of the dream. Of how he had felt when he had kissed her cheek. She rubbed the spot by her ear reflexively. If her dream had been a vision, then he was a lunatic. If her dream had been her mind making things up, she needed therapy because somehow, someway, she still found him alluring. She was probably going to need therapy either way.

She headed to the front desk, got directions to the microfiche room, and set to work.

The nice old lady who was in charge of the microfiche catalogue was extremely helpful. She looked like the kind of woman who probably crocheted potholders for people and made sure that the frog she found in her back yard had enough shade and water. Cora instantly liked her.

"It's so lovely to see a girl your age interested in local history," she said as she dug through the sheets.

"I just think it's interesting that so little is known about

Harrow Faire. With it reopening and all, I realized I never thought about it." Cora smiled.

"Oh? It's reopened?" The woman blinked. "That's exciting, though! Maybe we'll see a bit more of a summer crowd now. I hadn't heard anything about it."

"Neither did I. I just drove by it the other morning, and there it was, all fixed up." *As if by magic.* She opted not to say that part. "I've been twice now."

"Is it fun?" The woman smiled. "Oh, I haven't been to a fair in so many years. Maybe I'll go."

Cora felt her smile turn nervous, and she tried to keep from acting weird. She forced herself to sound as normal as possible. "It was great. Just, if they ask you to go through 'the Dark Path,' don't. That part, I hated."

"Is it like a haunted house?" The woman blanched. "I hate spooky things."

"Yeah. Exactly."

"Warning heard and appreciated. Ah! Here we go." The woman pulled out the folder from the back wall and turned to hand it to her. "Here are the newspaper articles from November 1st, 1934 like you asked. I'll keep looking around for anything else that mentions Mr. Harrow."

"Do you know what his first name was?" Cora asked as she headed to one of the microfiche machines. She hadn't used one of them in forever, since playing in old libraries with her dad as a kid, but they were pretty simple to figure out. She also knew almost nothing about Mr. Harrow, either.

"It was something odd. L-something, I believe," the woman replied thoughtfully. "Something biblical. I forget. I'll see if I can look up any other records we have on him."

"Thanks."

"Anytime." The woman smiled. "It's what I'm here for."

Cora smiled back and went to work, scanning through

newspaper articles. There were about a hundred on the slide, so it was hard to find at first. But when she finally got the hang of how they were arranged, she found it.

Harrow Faire Reopens: The Mysterious Grand Revival!

After its mysterious closure in 1910, the Faire reopened on Monday to great fanfare. The tower that had been neglected for twenty-four years illuminated the night sky to the delight of befuddled and entertained crowds.

When asked for an interview, Mr. Harrow politely declined, but sent this message instead—

Come one, come all, to Harrow Faire,
  To greet your sweetest nightmare.
  Rejoin your dreams and memories,
  Of carnivals and reveries.
  Seek the truth in mirrored lanes,
  That show you all the hidden planes.
  Enjoy the sights, see what we've made,
  Let all life's sorrows wilt and fade.
  For like all things, we'll call away,
  To all the gloom and shaded gray.
  Join us now, my friends, be brave—
  Laugh now. Laugh long.
  Soon comes the grave.

Cora had to stop. She rolled her chair back and rubbed her arm. Goosebumps had rushed over her. She took a sip of her hot coffee and hit print. She heard the machine by the wall whir to life. She'd finish the rest of the article later.

Holy shit.

She took a breath and let it out slowly.

Mr. Harrow was a piece of work. A morbid, terrifying piece of work. Great. Awesome. Add it to the list. She got up from the chair after a moment to fetch the printout. It came with a picture of the ticket booth. One entrance to the right…and the Dark Path to her left. Part of her expected to find Aaron in the photo. She was glad to find the booth empty of people. She didn't know what she'd do if she found a picture of Aaron staring at her from 1934.

She pulled out her camera and flicked it on. She hadn't gone through her photos from the day before. She had been a little too distracted to review them. The booth in the newspaper photo looked identical to the one she remembered.

She flicked to the first photo she had taken last night.

If she hadn't been wearing her camera on a strap, she would have dropped it.

The photo on her camera was of the ticket booth, all right. But not the one she had seen last night, or the night before. And not the one in the photo.

The photo on her camera was of a ticket booth that had been ravaged by time and neglect. Abandoned, faded, the cracked paint flaking off. People stood buying tickets from no one. The booth, once more, was devoid of people. But it had been fully staffed—she knew there had been people there when she took the photo!

She flicked through her camera and all the photos she had taken. One after another, all the images were the same. Neglected, abandoned rides and stalls, surrounded by laughing people. The figures were illuminated by lights that were shattered and broken.

The last image was different. It was of a funhouse attraction she hadn't seen. She hadn't taken this photo. It was a

The Contortionist

hall of mirrors. It was the only thing in the photo that looked intact. The next photo was closer, of the same hall of mirrors, and of the entrance.

Next to the entrance of the hall of mirrors was a sign that read *"Come find the truth of your soul!"* in garishly painted letters.

The words of the morbid poem echoed in her head. *"Seek the truth in mirrored lanes, that show you all the hidden planes."* She stared at the hall of mirrors, in a photo she hadn't taken, of a dilapidated and abandoned Harrow Faire.

No, no, no...

Feeling the color drain from her face, she sat in the nearest chair. Turning off her camera, she shut her eyes and fought the urge to scream or cry. Or both. She was firmly voting both. After a long breath, she turned her camera back on.

The first photo loaded.

It was normal.

Fully painted signs greeted her. The booth was still unstaffed, but the booth looked exactly like she remembered. Flicking through the photos, they all looked exactly as she expected.

There were no photos of the hall of mirrors. Not one.

I'm losing my fucking mind.

But I know what I saw.

"Oh, you're still here! Good. I found what you were looking for," the library attendant chirped happily as she walked back into the room. "Are you all right?"

"Yeah, yeah, sorry. Just a little under the weather today." Cora smiled, trying to wipe what must be a look of *full and utter existential dread* off her face.

"Poor thing. Well, it took some digging, but I went

through some tax records." The woman looked proud of herself. "His first name was Lazarus."

Cora kept back a groan.

Fucking perfect.

"Thanks." She flicked off her camera, picked up the newspaper article—for what good it was going to do her—and handed the woman back the microfiche sheet. "I think I have what I need. Thanks so much." *For fueling my panic attack.*

"You're very welcome. Come back any time. I hope you feel better."

Cora lifted her hand in goodbye as she headed out of the room. She made it halfway down the hall before she had to stop to lean against the wall, lowering her head and trying to sort through her thoughts.

The image of the hall of mirrors was stuck in her head, along with the creepy poem. It was important. It was trying to tell her something. *What is trying to tell me? Wait. That's stupid. The Faire isn't trying to talk to me. It can't be.*

Harrow Faire wasn't alive. It wasn't. It couldn't be. *Buildings aren't alive.* It wasn't possible. But neither was what she had just seen on her camera. Neither was a bizarre madman who appeared in her dreams and remembered them during the day.

Either the Faire was trying to talk to her, or she was going insane. And there was only one way to find out. If the Faire was talking to her—she couldn't even believe she was letting herself think those words—it wanted her to go to the hall of mirrors.

It also meant she would have to go near Simon. She chewed her lip. She would go—but she sure as hell wasn't going alone. She pulled out her phone and texted the group again. *"HF hat trick? Let's make it three days in a row. 5:30 pm?"* She paused in her typing. *"I need more funnel cake, damn it."*

Three little dots, and Trent wrote back *"Hells yes."*

She knew why he agreed, but it didn't matter. She'd take any company she could get. She didn't wait to hear back from the others. She needed a goddamn nap. Her shoulder hurt from this morning, and she hadn't slept well. Or she had, but it hadn't exactly been restful.

She wondered if it was considered sleeping if it was actually a vision. Getting into her car, she checked her camera one more time. The photos were still normal, and not the abandoned images she had seen the first time. But she knew what she had seen had been real. Just maybe not permanent.

I think I'm being haunted by a carnival.
Fuck my life.

9

SIMON WAS HUMMING, polishing one of his dolls. This one was empty of life, and that was probably for the best. It was a large dragon, with mirrored eye sockets that blazed when he lit the little gas lanterns inside them. He didn't want to imagine what it would be like to place a human soul inside something like this. While it would be entertaining to watch someone rampage around in a giant dragon puppet, it would also be extremely irritating to deal with their *fiery* mood swings.

He was tired—he had not slept—but it was worth it. Fatigue didn't stop the smile that spread over his features. It was an ever-present expression on his face, yes, but this time it felt different. It wasn't the usual one that came along with his typical madness. It was *excitement.*

"I don't think I've been excited in seventy years," he said to the dragon, patting it on the nose. It couldn't answer. That was also quite fine. It would probably just make weird grumbly noises at him. Whatever noises a dragon made, anyway.

"*Father?*"

The Contortionist

He turned his head to see one of his other dolls step out from the shadows. That one *did* have a life within it. Or whatever was left of one.

It had been thirty-eight years since he had made the doll that moved from the darkness onto the stage. It was the figure of a man, with chestnut brown skin and dark hair. He was also the last living doll Simon had made.

The last one he had promised he would ever build.

Or, rather, the one last one he had promised he would ever build under the threat of continued torture and imprisonment. Now he planned to break that promise. It wasn't that he had lied. Not exactly. At the time, he hadn't been lying, anyway. But thirty-eight years was a long time to hold someone to a promise.

And things had changed.

"Hello, Hernandez." Simon went back to polishing the dragon. "What do you want?"

"I want to go."

Simon paused and put down the rag, hooking it over the nose of his giant puppet. He turned to face Hernandez slowly. He furrowed his brow. "Why now?"

The puppet lolled his head to the side slightly, as if listening to something. *"It's time."*

He took a step closer to the wooden man. Hernandez wavered on his feet, as if dangling from strings. There were none that held him up. His living dolls didn't work quite that way. Simon reached out and took the man's wooden face in his hands. It was a careful reproduction of the man's features. Simon was proud of his work.

He was proud of it now. He had been proud of it then.

"SIMON!"

KATHRYN ANN KINGSLEY

Simon looked up from his workbench. Someone was calling for him from inside the main portion of the tent. Odd. He rarely received visitors. Especially one who didn't sound vehemently angry at him.

Upset, perhaps. But not angry.

The rest of the Family seemed to only seek him out when they wanted to yell at him...

Regardless, the wavering tone of the man's voice caught his attention. He put down his pencil on his sketchpad, pushed from his desk, and headed to his stage.

He stopped when he saw who it was and tilted his head slightly to the side. Surprising. Odd, wonderful, and intriguing. It also meant trouble was afoot. "Hello, Contortionist."

Hernandez stood in the center aisle. The man was trembling and wiping at his cheeks with his sleeve. He had been crying, judging by the color of his eyes. It looked like he might begin again at any moment. "Simon..." His normally bronze skin looked pale and yellowed.

"To what do I owe the honor, Hernandez?" Simon walked to the edge of his stage, folded a hand behind his back, and fashioned his most affable smile. "Business or pleasure?" He sniffed dismissively. "I assume the former, as no one comes to me about the latter. What do you want, Contortionist?"

"I need...I need this all to stop." Hernandez began to cry again, the wetness tracking down his face. This time he let them run their course. They were too numerous to fight. Best give up the battle and save the energy. And the damp sleeves.

"What do you need to stop?" Simon arched an eyebrow. "Be specific."

"Everything."

Now Simon's grin was a sadistic one. A hungry one. And he did hunger. "Are you asking me to end the pain, Hernandez?"

The Contortionist shivered. There was a faraway look in his eyes. There was no mistake—there was no devious ploy at work. Hernandez knew the cost of what he was asking. He knew what would become of him.

And it made his choice all the sweeter.

Brown eyes met his red ones, and with a wavering voice, he answered. "Yes."

"Well, then," Simon straightened, "I had better get to work."

SIMON REMEMBERED the day Hernandez had come to him in tears. The man could not take it anymore. The years of silence, followed by the chaos, and the noise. The poor creature had never enjoyed the act of feeding from the living. He had always cowered from it. He had always been a skittish, overly sensitive thing.

The Contortionist had wanted to be released from his place in the Family. So, Simon had agreed. But like all things, freedom came with a price.

He smiled. Everything came with a price.

I will have you soon, Cora Glass.

"I needn't remind you how I suffered when I made you, Hernandez." Simon grimaced, remembering the time he had spent hanging from his ankles. Creating a puppet from one of the Family was a deed that had not gone unpunished. Being strung up in the tower still haunted him at night. He remembered the *years* of screaming in pain. If he hadn't lost his sanity before—and he probably had—that agony had finished off what was left of it.

"I know. I am sorry."

Simon sighed and leaned in to rest his forehead against the wooden one of his puppet. There was a little life still left in Hernandez. Most of him had already faded away by the time he'd asked Simon to end it all. He was barely a flicker of what he had been when he had first set foot in the Faire.

Far be it from him to make someone to stay in a condition they no longer desired. That was a cruelty to which even he would not stoop. He knew it himself. "Goodbye, Hernandez. You made a good puppet."

"Goodbye, Simon."

Simon leaned his head up to kiss the smooth wood surface of Hernandez's forehead. And in that moment, Simon consumed the last bit of life left flickering in the wooden frame. He let the now-empty wood fall to the stage with a clatter, limbs twisted akimbo with no rhyme or reason or relation to human anatomy.

He would deal with it later. He needed to go for a walk. Hernandez had never been a friend—Simon was not in the business of keeping friends—but he had been a decent companion.

Simon's "children" were fine enough to talk to, to play with, and to keep his need for conversation from becoming too insultingly one-sided. He talked to himself enough as it was; he didn't need it to get worse.

There was no grief in his heart from losing another one of his dolls. But there was a bit of sadness in seeing another one of his "kind" fade away. Not because he cared a lick for any of them—the Family could all rot, for all he cared—but because it was a reminder of his own possible mortality. That someday he, too, might go the way of the dodo.

Such a shame about dodos.

He struck out into the Faire, walking the familiar paths, watching the patrons come and go. It was growing later in the afternoon, verging on early evening. The lightbulbs on the rides were just starting to be visible against the sunlight. Checking his pocket watch, it was just before six. It seemed

The Contortionist

like it would be a lovely night again. He did so much enjoy seeing the clouds.

Or any sky at all, for that matter.

He forced himself to think instead about a more charming, more suitable topic. Cora. He touched his fingers to his lips, remembering the sensation of her skin there. It had been such an enjoyable vision.

The fear in those big, gray eyes of hers had been beautiful beyond words. She really was quite stunning. Long, dark hair against soft skin that begged to be touched. And she was so delectable when she was afraid. And so confused! But instead of fleeing, she had brandished a knife. It had been so sweet he had wanted to hug her. Nobody had threatened him with a knife in *ages*.

He was whistling a tune now. It might have been Shostakovich. He had the urge to play his violin—another thing he hadn't wished to do in longer than he could easily recall. Something about her put a skip in his step. He would have fun tearing her apart, little by little. Peeling off each tiny part of her soul until there was nothing left, like the layers of a flakey pastry.

Cora Glass. Savory and sweet. And all *his* to consume.

He had not expected to want to kiss her. He did not make a habit of dallying with others—not like his fellows and so-called compatriots. They played their games, either with each other or the patrons. He kept to himself. Oh, now and again, a sweet treat would wander close and be brave enough to play with him for a night. Never twice.

Madness. It did not make for repeated bedfellows.

Placing a hand to his chest and striking the other out from him as though he had a dance partner, he twirled along with the waltz he was whistling. Oh, yes. He was excited, without a doubt.

His impromptu desire to dance ended rather abruptly as he smashed into someone. Someone who didn't budge at the impact. Someone Simon did not have to stoop to meet eye-to-eye. He glowered. "Hello, Ringmaster."

"Puppeteer." Ringmaster greeted him with nothing but distaste and firm dislike in his mouth. The big man was already glaring sternly at him as though he were a petulant child. "Hernandez is gone."

"Yes, and? He's been a ghost for years." Simon waved dismissively and went to step around the giant oaf in his bad clothes. Ringmaster was having none of it and grabbed him by the upper arm and yanked him back. Simon scowled back but knew better than to pick a fight.

One did not pick a fight with Ringmaster and win. He knew from experience. He still had an ache in his ankles some nights from those years dangling in the tower. But that didn't stop him from being indignant about having been restrained. Tugging his arm free, he smoothed out the rumpled line of his red suit. "You were angry when I made him into one of my dolls at his request. Now you are mad at me for freeing him from that state of being—*also* at his request. Am I to be strung up again for following the wishes of a tortured soul?"

"You freed him because he asked?" Ringmaster was still glaring at Simon from under his ridiculous top hat. His long mustache was hideous. Really, Simon hated everything about the man. "Why do I not believe you?"

"I don't lie! When have I ever done that? Even once."

Ringmaster snorted.

"Now, don't be catty, you overbaked loaf of bread." Simon pointed at him. "I manipulate, surely. But lie? Never." Simon pushed the glasses up his nose with the press of his ring finger on the bridge. "I am insulted. Now, if you've come

The Contortionist

to bother me about Hernandez, he's now well and truly dead. The matter is already quite settled." He moved to walk away but was yanked back by his upper arm. Again. He sighed. "What do you want?"

"Leave the girl alone."

Simon froze. *How does he know?* "What girl?" He tried to act innocent. He suspected it failed miserably.

"Barker and Bearded Lady came to speak to me."

Simon swore. "Rat fink *bastards.*"

Ringmaster rolled his eyes. "Leave her alone. You are not allowed to make another puppet."

"It's been thirty-eight years!" He was whining. He knew he was. But he didn't care. He ran his hands through his hair, slicking the stray strands away from his face. It was rather unruly at the best of times. "Thirty-eight years. Isn't that enough for you?"

"No."

"The girl is suffering. She's in pain. You want to curse her to a mortal life like that?" Simon folded his arms across his chest, playing the lofty one. "How cruel of you, Ringmaster. How utterly demonic, to let her languish in agony when I can cure her pain."

"No one would take your offer if they knew what price they'd pay when they did." Ringmaster stepped toward him, trying to intimidate him.

Simon held his ground...for a moment or two. He took a step back, but let a fiendish smile spread over his face. "That's where you're wrong, fat man. They all knew. Every single one of them looked at what they would become and took my hand all the same. Even your precious Hernandez. And she will, too."

"No, Simon."

"Why do you care? You never cared before. I preyed on

them for decades—nearly a century—before you ever tried to stop me! You didn't care until it was one of our own, so why care about a mortal girl now?" Simon tried to keep his temper down, but it was hard. He knew he was already shouting. He always felt as though he were chasing at the back end of a runaway carriage. His temper was always out of control. It went the way of his sanity, he supposed.

"You lost the right to feed on mortals when you took Hernandez. You *never* attack one of the Family. Ever. I put up with your random...spats of violence because I know you are not fully in control of your faculties." Ringmaster flicked his hands across the brass buttons of his green and black striped tailcoat dismissively. "But after that, after attacking the Family, you lost your rights. You will leave her alone."

"Don't pity me," Simon snarled. "And don't deny her the right to make her own mistakes. If she wishes to come to me—and she will—then that is her choice. You, who always rants and raves about how people must make their own decisions! You do not funnel everyone who comes here through the Dark Path because you want them to know what they give away. But you'll deny her the freedom to choose? Why?"

Ringmaster sighed heavily, and Simon watched as his argument worked. There was no better way to convince a righteous man to do the unrighteous thing than by using his own words against him. "Do you really think you can show her what she'll become, and convince her to join you?"

Simon flashed his best, most predatory smile. Even Ringmaster's eyes glittered in uncertainty. It was a honed skill, grinning like he could. It helped he did it all the time. "Oh, yes...I do."

"You will not take her against her will?"

"No." Simon stuck his hand out to Ringmaster. "We have

The Contortionist

a deal, then? I can have her if I can convince her to come to me."

Ringmaster's jaw ticked as he clenched it in anger and annoyance. "Fine." He turned away without shaking Simon's hand. "But you will never touch one of our own again, Simon. Ever."

"Cross my heart and hope to *die.*" He cackled.

"If you break your word...you might just."

The threat killed Simon's laughter. Something that angered him nearly as much as the words themselves. He wrinkled his nose and growled. He very much did *hate* that man. Turning on his heel, he struck off in another direction, once more wanting privacy. His excitement was dead in his chest, and he needed to go clean up the mess that the former Contortionist had made.

His excitement was dead.

Right until he saw her.

There she was. Cora. His interesting quarry had returned to the Faire despite all her strong words to the contrary! Walking next to that skinny little creature who had been thoroughly—extremely thoroughly—enjoying Strongman's company.

Heh. "Company." That's what they're calling it now, eh, Simon?

Such a curious thing she was from the outside. She would be vibrant and alive, if not for the sadness that draped over her like a shroud, hiding her true colors. She was fiery, she was feisty, and she had a mouth on her that entertained him greatly, when she was brave enough to use it.

And, oh, she was beautiful.

He had wanted to kiss her because he had, well, wanted to kiss her. Those gray eyes of hers seemed like liquid. They changed from light to dark and back again like the clouds in a stormy sky. Sometimes as pale gray as the beautiful, white, and happy fluffy things overhead, and sometimes as dark and swirling as a storm.

He did miss clouds so very much.

Cora had her hands tucked into her coat pockets, and she was glancing at every shadow like she might find it looking back at her. Her camera, a sleek,fascinating thing he wanted to play with—it had so many interesting levers and buttons, after all—hung at her side.

She looked scared.

She *always* looked scared.

He wondered what she would look like when she wasn't. *She won't get that far. She'll be a glassy, lifeless piece of porcelain before she ever stops looking at you in horror.*

Why did that disappoint him? Even just a little?

But it did, didn't it?

He furrowed his brow in confusion. No. That couldn't be. He wanted to consume her. To peel away her seity, a little bit at a time, and drink her like a fine wine. *It must be lust.* He chuckled to himself. That was it. Well, damn. His libido hadn't flared up for a long time. But there it was, clear as day, waving at him like his damn shadow, and it was desirous of the girl with the eyes that changed colors.

She was thin, but there were curves beneath her loose clothing, just hidden enough that he wanted to reveal them. He wanted to touch her. He wanted to play with her.

Oh, yes. That was definitely lust. He wanted her. He wanted to have her. In more ways than he was expecting. She was interesting. Maybe just a little bit. But his life was so very boring, after all.

He stood in the middle of the path, waiting for Cora and the skinny man to come close enough that he could block their paths without them noticing. It was a trap he was accustomed to setting. The two of them pulled up in shock as they realized he was there.

Folding his hands casually behind his back, he used his considerable height to his advantage and bowed, ever so slightly. "Hello, Cora dear." He looked to the scrawny one. "And you are Ludwig's new chew toy...and your name is?"

His eyes widened as he found a gun pointed into his face. Cora held it aloft, pointed straight to his nose.

She was glaring at him as though she wished him to burst into flame. "Get the fuck away from us, Simon."

Oh. Now she was *very* interesting.

10

It all happened so fast Cora didn't even register any of it until it was too late.

Going back to the Faire was nerve-wracking at best. She was glad to have Trent there with her. Emily and Lisa had bowed out for the night, which was fine. Three trips to a carnival in three days was a bit much. But she and Trent had other motives.

Very different motives—extremely different. But motives all the same.

She just wished he'd shut up about Ludwig. Okay, great, fine. She was happy for her friend. This seemed like more than a casual fling to him, and there was no problem getting emotionally invested in someone. But the conversation was getting tiring.

"He's just such a sweetheart. He's so quiet, and calm, and —oh, he's just different." Trent was beaming as he walked beside her. He was glowing. Absolutely radiant. "And he's good. Really good. And really—"

"Nope. No more. No details." She wrinkled her nose. "I don't need to know."

"Oh, come on, you could use a little vicarious love life." He shoved her arm with a laugh, and she found herself laughing along with him.

"Yeah, that's true. But I have books for that. I don't need to hear about your exploits with Ludwig the Leopard."

"Lion."

"Whatever."

Cora couldn't have been any farther from where he was on the emotional spectrum. Every time she saw someone who worked for the Faire, she glanced at them nervously and tucked her hands tighter into her pockets.

This place is alive. It's eating people.

It took a piece of me.

She knew she should warn Trent. She knew she should make sure nobody she knew ever came back to this place. Or maybe go on an arson spree and burn the place down. But she knew Trent wouldn't believe her. Nobody would. Fuck, she didn't even know if she believed herself. And screaming like a lunatic and holding up a sign outside was a great way to get carted away.

She kept it to herself.

For better or worse.

They passed a performance stage. On it was a woman, a beautiful and incredibly fit blonde, sitting in a hoop of metal that was hanging from some overhead rigging. She was dressed in a vintage circus outfit and was dangling precariously from the bottom of the hoop by one knee. The crowd watched her in awe.

What are these people? Are they even human anymore?

The other ones she had met—Aaron the Barker, Bertha the Bearded Woman, and even Jack—whose job she didn't know yet, but apparently in the circus jobs served as titles—

had all been nice to her. Concerned. Kind. They treated her like family. All except Simon.

Her thoughts circled back to him with the gravitational pull of a black hole.

And just like the old proverb, although she didn't have to even speak of him, the devil appeared. It seemed as though he came out of nowhere. One second, there was just a crowd. And the next, he was there. Towering over them, that same sick, sinister smile on his face. Cora and Trent were forced to pull up abruptly to avoid crashing into him.

"Hello, Cora dear." Light flashed off his sunglasses, making them blink amber. It didn't help him look less monstrous.

Fuck you, buddy. She pulled the gun from her coat. It wasn't anything impressive. It was a stupid little .22 pistol. She had a license for it, and to conceal carry, so *technically* this was legal. The Faire didn't post any signs about no firearms permitted on the premises, and it was New Hampshire, after all.

She had barely even clicked off the safety before it happened.

His eyebrows lifted in surprise, and his smile warped into a sadistic grin. Lifting his hands in a show of surrender, he suddenly flicked his fingers and the gun flew to his palm.

It felt like her hand had been hit by a car. She yelped in pain and cradled it against her chest.

"What the fuck—" Trent jumped back from them both.

"Ever full of surprises, aren't we, Ms. Cora?" Simon held the pistol and looked down at it with idle curiosity. He flicked the safety back on after a second and slipped it into the inner pocket of his coat. "There. All better."

"Give it back," she snarled at him.

"Give what back?" He answered her anger with a sweet,

if entirely fake, expression. "I don't know what you're talking about."

"What the fuck, Cora?" Trent was standing several feet away from them now, his hands up like she had been pointing the gun at him. "You brought a gun?"

"What gun?" Simon turned to address Trent and acted innocently confused. "There was no gun."

"But she—you—" Trent stammered. "It's in your pocket."

"Is it?" Simon opened his coat and pulled the lining of his pocket out, showing it to be empty. "I don't have anything, dear boy. Are you feeling well?"

"I...but..." Trent had seen something impossible. Cora sympathized. Simon had just magically ripped a gun out of her hands, despite the several feet of space between them, then apparently made it disappear. He had barely moved. Trent wasn't taking it well. He threaded his fingers into his hair and looked at Simon and Cora in vaguely concealed panic.

"If she had one, how did I take it away?" Simon shrugged. "I think it must be the whirling lights and over-abundant exercise you've been getting, hm? Perhaps the smell of the gasoline-powered rides is affecting you. Go see Ludwig. He'll take care of you."

"But—but—" Trent shook his head. "No. Cora. What the fuck just happened?"

Simon didn't give her a chance to answer. "Cora and I have some business to attend to. Everything is fine. Isn't it, Cora?" He looked to her then, and there was a very thinly veiled threat in his words. "There's nothing wrong...*correct?*"

She felt her heart pounding in her ears. But she swallowed down the panic and nodded. It was stilted, and strained, but it was the best she could do. She looked to

Trent and forced herself to smile. "It's all right. Go on, Trent. Go see Ludwig."

"But—I saw—you just..." Trent shook his head. She watched him go through the same thing she'd been experiencing over the past two days. He saw something impossible, and instead of accepting it, went with the easier answer. That his eyes had just been playing tricks on him. "I guess. That was super weird..." He rubbed his hand over his face. "I guess I do feel kinda lightheaded."

"Poor thing. Tell Strongman to go easier on you, hum?" Simon smirked.

"It's okay, Trent," she insisted firmly. "You should go see Ludwig. Simon and I need to talk."

Trent took a step back, shaking his head. He clearly didn't understand what was happening. He chewed on his lip. She understood. She really did. But she didn't say anything. Trent finally gave up. "O—okay. I'll...I'll see you later, Cora." And with that, he left.

A hand settled on her shoulder. "It's so easy to convince mortals that what they've seen is false. They'd rather ignore the impossible than rethink their understanding of reality. Isn't that true, Cora dear?"

She jerked away from him and took a few steps back. Not that it would help her if he wanted to do anything. He'd shown her very quickly that his bizarre strings were not just in her dream. "How did you do that?"

"The same way I restrained you last night when you tried to stab me." He stepped toward her. "Charming notion, by the by. I was very flattered by the thought."

"Give me my gun back."

"Why?" He raised an eyebrow.

"I might need it."

The Contortionist

"I don't want to hurt you. As for Trent...eh." He shrugged.

"Don't you dare hurt him."

"Why would I?" Simon chuckled. "He's perfectly boring. Let him and Ludwig have their fun, I say." He clasped his hands behind his back again. "You, on the other hand, are quite interesting. Come, Cora. Let's discuss our negotiation."

"No. That's not why I'm here." She walked away from him, heading in the direction of where all the funhouses were set up. "I don't want anything to do with you."

"Really?" He was walking next to her, easily keeping up with his long legs. "That's disappointing. After our chat last night, I thought you would have changed your mind."

"No."

He sighed, shrugged, and kept walking alongside her. When he began whistling a tune, it was very clear she needed to try harder to get rid of him.

"Go away." She glared at him. It was bad enough she was back inside the man-eating murder-circus. She didn't need the maniac next to her grinning like he wanted to eat her whole. He probably did.

"No-*pe.*" He popped the last half of the word again. "Oh, don't look so glum, Cora dear! Now. If you aren't here to talk to me, why come back? I thought you said you'd never set foot in here again."

"I'm not going to tell you." She tried to walk faster to get rid of him, but he was so damn tall, and his legs were so long, it was useless.

"I can help you with whatever it is you're here to do. I do live here, after all." He leaned in a little closer. "That's what friends do, isn't it?"

"We aren't friends." She shot him another vicious look.

He staggered and gripped his chest as if she had actually shot him like she had threatened to. Cackling at his own melodrama, he caught back up to her quickly. "Come, don't be stubborn. Accept help where it's offered! And this assistance comes free. Whatever are you hunting for tonight, Cora dear?"

She debated not telling him. But he wasn't going to go away, and he was going to find out eventually once she found it. "I need to find the hall of mirrors."

His brows scrunched together. "Whatever for?" When she didn't answer, he grabbed her hand and suddenly yanked her around to face him. "What mystery do you think you're solving, darling? The secrets of the Faire?" He chuckled. "I have all the answers you could possibly need. What do you wish to know?"

"And why the fuck would I trust you?" She tried to pull her hand away, but he only tugged her closer. When he wrapped an arm around her, she shoved on his chest with her free hand. He might as well have been a wall. The smell of antiques, warm and welcoming, slid over her again, mixed with an equally old-fashioned but enticing cologne. "Stop it!"

"Talk to me. That's all I ask."

"Let me go."

"Talk to me, and I will."

"Fine!" She shoved him. He released her obediently and she quickly put distance between them. He stood there, eerily smiling, the lights flashing off his sunglasses, and waited for her to explain herself. She sighed. "There's no getting rid of you, is there?"

"So many people have asked that question that I'm starting to take it personally."

That almost made her laugh. She might have if she didn't want to also smack the shit out of him. She started walking toward the funhouse area again, and Simon fell into step beside her. "I found an article in an old newspaper. It had a poem in it that was interesting." She took it out of her coat pocket and handed it to him. *And the Faire showed me photos.* But she didn't know if she wanted to admit that part just yet. She might not be able to get rid of him, but she certainly couldn't trust him.

"Interesting how?" He took the photocopy and lowered his glasses down his nose to read it. She wondered if the tinted glasses ever bothered him since he seemed to wear them all the time, but promptly decided she didn't care.

"It might be a clue to what's going on here in the Faire."

"There's no mystery to solve, cupcake. I've told you everything you need to know. But does this mean you believe what's going on now?"

She slid her camera in front of her on the strap and turned it on. The photos were still as she would have expected them to be. Freshly painted signs and brightly lit bulbs. But she still knew what she had seen with the abandoned photos. Simon and his strings...and everything else. It was just too much to ignore. "Yeah...I guess I do."

"Oh, huzzah. What a relief!" He read the article, mumbling the poem to himself. "Seek the truth in the mirrored lanes, that show you all the hidden planes. I think, my dear, that you're on a bit of a wild goose chase. And this poem is downright atrocious." He handed the article back to her and pushed his glasses back up with a ring finger.

"I want to know what this place is. And why."

"I can tell you the what, my dear. I already have. As to the why? Nobody knows. Nobody except Mr. Harrow himself. But he is...a bit of a recluse."

"He's—he's still alive?" She looked up at Simon, stunned.

He smiled thinly. "How old do you think I am?"

"I don't know. Thirty?"

"I was thirty-one when I came to Harrow Faire on that fateful day that ensured I would never leave again. So, I will give you credit for your guess. But the year, my darling, sweet, and wonderful Cora…was 1885. And I am not the oldest who remains 'employed' by Mr. Harrow, if you would like to call it that."

"You're trying to tell me you're a hundred and…" She did some math in her head. "Sixty-five years old?"

"Sixty-six." He corrected with a smile. "And indeed I am. Save for Mr. Harrow himself, Ringmaster is the oldest of us. This year marks Ringmaster's two hundred and tenth. Well. In normal years."

"What do you mean, normal years?" This was all insane. But she would play along for now.

"It's hard to explain." He waved his hand dismissively. "And unimportant. Anyhoo, Mr. Harrow is very much alive." He paused. "If we're alive. I'm not quite sure, honestly. I mean…we bleed, we sleep, we eat, we can still make love, as your friend Trent is *very* well aware. Save for the part where we cannot die, everything else is quite standard. That makes us alive, yes?"

It sounded like he was really asking her. She shook her head. "I don't know. Sure. Good for you. Can I talk to Mr. Harrow?"

"Sadly, no. Nobody talks to him, save for Ringmaster." Simon's expression flickered to one of anger. "Believe me… I've tried."

"Is Trent in danger? Has this place…fed on him?" It was hard to say that out loud and not cringe. She still felt like she was going insane. "Ludwig isn't dangerous, is he?"

"That genetically altered, overblown hamster?" Simon

The Contortionist

let out a loud *hah* of laughter. "Hardly! And the Faire has all it has planned to take from you, as well. I am the only one here with any continued interest."

"And why do you have interest in me?"

"I told you. I want to help you."

"Sorry, but you don't seem like the charitable type."

"I stand to benefit, as well. Don't worry."

Cora rolled her eyes. She could see the hall of mirrors just up ahead. It looked like one of the oldest attractions in the park. Wiggly panes of the reflective surface were arranged to either side of the entrance. On a sign next to it read *"Come find the truth of your soul!"*

It would seem like terrible marketing to anyone else. But to her, it was another clue. This place *had* to mean something. Simon might be able to give her answers—but like hell if she trusted anything that came out of that man's smirking face.

When they reached the entrance, he leaned against the railing. "You won't find anything interesting in there save your own reflection. But if you wish to chase this red herring down the stream, by all means." He gestured. "I'll see you at the exit, then I can answer all your questions." He glanced to her camera. "And maybe pose for a photo or two." His face lit up as though he were actually excited to have his photo taken. "I've heard a rumor that I'm tall and sexy."

She glared. "You're insane."

"That is not news." He jerked his head toward the entrance. "Go on. See for yourself."

With a beleaguered sigh, she stepped into the hall of mirrors.

11

The winding rows of mirrors reflected all the surfaces around them. Again, and again, fading off into infinity, she saw herself stretching out in all directions. Every post, every light, whirled around her in an endless array of shapes.

It was meant to be disorienting. It was incredibly effective.

She had to put a hand in front of herself to keep from ramming into the reflective walls. There were no arrows or guides to tell her which way to go. *The fire marshal must have a field day with this place.*

Then again, a supernatural, man-eating murder-circus probably didn't need to worry about building inspectors and fire code. She wound her way through the maze and was fairly certain she had gotten turned around more than a few times.

She could still hear the faint music of the park. The never-ending pipe organ and hurdy gurdy tracks that were beautiful, joyful, and inherently creepy.

"Okay. I'm here now. I don't know what you want from me," she said to the empty air. There was nobody else to

The Contortionist

judge her for talking to the freaking circus as though it were conscious. The floor creaked as she walked, the old surface made of wide planks of wood, heavily polished and smooth with age. The hall of mirrors looked to be over a hundred years old. "I don't know why you showed me those photos this afternoon. I don't know what you're trying to tell me." She picked up her camera and, flipping it on, took a few photos of the infinity mirror around her.

Click. Click. Click.

"But I'm here now. I'm listening. Tell me what you want."

She checked the images. The first two seemed normal.

The third...was not.

The third had no right to be on her camera. It had nothing to do with where she was. It was Trent...and he was lying on the packed dirt walkway of the Faire. A halo of red around his head. His eyes were open, lifeless, and glassy. He was dead.

"Oh, God..." She put her hand over her mouth. "No, please." It was a warning. She knew it was. But what could she do about it? She flicked the switch back to photo mode, bit down her horror, and lifted the camera. She took three more photos. "Not Trent."

Click. Click. Click.

She reviewed the photos. All three were of Trent. All three were him dead in a different way. But each one was her best friend in the world, butchered and lying dead in the dirt, covered in blood.

She wailed. She found the jamb of one of the mirrors to lean against to support herself. "This can't be real. It can't be!" She took three more photos.

Click. Click. Click.

Three more images of Trent's murdered body. Each in a different pose. One with his eyes gouged out. One with his face split open. Another with his entrails on the ground around him.

She bit back her tears. Her voice cracked as she spoke. "Tell me how to stop it."

Click. Click. Click.

She flicked over to review the photos. They were all blank. Just three empty black squares. "No. You can't do this! Tell me how to stop this from happening. Tell me how to protect Trent."

Click. Click. Click.

Three more photos, and three empty black squares.

"No, please...don't do this to me. Tell me what I can do!" Fear was making her voice crack. She thought she might cry. She was begging. "Please. I—I'll do anything. I'll give you anything. I'll do whatever you want. I just..." Images of growing up with Trent flashed in her mind. Of him crying on the playground because a bully had called him a fag and split his lip. She had held an icepack to his face and told him he was still prettier than she was. It had made him smile. The images of him bleeding out on the ground had reminded her of those days. She protected him when they were young. She had to protect him now. "Tell me what you want me to do."

She took three more photos.

Click. Click. Click.

She reviewed the images. They weren't blank, at least. But she didn't know what they meant.

The first photo was of a mirror in a frame, but not any of the ones around her. It was decorated around the edges with text that loudly proclaimed, *"See into your soul!"*

The second was of Simon's puppet show tent, the red and black stripes standing out boldly in the image.

The third photo was of somewhere in the Faire that she

The Contortionist

didn't recognize, but she could make out the Ferris wheel in the background. It was of an old circus train car. One that performers would have lived in while traveling. The grass that had grown long by the wheels showed it hadn't moved in a very long time. Stairs led up to a door on the back of it, which was painted with the number zero in gold.

"I...I don't get it. But I'll figure it out. I'll try." She wiped her cheek, pushing away a tear that had slipped out. "I'll do anything to save him. Anything. He's like my brother." She went back to winding her way through the mirrored halls.

When she came to the end of the maze, it seemed like there was one more thing to see. The rest of the room was all blacked out, with a spotlight down on a location in the center. And a large mirror, decorated with text, stretched from floor to ceiling by one wall. *"See into your soul!"*

"Oh, fuck."

She ran her hands through her hair slowly, scratching her scalp, trying to think through what she should do. Run? Not look? She had the sinking feeling that whatever the mirror was going to show her wasn't going to be normal. It wasn't even going to be wibbly-wobbly like funhouse mirrors should be.

This was going to be bad.

But Trent's life was on the line. With a groan, she stepped into the circle of light and looked at her reflection in the glass.

It was her.

But then again, it wasn't.

She didn't recognize what she was wearing. A skin-tight outfit of white and black lace accented with matching striped leggings. Her hair was carefully curled and done up in a way she never had the time for. Loud makeup made her look like...a circus performer.

Her reflection smiled at her despite the fact that she herself wasn't smiling. Cora whined in fear and put her hands over her mouth. But she couldn't look away. Her reflection turned to the side, posed, then...bent in half backward like a contortionist. The image of her had one arm elegantly outstretched, even as the rest of her was bent at unnatural angles.

She cringed. That had to hurt. It made her joints ache just watching it. The reflection of her straightened back up and took a bow. When she straightened, the outfit her reflection wore was no longer white and black.

It was covered in blood. Like Lady Macbeth on a stage, her reflection wiped her hands down her arms, coating herself in the substance, then held her palms out for her to see. All the while smiling in excitement and joy. As if she was showing off what she had done.

Cora had seen enough. She turned to leave out the exit—

And screamed.

There was a disembodied shadow against the wall, a wild and animalistic grin plastered over its face like a shark. It opened its maw, showing off its sharp and ghoulish teeth.

Cora ran. She ran back the way she had come and into the mirror maze. She was too scared to really think about where she was going. Or that she was barreling head-first into a place where the walls weren't always where she expected them to be.

She crashed into a corner and screamed in pain as it rammed into her shoulder. She fell to her knees, cradling the dislocated joint in her other hand. It was really far out this time. She had gotten it good. It was the last straw. It was insult to injury—or, rather, injury to insult.

First, the trip through "the Dark Path." Then the dreams.

The Contortionist

Then Simon. Then the photos on her camera. Seeing Trent's murdered body. Seeing herself—like that—bloody and warped and twisted—and then Simon's stupid freaking shadow. And now this.

She was done. Stick a fork in her, she was done. She doubled over at the waist and cried. She didn't care anymore.

"Cora?"

Someone knelt down close to her. It was Simon. A hand stroked her hair. "Cora dear, what's wrong, cupcake? Oh—oh, dear me. That's not normal, is it?" His other hand touched her shoulder tenderly. She hissed in pain. "Ah. Yes. Sorry. Sorry." He sighed. "Can you stand, sweetheart? Let's get you out of here."

She nodded weakly and pushed to her feet with his help. He kept his hand on her uninjured elbow and gently led her out of the maze and down the steps of the entrance. She made it to a grassy spot by a tree nearby before her legs gave out, and she sank to the ground. She wept.

"Are you crying from the pain?"

"No," she said through gritted teeth. "I'm scared and I'm angry."

"Ah. Hm." He stood in front of her and scratched the back of his neck. "Not much I can do to help you there, I'm afraid. I'm generally frightening and infuriating." He smiled, and when she didn't laugh at his joke, he sighed. "What can I do about your shoulder?"

"Help me put it back in." She tried to straighten up and cringed as the tendons pulled angrily on the joint. "I need you to kneel behind me."

"A woman asking me to kneel. How uncommon and enticing," he purred. When she glared at him, his expression fell. "Poor timing, I agree." He walked behind her and knelt as she had asked him to.

She reached her bad arm out to her side as far out as she could go on her own. "I need you to put one hand on my scapula. Take my wrist and pull it up a bit and back. It's going to crunch. It'll be disgusting."

"I've done worse." He took her wrist as she instructed. She felt his other palm against her back. He pulled her arm back and up at a small degree until he met resistance and paused. "Ready?"

"Yeah, just get it—"

He tugged. Her shoulder crunched back into place with an audible and bony *pop*. Cora gagged in pain. It hadn't been that far out in a long time. She couldn't even make a noise. Her vision whited out, and when she came to, she was lying on her back in the grass. Simon was over her, stroking her hair. "Welcome back, dear."

He actually looked concerned. His expression was one of sympathy. He had taken his glasses off, and she could see something like real empathy in his freakish, inverted, and inhuman eyes. Kindness wasn't what she would have expected. For once, he wasn't smiling.

"Did I pass out?"

"Only for a second or two." He stroked her hair again. "Your dignity is safe with me."

She huffed herself to sitting, and he placed a hand on her back to help support her. "Thanks. Most people aren't capable of doing that. They get too freaked out. Trent had to help me once, and he was the one who passed out."

"It was my pleasure."

She shot him a look.

He blinked and realized what he said. "Ah, yes, well, not like that. Or, well, that's a bit of a lie, perhaps but—now,

The Contortionist

there's no reason to glower at me harder. Do you want me to lie to you? Or—"

"Puppeteer! Get away from her."

Cora looked up to see Aaron standing at the edge of the grass. Jack, the man she had met on the very first day, was standing next to him. Both of them were glaring at Simon.

The Puppeteer put his hands up. "I have done nothing wrong, for once."

Jack took a step forward, his fists clenched. "You're a lying, evil, manipulative son of a bitch. Get the hell away from her. We're not going to let you trick another person into one of your sick *deals.*"

"Is this about Hernandez? Still?" Simon rolled his eyes. "Oh, please. Find another drinking buddy, Jackie boy, and get over yourself. It's been thirty-eight years! As for the girl, I have not harmed her."

Aaron looked at her. "Are you all right? We heard screaming."

She nodded weakly, rubbing her sore shoulder. It was going to be absolute misery tomorrow. "He was helping me. I dislocated my shoulder in the maze when I ran into the wall. He was just putting it back into place. I asked him to do it."

"See?" Simon pointed at her. "I didn't do a thing. She *asked* me to hurt her." He smiled. "She's into that kind of thing." She used her good arm to smack him in the chest. He laughed. She almost smiled. And if it had been a normal day, and she hadn't just had her friend's life threatened, and if she hadn't just been terrorized by a man-eating murder-circus, she might have. She might have even laughed.

"Leave her alone." Jack was still glaring a hole into Simon. "Get away from her. Now."

"Oh, my dear, sweet Rigger." Simon sat in the grass next

to Cora and, bending a knee, draped an arm over it. "I would very much like to see you try to make me."

What happened next Cora didn't quite understand. Two men, one of whom looked like the kind of muscle-bound a person gets from working with heavy equipment all day, just stared at Simon and...backed away. As if Simon had called their bluff.

Two guys versus one. Sure, Simon had the weird...string thing. But now she was beginning to suspect all the people who "worked" at Harrow Faire were a little more than normal.

But it was fear she saw in Aaron's and Jack's faces. Fear of the man who was sitting casually in the grass next to her like they were having a spring picnic.

"Ringmaster will hear about this," Jack said in an angry hiss.

"Ringmaster already knows." Simon lay back in the grass and folded his arms behind his head. "We have a deal. But go and ask him yourself if you're so desperate to see me foiled at every turn." He gestured a hand to shoo them away. "Go on, now. You're ruining the mood."

The two men glanced at Cora before turning and walking away. She was too confused and overwhelmed to really absorb what had just happened. She felt sick. Her shoulder burned like it was on fire. "Simon?"

He sat back up. "Yes, darling?"

She rolled her eyes at his overeager tone. "I could really use a drink."

"Ah! A perfectly reasonable request. And quite prudent, considering the amount of pain you are clearly in." He got up, brushed the bits of grass off his suit, and bowed extravagantly. "As the lady commands, so shall I do. I will return shortly. Try not to pine over me too much while I'm gone."

The Contortionist

She rolled her eyes.

He walked away, leaving her there by herself to think. And sulk. Mostly, she was sulking. She pulled her camera around and was glad to see she hadn't shattered it in her mad dash through the mirror maze. Flicking it on, she only found photos of the maze. None of the weird phenomenon it had shown her inside.

Scooting back until she had her back up against the tree, she sighed. Trent was in serious danger, and she didn't know how to help him. But it had tried to tell her. She shut her eyes as she tried to picture the images that had been on her camera. The first one, she had already played out.

The mirror had shown her an image of herself that she had barely recognized. Not only because of the weird outfit and the contortionist tricks, but the smile. It had been a real one. A *happy* one.

Cora couldn't remember the last time she had smiled like that.

Chronic pain led to many things. Loss of sleep. Loss of hobbies, and for her, her livelihood. And it also tended to result in things like anxiety and depression. And she had both in spades. But the girl in the mirror had looked unrecognizable to her, not because of the outfit, but because of how much life burned in that version's gray eyes.

The second photo had been of Simon's tent.

The third was of a weird caravan, circus train, boxcar looking thing. With a number zero painted on the door.

*Does this place want me to make a deal with Simon? Is that what this is about? It wants me to trade something to him in exchange for Trent's life...*She sighed. She wanted to cry again.

"My lady! Alcohol has arrived."

She jerked in surprise. Looking up, Simon was standing there with two large paper cups with straws sticking out of them. He handed her one. It smelled like lemonade and vodka. She forced herself to smile at him. "Thank you."

He sat on the grass next to her and sipped his drink. "I thought you might like it. Since you seem to enjoy it made with limes. I will admit that is superior, but we only have the lemonade here."

"You really were in my dreams last night?"

"Mmhm," he said through the straw as he sipped it again. He stirred it for a second. "I know this is all a great deal to absorb. What did you see in the hall of mirrors that frightened you so badly?"

"Your fucking shadow."

"He wasn't—" He growled. "I have told him inappropriate actions with unsuspecting people is unacceptable."

She blinked. And then laughed. "No. That's not what I meant. But that's also disgusting, and I don't want to think about it too hard."

He smiled. "Ah. You meant it as an insult. Forgive me. It's hard to tell with him sometimes." Simon sipped the drink. "He is harmless. A good startle and general irritation are all he is capable of mustering."

"It wasn't the only thing I saw. I took some photos, but they changed again, like earlier today, and—" Whoops. Oh, well. Cat out of the bag and all that. She sighed.

"What do you mean, earlier?"

Too late now. Might as well spill it. Maybe Simon could actually help her. "I...took photos here yesterday. And when I looked at the photos today, they were all screwed up. It was like the Faire was abandoned again. But there were photos in the mix that I didn't take. Ones of the hall of mirrors. It was...asking me to go there."

He was watching her silently, expression unreadable. After a long pause, he spoke. "You didn't tell me the whole story earlier. You lied to me, Cora girl. You said you only had the poem to lead you there."

"I don't trust you."

"And here I sit, insulted." He sipped his lemonade and vodka. Something glittered in what she could see of his eyes. Something excited. "What do you think was talking to you, cupcake?"

"I don't know. The Faire? It sounds like nonsense."

"Not at all. Believe me."

She sighed. She pulled her camera off from where it was slung across her neck and under her left arm and put it in her lap. Flicking through the photos, again, it was just of the maze. Nothing strange was there. "Every time I see something weird on here, it goes away."

Simon leaned close to hover over her as she went through the images. "That's incredible. It has a tiny little screen!" He reached down to poke it and set off the touch screen. "Oh. Hah. Fascinating." He poked it a few more times and figured out how to scan around the image. "Can I play with it?"

She smiled despite herself. He looked like a kid in a candy shop. "Sure." She handed the camera to him and took off the lens from the front. "The knob on the top switches modes. The button with the little right arrow there goes back and forth between taking pictures and looking at them."

"What did the Faire show you that scared you so badly?" He picked up the camera and started clicking switches and pushing buttons. He put it into camera mode with the screen on and started waving it around, watching the image change.

"Trent. Dead on the ground. He's in danger. I asked it what I could do to stop it, and it showed me three images.

The first one was of the mirror in there. The last one that says 'see into your soul.' It told me to look into it, and I did."

He paused in his fascination with the camera and looked over to her. "I've never known that mirror to be anything but a cheap trick. There's a weight sensor in the floor that triggers an illusion. It's a two-way piece of glass that lights up a fake monster dummy on the other side. It's just an old jumpscare."

"That's not what happened to me." Cora sipped the drink. She needed it to settle her stomach, as well as help dull the pain in her shoulder. "It showed me dressed in some freaky circus outfit, and I was covered in blood."

"Oh, my." Simon looked off thoughtfully. He picked up the camera and took a photo of something in the distance. It was terribly out of focus. He began twisting the lenses to try to fix it. "Then my shadow made an appearance, I take it?"

"Yup."

"The good old one-two punch." He took another shot. It was much better. "Am I wasting your film?"

He really was a hundred and sixty years old, wasn't he? "It's digital. You can take about a thousand photos. There's no film in there. It all goes to a little plastic memory card."

"I understood those three words, but I have no clue what they mean together." He smiled. "Technology is so fascinating." He took a few more images, now clearly unafraid of using up her film. "What else did the Faire show you?"

"The second image was of your tent. The third was of an old-fashioned train car with a number zero painted on the door."

Simon froze. When he looked at her again, his freakishly colored eyes were wide. "When you saw yourself in the mirror...what did your reflection do? Anything at all?"

"I...bent in half backward, like a contort—"

The Contortionist

She broke off as Simon jumped up to his feet. She caught her camera before it crashed to the ground. He was suddenly pacing around in front of her, back and forth in rapid succession. He was muttering wildly to himself.

"Simon?"

He didn't answer her. He just kept pacing, rapidly talking to himself.

"Whatever." She dropped her voice to mutter, "Lunatic." She sipped the drink. Once she felt like she could walk without throwing up or passing out, she was going to go home and convince Trent never to set foot in the Faire ever again.

Suddenly, he had her by the good arm and was dragging her up to her feet.

"Hey! Let me go!"

"No." He started pulling her down the path. "This is important."

"Stop. Right now. Stop it!" She kicked at his leg. "Don't make me scream rape, you giant strawberry popsicle stick. Let me go!"

He stopped and turned to face her. "I'm a what?"

"Let me go. Right the fuck now, Simon."

He sighed heavily. "You need to come with me."

"Why?"

"Because we're going to go see Mr. Harrow."

12

Cora stared at him, stunned. "I thought...I thought nobody talks to Mr. Harrow."

"Nobody does. And nobody talks to the Faire either." Simon took a step closer, towering over her. His fingers were still wrapped around her wrist. They tightened. Not enough to hurt, but enough to make sure she was paying attention. "Let me explain something very crucial for you to understand in the following few minutes. Are you listening?" The amber lightbulbs of the nearby rides flashed off his mismatched sunglasses. She could just barely make out the black-red-white coloring of his eyes.

She blinked. Christ, he was terrifying. "Y...yeah."

"Good. The rules are simple—the Faire only talks to Harrow. And Harrow only talks to Ringmaster. That is how it has always been. *Those are the rules.* And yet here you are...and the Faire is whispering to you. And I want to know why. Why it picked *you*, when—" He broke off. "Come on." He turned and started walking, dragging her behind him.

She dug in her heels hard enough that he growled and

The Contortionist

turned back to her, irritated she wasn't playing along. "When what?"

"Hm?"

"You said, 'why it picked you, when,' then you stopped. When what, Simon?"

"It's not important." His jaw ticked. "Just follow me like a good girl, please."

She narrowed her eyes. "How hard do you want me to knee you in the balls, Simon? No. Step one, let go of my wrist. Step two, tell me what you were going to say."

Simon sighed. "You modern women are so irritating sometimes." He let go of her wrist. "The simple fact is that I misspoke. Now, come with me. You want your chance to talk to Mr. Harrow, don't you? This is your opportunity."

It was painfully clear he was hiding something. He didn't want to tell her what he was about to say. *I can't trust him. Not now, not ever.* "You know something, and you're not telling me."

"Oh, most certainly. Several things, I would imagine." Simon grinned, a vicious flash of white teeth. "But that is neither here nor there. Come, Cora. Let us go see Mr. Harrow like you wanted."

When he turned and left her there, she knew he was calling her bluff. With a groan, she followed him. She had to run to catch up. "Next time you want to take me somewhere, just ask, Simon. Just ask."

"Not something I'm accustomed to. I'd be dragging you by my strings, but I think your high-pitched shrieking would upset the patrons." He slowed his steps by half a beat. Whether it was because he wanted to gloat or because he took pity on her shorter legs, she didn't know.

"I do want my gun back, by the way. How did you hide it?"

"Double-lined pockets." He smiled. "Simple trick. No dark magic involved."

"Magic is real." It was a statement more than it was a question. "I'm still processing that fact."

"You are a little slow. I understand."

She glared at him.

He didn't seem to care. "Before you ask, I'm not sure if magic is real elsewhere. But I know that here, in the Faire, it very much is." He tucked his hands into his pockets as he walked, slowing down another beat. He seemed to like to talk and was suddenly in much less of a rush.

"Does everybody have…freaky superpowers like you?"

"Hm? Super-what?" He paused. "Ah. I get it. No. Well, yes. But most of them have far less…useful and spectacular gifts. I lucked out, all things considered. However, I did go entirely bonkers. I suppose there's that to take into account." He cackled.

A liar and an admitted madman. She had to remember that. "I really do wish you'd give me my gun back."

"Later. You don't need it. You could put as many holes in me as you want, and you'd just ruin my nice clothes and scare the patrons." He grinned. "But later, I can strip naked, and you can pop me with your little toy as many times as you like."

She grimaced. "Hard pass."

"Damn."

She really almost laughed that time. "So, you can't die?"

"No." His expression grew strained. "It is not as fun as you might think." He switched back to his usual manic self like a flick of a button. "Although! It does take the risk out of certain things. I have no fear of high places anymore. I suppose the circus acts would be rather more disappointing if the audience knew how many times the performers had

The Contortionist

fallen without the net, only to get up and brush themselves off afterward." He snickered.

"Does it hurt, though?"

"Oh, yes. Wonderful motivator, pain. Wouldn't you agree?" His eyes glinted in mischief as he looked down at her askance. "Don't forget our deal, Cora dear. The offer still awaits your reply."

"You haven't told me what I'd be trading." She took a step to the left to walk a little farther away from him. She knew the distance was pointless, but it was comforting. "And I'm more interested in saving Trent right now."

"Well...if the photos you described to me were as you say, then it seems that you may be able to kill two birds with one stone. The Faire showed you my tent, didn't it? I propose this—we go to see if Harrow will speak to you. If he does not, then...come to my tent. Let us discuss the terms. Perhaps you can save your friend, and I will have what I want, and all will be right with the world."

Why did the idea of setting foot inside his tent seem like a terrible point of no return? Probably because...it was. She wasn't usually one to listen to her instincts, but this time she tried to pay attention. Her usual understanding of everything in the world had been thrown out. Logic. Reason. Science. *Poof*.

Magic was real.

Instinct might be all she had left.

"I'm not going to agree to anything until you make it perfectly clear what I'm agreeing to, Simon."

"Of course! I would never think of tricking you. Really, I'm insulted. I am beginning to suspect you are listening to the Barker and the others." He huffed. "Lies and slander."

She watched him for a moment. He moved with a grace that she wouldn't have expected from someone of his size.

He was all sharp lines and high contrast. His suit was tailored to make him look...well, eccentric. With the crimson fabric and black pinstripes, the odd-colored glasses, and the ruffled, wavy black hair...he looked like the devil himself. "They all hate you, don't they?"

"Mmm, hate is a strong word." He grinned. "I think 'loathe to the point where they wish I would burst into flames and spend the rest of eternity screaming in agony' is a stronger and far more appropriate descriptor."

That time, she did laugh. It was small, and it was weak, but it was there. "Why?" Oh, she knew she couldn't trust a word that came out of his mouth. But she was curious what reason he'd give.

"Jealousy, perhaps. I'm honestly not quite sure. I've never done anything wrong." He shrugged. "You would have to ask them, to be blunt."

"Right."

"You don't believe me!" He threw up his hands. "That is hardly fair, Cora. I haven't done anything to you. Not a damn thing. Barker and Rigger are off running to Ringmaster now to complain that I've hurt you, when it was *you* who asked *me* to put your shoulder back in its joint. That is the story of my life. People ask me to help them, and when I do, I'm blamed for it!"

She blinked at his angry rant. Angry, and just a little desperate. "I'm sorry."

The frantic expression on his face vanished as quickly as it had arrived. "Apology accepted."

"Maybe if you weren't so fucking creepy, Aaron would like you more."

"No, I suspect it has very much more to do with the fact that I've dismembered him a few times." He smiled sweetly.

"Dismembered?" She took another step farther away

The Contortionist

from him as they walked. "You said you've never done anything wrong! I'm pretty sure that counts."

"Cora, Cora Cora..." He sighed and suddenly stepped into her, wrapping an arm around her shoulder to hug her to his side. "You really are adorably slow. You should be so happy that you're beautiful. You heard me when I said we cannot die. I fear that without the threat of permanent harm, arguments become a bit more spectacular." He grinned viciously. "I would never dismember you. There are many things I would like to do with you...Oh, such a list I've created in my head." His fingers on her shoulder spread, caressing her. "But you're safe with me."

Says the shark to the fish. She pushed away from him. She didn't like the feeling of his arm around her. Not because it felt wrong.

But because it felt just a little too nice.

He was, like she supposed the devil would be, fiendish and cruel—but alluring. She knew she was attracted to him on a surface level. But the threats of violence, Trent being in danger, and the fact that he was a supernatural, immortal, murdering lunatic kind of tipped the scales out of his favor.

"What's with all the titles?" She quickly changed the subject. "Barker, Rigger, whatever? You people have names, so why not use them?"

Clearly disappointed at her dodge, he looked off thoughtfully then shrugged. "No harm in explaining it, I suppose. There are twenty-two of us in total. And only ever twenty-two. Sometimes there are fewer, but never more. We are each an aspect of the system that Mr. Harrow created to build and sustain the Faire. Think of this place like a sea anemone. Alive, instinctual, but not sentient. Mr. Harrow, therefore, is like the cultivator of an aquarium. All of this"— he gestured his arms out wide to the carnival around them

—"is Mr. Harrow's design. And we are the adorable little fish in the tank that help feed and care for the anemone that also sustains us."

Cora didn't know what to say. "This place was abandoned a few days ago. Now it isn't. What happened?"

"That is a far more complicated topic better saved for another day. One thing at a time for your overwhelmed mind."

"I'm not stupid, Simon, and I really don't like it when you say I am."

He chuckled. "I don't mean it as an insult. When I came here, it took me years to accept what had happened to me." His expression fell again, the humor leaving him. "It took me years to understand."

"How did you...uh...join?" She didn't know what else to call it.

"I was taken. Some choose to be here. Others...do not." He grimaced, and agony flashed over him as though a memory had caused him visceral pain. It faded. "No matter. It's a deed long concluded. I'm here now, you're here now, and we have business to attend."

They reached a part of the park she hadn't seen before. It was behind a few of the tents, tucked way back, and behind a fence. A gap in the fence had an archway over it, which read "staff only."

It was a collection of little buildings, haphazardly placed around in a smaller portion of the huge field and bordered by the woods on three sides. One large, open-air tent had a scattering of park benches underneath it. It definitely lacked the loud signs and the flashing lights of the rest of the circus, although bits and pieces of painted facades and props were laying around on boxes or up against walls.

Everything looked, like the rest of the park, like it hadn't

The Contortionist

been updated in a long time. It was in pristine condition, but still vintage. *No. It's old. And alive. This isn't a reproduction. It's meant to be like this.*

Simon led her through the buildings and tents until they reached an array of—

She stopped. They looked like old caravans. Or train cars. The wheels on them were designed to have ridden on metal rails, although she could tell they had clearly not moved in ages from the grass and vines that were wound around them. They were wooden, antique, and all identical. Each one was about forty feet long and maybe sixteen feet wide, with windows running along all sides.

Some were lit from inside, but most were not. Some had curtains drawn, others didn't.

They were exactly what she had seen in her photo.

At the back end of each car, a little set of stairs were folded out to climb up to their doors. And on each door was painted a number. Seven, twelve, nineteen, eight…her eyes settled on one in particular. Its lights were off. The curtains were drawn. Grass and vines had begun to climb up the stairs as though no one had walked on them in a very long time.

It was painted with a zero.

A hand settled on her back. She jumped, gasping, and looked up at Simon. She hadn't expected him to be there at her side. He was watching her with a strange and eager fascination. "This is what you saw, isn't it?"

"Y—yeah." It was the third photo the Faire had shown her. The first was that terrible mirror. The second, his tent. And the third was there, right in front of her. She felt cold. She shivered.

"I almost didn't believe you, until I saw the color drain from your cheeks just there." He sighed. "For shame. I was hoping this was all an elaborate hoax the others were playing on me."

"Huh?"

"I thought perhaps Barker and Rigger had secured your affections and were using you to play a prank. They're always trying to take from me what I want. I do not know if I'm happy or sad that my theory was wrong." He lifted a shoulder in a half shrug. "Come along, Cora dear. Mr. Harrow's boxcar is this way."

It took her a solid few seconds to snap herself free of staring at the boxcar with the gold zero on the door before she followed after him. "Have you ever seen Mr. Harrow?"

"Never. He doesn't leave his boxcar. Ever. Ringmaster speaks to him via a series of notes passed under the door." Simon's expression darkened. "I have tried to bash in the door a thousand times. I have tried to set fire to it. I have tried to shatter the glass. Nothing works."

"Why were you so desperate to talk to him?"

Simon winced. "As I said…I was taken. I am not here by choice. It took me many years before I gave up and grew to enjoy my new life."

"I'm sorry."

He looked at her, an eyebrow quirked up. "Are you really?"

"I—" *What the hell kind of question is that?* "I mean, yeah. I'm sorry that happened to you. It sounds terrible. I don't know what I'd do in that situation."

There was an odd, knowing smile on his face. But it was paired with a strange, unsettling, overeager twist that made her uncomfortable. "I will do my very best to ensure that does not happen."

When they rounded a corner, Simon stopped short. She did the same. His shoulders lifted, and he went tense. Anger

The Contortionist

came over him so quickly it was almost palpable in the air. She took a step away from him reflexively. But luckily, it wasn't pointed at her.

They weren't alone.

Set away from the rest, nearly touching the woods, was a boxcar labeled twenty-one on the door. Standing at the base of the stairs was an enormous man with bronze skin and a dark mustache, wearing a green, gold, and cream striped tailcoat. He wore knee-high black boots, and canvas-colored pants tucked into them.

He looked just a little past his prime. He was handsome and had probably been an absolute showstopper in his youth. He also looked like he had once been muscular, but it had started to slide a little. He wasn't out of shape, per se. Age had just happened to him. His skin was bronze, his hair was short and dark, with a dusting of gray at the temples, and he boasted a broad and long mustache. His features gave her the impression he was probably somewhere from the Middle East or the Eastern Mediterranean.

There was no doubt he commanded whatever room he was in. He must have been as tall as Simon, but easily twice the Puppeteer's bodyweight. The tall, black top hat he wore made him seem that much more imposing. He held a coiled leather bullwhip in his hand.

And beside the man she assumed was "Ringmaster" stood Aaron and Jack.

It was clear that none of them were fond of Simon, and the feeling was mutual.

"You ran to Daddy, I see," Simon seethed. "Hello, Ringmaster. Hello, boys."

"Leave, Simon." Ringmaster walked toward them. "Go back to your tent, or to your boxcar, I don't care which. But leave Cora alone." The man turned warm, dark eyes to her.

There was such a look of sad sympathy in them that she was taken aback. He was looking at her like someone might look at a person dying of cancer. "Your game ends here."

"No!" Simon snarled. "She belongs to *me!*"

What?

She took a step away from Simon. That was it. She was done. *Sorry, Trent.* She tried to leave, but suddenly, she couldn't move. She struggled, but it felt like there were a thousand tiny wires surrounding her. She caught the faintest reflection of light off silvery, spider-like strings in the air around her.

Simon twitched his fingers, and she lurched, moving beside him. It was not of her own doing. Her feet moved, and she had nothing to do with it.

She wailed. "Oh, God—oh, God!"

His arm snaked around her, yanking her against him possessively, flush to his side. The smell of antiques and cologne washed over her. Now that she was this close to him, there was the scent of something like paint buried deep in there as well. "Be quiet, Cora." He was not looking at her but glaring a hole at Ringmaster. "We had a deal, fat man."

"Let me go!"

"Shush, Cora!" Simon snarled down at her. "Not now."

"Why have you brought her here, Simon?" Ringmaster narrowed his eyes, matching Simon's expression of rage with one of taciturn disapproval. "What is going on?"

"It isn't any of your business." Simon squeezed her again, as if afraid she'd be ripped away from him.

She still couldn't move. She couldn't lift her arms, turn her head, nothing. She would be shaking, but she didn't even have that range of movement. Her heart was thumping so loudly in her ears she missed part of the conversation.

The Contortionist

Panic was welling up in her chest. She wasn't claustrophobic —but being unable to control her own body was something new entirely. "Please," she whimpered. "Please stop..." She felt lightheaded.

I think I'm going to pass out. I never thought I was the passing out type.

Here we are, though, twice in one day.

Huh.

Simon's grasp on her was harsh and reeked of ownership. Like she was a toy and Ringmaster was threatening to take her away from him. She felt like an object on a shelf. She felt less than human. She also felt like she was strapped into a rollercoaster and watching a solid wall come rushing toward her. Unconsciousness was probably better than this. Sure, why not.

Something loud snapped her out of the sinking tunnel that she was drifting into. Something that split the air like a gunshot.

Crack!

Cora collapsed to the ground in a heap.

13

Everything was a blur. The last thing she knew, she had been about to pass out. Simon had her trapped with magic strings. Magic was real, and that was something she couldn't quite accept. Her mind kept skipping over that fact again and again like a broken record.

This can't be real.
This can't be real.
This can't be real.
But it was.

She had seen too much to do anything other than accept the fact that either it was real, or she had lost her mind and was now hallucinating the entire world around her. Right now, she felt detached enough to believe it was the latter.

Cora never figured herself as one for suffering panic attacks, but the events of the day were proving otherwise. Apparently, she just never had anything worth having a panic attack *about*. Strange disappearing photos on her camera, Trent being threatened by a man-eating murder-circus, a bloody apparition of herself in a mirror...and magical strings controlling her movements.

The Contortionist

Check, please.

But then, something had split the air, deafening and loud, and the ground had rushed up to meet her. Her head was spinning, and she felt both hot and cold at the same time. She was struggling to catch her breath. People were shouting, and someone was on the ground near her, a heap of red fabric. A heap of angry red fabric.

Simon. He was swearing and cursing about something, but she couldn't really make out his words. He had a hand pressed to the right side of his face.

Her fingers touched something unexpected on the packed dirt. Something small, and metal, and delicate. They were a pair of circular, antique sunglasses. One lens was tinted red, the other black. She gently took them into her palm and held them. She didn't know why. It was an impulse. Something about her mind struggling for anything to grasp onto. Anything at all.

Hands on her arms plucked her up from the ground, and the world was moving again. She nearly toppled over a second time, but someone held her steady. She blinked, trying to straighten out her vision.

She slipped the glasses in her pocket. She really didn't know why. In the back of her head, she just didn't want them to get stepped on and broken. It was a weird reflex, but she couldn't really argue with it at the moment.

She looked up at the concerned face of Jack as he pulled her away from whatever was happening. There was more shouting going on behind her. When he brought her to a nearby wooden storage box and sat her down, she could finally make some sense of what was going on.

"She is *mine!*" Simon howled. He was on his knees, shouting up at the imposing man in the green and gold striped tailcoat. The right half of the Puppeteer's face was a mask of blood. He might have even lost his eye. He had a hand pressed to the socket, and the crimson that was flowing from him stained the red of his clothing an even darker color. "You have no right to intervene—"

"I'm in charge. Therefore, I have every right," Ringmaster snarled. His long leather whip was snaked around behind him. As he moved the handle, it jerked around so quickly it was almost like a living thing.

Simon began to push to his feet, but Ringmaster was having none of it. He swung the bullwhip over his head. *Crack!*

That was the noise she had heard.

"Stay on your knees, Puppeteer, or you'll stagger back to your boxcar with *both* your eyes missing." Ringmaster flicked his wrist and caught the tip of whip in his hand as it came up to meet him, creating a loop. He decked Simon across the face with it, rocking the other man's head back with the blow.

Simon spat blood onto the ground. But he stayed on his knees. "She's mine, Ringmaster. Not yours. Not anyone else's. Not the Faire's. *Mine."*

"The agreement was that you could have her if you could convince her. I don't see a woman who was ready to be turned to one of your abominations, Simon. Have you even told her the cost of your games?"

"We were about to begin broaching the subject when you interrupted."

She felt like a passerby. Like she was watching a movie, not *in* it.

"Liar!" Jack interjected. "You weren't going to explain shit, and you know it." Jack was still standing at her side, a reassuring hand on her shoulder. He turned to look down at her. "Cora? Why was he bringing you here?"

The Contortionist

"Don't tell them anything, Cora. Don't trust them!" Simon moved to get up on his feet, but Ringmaster wouldn't allow it. He pulled back the handle of the bullwhip and smashed the Puppeteer in the face with it, knocking him back flat to the ground with a thump. When Simon removed his hand to catch himself, she saw the whole right side of his face was a massive gash from his chin to his forehead. The wound had clearly been put there by the first swing of the bullwhip. She turned her head away from the gore. She might have seen bone.

"Trust? That's rich coming from you, *traitor.*" Aaron shot the words over his shoulder as he moved to stand by her. He knelt at her feet, looking up at her with nothing but pity and sincerity. "It's okay, Cora. You can tell us."

"Traitor?" Simon laughed and shuffled back to his knees, putting his hand back over the slash on his face. "And how am I that? Is this still about your lover? Is this still about Hernandez?" He sighed dramatically. "For the last time, he came to me. He wanted all this to stop. He needed the pain to end. And he knew I could help him. I'm sorry your constant humping wasn't enough to console him." Even through the obvious pain he was in, Simon grinned. His teeth were stained red. He looked to her with his one remaining bizarrely colored eye. "Tell them nothing, Cora. Nothing at all. If you think you are in danger from me—you know nothing about what they're capable of."

"I..." She felt so small. She was so sore. She was so tired. "I just want to go home, please."

Aaron picked up her hand and gently held it between his. "You're safe. We're not going to hurt you. Don't listen to anything he says. He's a liar, a cheat, and a manipulator. I know it's easy to believe he's a friend, but he's only ever looking out for himself. He wants something from you. You heard him—insisting you belong to him. You don't. Don't fall into his web."

She didn't know what to do. She shook her head numbly. "Please...I just...this is all too much."

"Jack." Ringmaster jerked his head toward Simon. "Keep him down."

Jack obeyed, leaving her side to go to where the bloody man was still on his knees. "Gladly." He rounded a kick into Simon's side, sending the Puppeteer sprawling to the ground with a heavy groan.

"How noble." Simon coughed a glob of blood into the dirt. "See how they treat me, Cora? See how they'll treat you, too?"

"Shut the fuck up, Simon," Jack kicked him again, "or I'll break your ribs."

"Only way you can win a fight with me is when I'm already beaten. Enjoy yourself, Rigger. This'll be your only chance in a long time." Simon rolled onto his back, wheezed, and let his arms sprawl out in the dirt.

She had to look away from the gore again. She could see his teeth through the split in his lip. The cut definitely went down to the skull. "Please, stop. Please." She didn't know who she was begging, or for what. She needed everything to just take a second.

"Listen to the nice girl, Jackie-boy," Simon taunted from the ground. Where he found the strength to mouth off when his face was destroyed, she didn't know. *He says he can't die. Maybe he'll just magically heal.*

None of this is real.

But here it is.

A shadow fell over her, cast by the glowing amber lights mounted on posts that illuminated the "staff" area of the park. She looked up at the imposing figure of Ringmaster.

The Contortionist

He took off his hat and smoothed a gloved hand back over his black hair. He was as tall as Simon, but twice as broad. With his dated Ringmaster outfit and handlebar mustache, he looked like he had stepped right out of a vintage poster. Of course, so did everyone else around her.

"Hello, Cora," he greeted her gently. There was warmth and sadness in his brown eyes. "I'm afraid you've had a rough few days, haven't you?" He felt somehow...safe. Like a hot cup of cocoa after being stuck out in a terrible winter storm. Where Simon was thin, this man—the Ringmaster, apparently—was double wide to make up for it.

She nodded.

"They call me Ringmaster. Or Turk, to my friends. I'm afraid I don't quite remember my real name." He smiled. "I think Simon has been playing a terrible game with you, and I'm sorry. He is a monster, but he is still part of the Family. How much has he explained to you?"

"Some. I don't know. I still can't wrap my head around it."

"I want to help you, Cora. And I can. I can set all of this straight. But you have to talk to me." He coiled the whip and hung it on what looked like a little hook with a leather strap on his hip. "Why did he bring you here?"

"Don't do it, cupcake," Simon warned her. "If you tell him, it'll doom you forever." Jack kicked him in the ribs again, and Simon rolled onto his side with a wheezing groan.

"That's rich, coming out of you," Jack snarled and kicked Simon in the back. "You're planning on making her into a doll!"

Make her into a what?

Cora really hoped Jack didn't mean that literally, and she was starting to suspect he did. Fear settled over her like a cold breeze rolling down her spine. She shivered, and if she could have sunk into the box or into the ground itself, she would have.

Aaron squeezed her hand reassuringly. "It's all right, Cora…you can talk to us."

She swallowed the lump in her throat. She didn't know who to believe or what to do. But she certainly didn't trust Simon. "I…I need to talk to Mr. Harrow."

"Why, Cora?" Ringmaster asked quietly.

She paused for a long time before she worked up the nerve to speak. She didn't know what else to do. "Because my…my friend Trent is in danger. Something here is going to kill him."

Simon began to laugh. It was a quiet, sadistic sound that grew in volume and its manic quality. It only stopped when Jack kicked him in the ribs again. When the Puppeteer could breathe, he lifted his head to look at her. "It's all over now, Cora. I could have saved you. I could have helped you. But you made your choice." He laid his head back down on the dirt. "Nobody ever listens to me."

His shadow was drawing a sharp and unnatural line across the dirt, cast in the wrong direction from the light. The creature was on the wall, all teeth and anger pointed silently and uselessly at Jack.

"How do you know all this, Cora?" Ringmaster's tone was quiet and insistent. But for some reason, she felt like she was in trouble with her dad. She was a little girl in front of the enormous man.

"The Faire is…is talking to me." She chewed her lip and picked up her camera with her other hand. It was still somehow not broken, despite the fact that she fell on it again. "Through this. Through pictures."

Simon was still grinning like a maniac even from where

he was lying, bloody and beaten in the dirt. "Now Mr. Harrow isn't the only one to hear the will of the beast."

The feeling in the air seemed to change. Ringmaster, Jack, and Aaron all glanced at each other with their faces various pictures of wide-eyed concern. Fear, worry, and the expression that came along with learning that the impossible was now *very* possible.

She knew the look because she was wearing one of her own. Maybe just for different reasons. Aaron let go of her hand to stand and face Ringmaster. "Turk. He's lying. He has to be."

Ringmaster glanced to Simon then looked to her. He stroked his hand over his mustache. "Is he, Cora?"

She shook her head meekly.

Ringmaster let out a long and heavy sigh. He shut his eyes, and his fists clenched for a moment before he released them. "What is it telling you?"

She looked down at her camera. It had definitely taken a bit of a beating in the past few hours, but it seemed okay. "It's been leaving me photos. It showed me this place when it was abandoned. It showed me the hall of mirrors, and I knew I had to go there. When I did, it showed me photos of Trent, dead. Murdered. When I asked it—begged it—to tell me how to stop it from happening, it—" She stopped.

Why did she feel in danger? Why did she suddenly look up at Ringmaster and feel as though Simon wasn't the only monster who wanted to hurt her? There was nothing in his expression except a stern and resolute kind of regret. He wasn't threatening her.

But it felt wrong.

This felt like it could all go very poorly.

The image in the mirror of the funhouse was personal. Maybe she shouldn't have told Simon about it—but suddenly, she knew telling Ringmaster about it was a very, very bad idea. Telling Simon about it, combined with the boxcar painted with a zero on it seemed to have made him frantic about something. She didn't want a repeat performance with "Turk."

"It what?" Turk urged her to finish.

"It showed me a photo of a boxcar." It wasn't a lie. It wasn't the whole truth either.

Simon laughed. She knew why, but she hoped nobody else did. She didn't want to lie to them, but she had no desire to go over whatever cliff she found herself standing on. Proverbial or otherwise.

Ringmaster studied her for a long moment. She could only pray he couldn't see through her half-truth. He looked toward the boxcar painted with the twenty-one on the door. There were no lights on inside. "The Faire only speaks to Harrow. And Harrow only to me."

"Not anymore." Simon rolled onto his back again. His face was…healing. She couldn't see the teeth through the gash in his lips. She couldn't see it happening from that far away, but the results were clear. *Magic is real.*

None of this can be happening.

She managed not to wail again as she squeezed her eyes shut for a moment. She felt sick. "Please, I just want to go home."

"I think that would be for the best." Ringmaster walked away from her. "You're free to go, Cora. No one will stop you on the way out of the park." He crouched down and snatched Simon up by the hair. The Puppeteer yelped and was forced to his feet. "You and I are going to speak in private."

"No—you can't let her leave, fat man!" Simon swatted at the hand in his hair, but he received a hard punch in the

The Contortionist

face from Ringmaster for his trouble. He grunted, and his knee buckled. "Ow. Fine, fine...I'll come. Cora. Cora! Come back to see me tomorrow. We need to talk."

That freakish, unnatural shadow of his was now trying to bite Ringmaster's own shadow. But it seemed he really was harmless and could only make threatening gestures and chomping faces.

As for talking to Simon? No, they didn't need to do anything of the sort, and she had no plans on returning. She was going to put the Faire in her rear-view mirror and never come back.

But what about Trent?

She swore under her breath. "Wait. Ringmaster, I need your help."

Ringmaster turned to look at her, an eyebrow raised. "What is it, Cora?"

"My friend Trent is in danger. I know he is. I have to find a way to stop this place from killing him."

"Do you know how he dies?" Aaron asked from where he stood a few paces away, his expression a mix of confusion and muddled shock.

"No. It showed me a bunch of different ways." She cringed at the images in her memory. She knew they'd haunt her for a long time.

Aaron shook his head. "Not sure how to stop something if we don't know how it happens."

"The Faire, if it was whispering to you, showed you whatever it wanted you to see. It doesn't mean it's real. This place is a world of illusions and lies, Cora Glass. Leave here, and if you're wise, you'll never return." Ringmaster began walking, dragging a staggering Simon beside him. "Your friend's fate is his own. This place only means to hurt you, Cora. Stay away."

That was advice she had every intention of following.

But as she slipped her hand into her pocket and found a pair of sunglasses folded and tucked away, she had the feeling her business with Harrow Faire wasn't nearly done yet.

I need to save Trent.
I just need to figure out how.

14

SIMON CRASHED into the chair into which Ringmaster hurled him with no pomp or circumstance. But he was glad to be sitting. He was also glad for the chance to take his handkerchief from his pocket to try to wipe some of the drying blood from his eye and his face. His eye had healed on the way to Ringmaster's office at the back of the big top tent, but he hadn't had the opportunity to clean himself up enough to use it.

He squinted his best glare up at the man who had pushed him there. "You're being very rude, fat man. You—" He let out a rather undignified noise as Ringmaster grabbed him by the front of the shirt and half-hefted him back up out of the chair where his "boss" had just deposited him. "Rude and indecisive. Do you want me in the chair or out of the chair?"

"Shut up, Simon. Before I knock your teeth all over the floor." Ringmaster dumped him back down roughly into the wooden chair. It creaked from the impact but at least didn't shatter. That would be more insult to injury—picking wooden shards out of his clothes. "Tell me everything you know about Cora Glass."

Simon smiled and stayed silent.

When Ringmaster reeled back a fist, intending to punch him in the face—again—Simon cringed and turned his head away. He hated getting hit in the face. It seemed to happen fairly frequently, all things considered. "You told me to shut up. Now you want me to talk. You want me to sit. You want me to stand! You want me to sit again. Make up your bloody mind!"

"What else has the Faire told Cora?"

"I didn't see any of the photos myself." He had no reason to tell the oaf what he knew. And it was true, he hadn't seen any of what Cora had told him. The clever child had been smart enough to see she had no friends in that unexpected quarrel only a few minutes prior. She didn't trust him—which he resented a little but understood—but she also didn't trust Ringmaster and the rest.

He could use that particular development.

The big man was pacing around the room, concern etched deep on his face.

Simon watched Ringmaster walk back and forth for a moment. He cleaned some of the blood off his face while he thought about how best to use this to his advantage. "If the Faire is talking to her, she's a threat to Mr. Harrow."

Yes, there was definitely a way to get what *he* wanted out of all of this. He wanted Cora.

All of her.

Ringmaster was facing him now, consternated at best. "I realize that."

"Then, if you want to protect our mutual employer...I have a suggestion." Simon grinned. "If she comes back here, let me have her. She won't be a threat if she's one of mine."

The Contortionist

The big man sighed and turned away, walking to his desk to place his heavy hands on the wood surface. "You're asking me to doom that girl to a terrible fate."

"I'm only asking you to do it *if* she comes back. If she stays away, then she gets to live out her unhappy little life. But if she sets foot in here again, and you want to protect Mr. Harrow? Then she has to go." It hurt to grin. His face was sore. But he couldn't help it. Everything was so terribly funny. For a minute, it had looked like he was going to be denied what he wanted. But this was also going to be fun. It was the long way around, but he didn't mind a scenic route once in a while.

"What else do you know, Puppeteer?"

"You split open my face, you've punched me, what, four times tonight? You let Jack kick me for a laugh. Why, in the name of all the pits in Hell, do you think I would tell you anything? Even if I knew the details?"

"Because if you don't, I'll hang you from your ankles in the tower for another five years," Ringmaster snapped at him before slumping down into his chair. He looked exhausted. "And I will enjoy every second of your screams. You know I will." The threat was lacking the big man's usual bluster. It was the half-hearted complaint of a man who knew he was already losing the advantage in the conversation.

"I'm afraid to say that all I have is theories to go on. I have no idea what the Faire wants with Ms. Cora." Now, that was a bold-faced lie. He had a very good *idea* of what the Faire wanted. But it was still a theory, even if it was backed up with evidence. The Faire wanted her...and it wanted to keep her for itself. He found himself at odds with the very creature that kept him alive.

But he'd be damned a second time before he let the

Faire take anything else away from him. It had taken everything—literally everything—that was valuable to him. He would not let it take this newest prize from his fingers.

The Faire owed him one.

And he wouldn't let Ringmaster, Mr. Harrow, or even the very ground beneath his feet deny him Cora, so he did something he honestly hated to do, despite what everybody claimed. He lied. "I only know what she told you. That her camera has shown her bizarre photos, including one of a boxcar with a painted digit on the door."

He just wouldn't tell Ringmaster which digit in particular. Let the fat fool believe himself to be the smartest man in the room. Let him come up with his own theories. Simon had his.

The Faire has a hole to fill. And it wants her.
But she belongs to me.

"What else is there, Simon? What else has she told you?" Ringmaster narrowed his eyes, as if that might let him see past his deception. Honestly, Simon was certain Ringmaster always expected the worst from him. And he usually wasn't wrong.

"Cora is confused and scared. She's worried about her friend and asked the Faire what she had to do to save him. It gave her a riddle. When she told me she saw a boxcar with a painted number, I assumed it must be Mr. Harrow. I was taking her to see him. I assumed he might have something to say to her." That was all true. Mostly true. He left out giant details. He owed Ringmaster nothing. Simon shrugged innocently. As best as he could do anything innocently, anyway. "I think you should be talking to Mr. Harrow, honestly. It's his reign of Master of the Faire that's being challenged, not anything to do with me."

The Contortionist

"And why would you protect Mr. Harrow? You hate him."

"To set the record straight, I hate all of you." He laughed. "But I only want one thing in this endeavor, and I've made that perfectly clear. I have no interest in letting anyone take her from me. So, if these means serve my ends, then I'm happy to play along."

Ringmaster rubbed his hand over his face. "Why do you have to be so difficult, Simon?"

"See previous comment about hatred." He smiled sweetly. "Now, if you'll excuse me, I'm going to go to my boxcar and clean up. I need a change of clothes, as these are sticky and ruined, and I seem to have lost my sunglasses. I do hate to terrorize the patrons. Well, at least when I'm not trying to." He stood from the chair and brushed himself off. He was a disgusting mess. Blood had really soaked his clothes. "I should probably take the back way, speaking of terrifying the patrons..."

"If I find out you know more than you're telling me, Simon...you will regret it."

"When have I ever regretted a single thing in my life?" He shrugged as he walked toward the exit. "Have a lovely night, you giant tub of lard." He whistled to himself as he left, grinning once more. He rubbed his face as he felt the muscle twinge, and it still came back sticky. He needed a shower and a stiff drink. He wished he could share both with Cora.

The mental image of her naked and pressed up against the tile of his shower wall made him shudder. Lust was entertaining, and it was an emotion he hadn't felt in a very, very long time. He savored it. He wasn't sure if he'd ever get to act it out, since he was going to steal her life and place it into one of his dolls. But perhaps she might entertain the idea in their dreams.

After she forgave him. Which she would. Eventually.

Maybe.

On his way back to his boxcar, he passed the one with the painted zero. He paused to look at it. It was overgrown and abandoned. No one had lived in it for thirty-eight years. All that remained of the Contortionist was now dead and gone. But, just like all the times a slot in the Family had gone empty, the Faire sought to fill it. Usually, it was Mr. Harrow who issued the order. It had never come directly from the Faire itself, not for as long as Simon could remember. But it seemed Simon wasn't the only creature overeager to play with his fiery little Cora Glass.

All the others shunned the empty and vacant boxcar of the previous Contortionist. So many other Family members had come and gone in the century-and-change that Simon had spent as Puppeteer. Although nobody else had gone in quite such a spectacular method as Hernandez. All the rest simply faded out until they were gone like a spent candle waiting to flicker its last bit of light.

And they were always quickly replaced. There had to be twenty-two of them. And Mr. Harrow was ever eager to draw a new fly into its web. But they had never had another Contortionist in all those years…and now he knew why.

Because Hernandez was still here, wasn't he? It was no coincidence that the last dregs of that pathetic man had asked for his freedom at the same time that Cora set foot into Harrow Faire. The Faire itself had pushed out the last remains of the old to welcome in the new.

It wanted her. The moment she told him about what she had seen in the funhouse mirror—that strange vision of herself as a contortionist covered in blood—he knew. It

The Contortionist

had erased any doubts in his mind about what was going on.

"You won't get her," he muttered under his breath. He often talked to himself or his shadow. No one would pay him a second glance for talking to himself now. "She's mine. Do you hear me? I haven't wanted anything in a long time—a very long time—and now that you let me taste her, I know you want to rip her away. I won't let it happen, you stupid, glorified sea urchin."

I will find a way to burn this place down if you dare take anything more away from me. Never again.

"She belongs to me." He said it as a threat. He said it as a promise.

Now, in order to make good on it, he just had to find a way to get Cora to come back to him. He let his eyes drift shut. He was so tired. And that poor girl must be exhausted. He smiled as it gave him another idea. He had many gifts in this world, and one of them was talking people into giving him what he wanted.

And oh, how he wanted her.

And he knew just how to get her.

———

CORA MADE it home before she burst into tears. It wasn't until she closed the door behind her and leaned against it that she let it happen. Mostly because she was frustrated. Partially because she was in a great deal of pain. And also, y'know, because she was having a major existential crisis.

I guess I'm allowed.

She wiped her sleeve over her eyes. Nothing made sense anymore. Why was the Faire whispering to her? Why was it showing her all those weird images? Why was it after Trent?

She decided she needed a drink. She moved to pull off her coat and paused. She had put her hand in her pocket, where she had put Simon's sunglasses.

They were gone.

She checked her other pocket and blinked. They had definitely been there. Things didn't fall out of her coat—she hated when that happened, so she always bought ones with super deep pockets.

Mysteriously disappearing sunglasses definitely went on the bottom of the list of weird shit she had seen that week. She shrugged it off. With a long sigh, she took off her coat and hung it on the peg on the wall. Heading to her kitchen, she grabbed a beer, popped the cap off, and sat at her table with her camera. She flicked it on and almost dreaded going through the images.

But she had to know if there was anything there. If there were any more clues to the riddle she was trying to solve. One she was pretty sure Simon had the answer to, but never got to tell her.

Not that she trusted that tall creep.

She ran through in her head what the camera had shown her. The images that were now gone. An image of the funhouse mirror. An image of Simon's tent. And an image of the boxcar painted with the gold zero. That was what it had shown her. The first had come true already, showing her an image of herself, twisted and warped. The second...she couldn't tell if it meant for her to avoid Simon or go to him.

Am I supposed to sacrifice myself in trade for Trent?

The memory of her reflection covered in blood ran through her mind. She sipped her beer and cringed, switching hands. Her right shoulder was a hot mess. It was angry at her for ramming it into a wall. It would be barely usable tomorrow.

The Contortionist

She scanned through her photos. Images of mirrors, followed by the silly images Simon had taken, most of which were blurry or pointed at the wrong thing. She started to speed up, since the man had managed to take somewhere around a hundred and fifty photos in a ten-minute span of time. Halfway through the stream, she saw something odd. Something that was the wrong color for every other photo around it. Backing up, she groaned.

She leaned back in her chair.

It was certainly the wrong color to belong with the rest. It was also the wrong time period. The image was faded and old, distressed like it was taken a hundred years ago. And picking up the camera, she instantly recognized the man in the image.

Simon. Posing with a young woman with long blonde hair. They weren't smiling—but she knew it was because the technology at the time took too long to expose the film for the subjects to hold an expression. They were both painfully beautiful and well-dressed. He wore no glasses, and he was missing the manic and terrible grin on his face that he always seemed to wear. It seemed Simon had originally come from money. Photographs were exceedingly rare and expensive at the time. And they were both dressed incredibly well. He was standing behind the woman, who was sitting on a stool in front of him, his hand gently resting on her shoulder.

She picked up her camera and looked down at it. But who was she? They didn't look related. And why was the Faire showing her this? At least it wasn't the dead body of her friend or her own self covered in blood. She'd take a weird old vintage photograph.

But why?

The Faire was telling her something about Simon. Was it

telling her to go to Simon? But then why show her a vintage photograph of him and some random lady? She clicked through the rest of the images in case there were any others hidden in the pile, but she couldn't find any. Going back to the one she had found, it took her a second to realize anything had changed.

But when she did, she nearly dropped her camera.

The image had changed.

Simon was once more as she recognized him. Sadistically smiling at the camera, his mismatched glasses on his face. His clothing was the sharply and eccentrically cut pinstripe suit. She knew it was red, even if the image was still a sepia black and white.

But that wasn't what almost made her drop her camera. Simon had his hand wrapped around the throat of the woman sitting on the stool, pressing her back against his chest.

And the woman sitting on the stool wasn't a beautiful blonde…it was Cora.

She turned off the camera and shoved it away. She downed the rest of the beer and decided she needed something stronger. "I'm not going back there. I'm not." *He wants to make me into one of his "dolls," whatever that means. I'm going to just go with the nicest possible option and hope it's sexual. The other options are worse.* "I don't care."

But what if it meant that Trent died? She leaned her head on her cabinet doors and let out a long, beleaguered groan. She fixed herself a gin and tonic. She collapsed on her sofa, wincing again at the stabbing pain in her shoulder, and tried to calm her racing heartbeat.

Simon is going to do something terrible to me.

The fucked up, man-eating murder-circus is going to kill my friend.

The Faire never said that it was a trade. I asked it what I should do to save my friend, but it never specifically said that was the deal we were making. This could all just be a trick. She sipped her gin and took a deep breath, held it for a second, and let it out slowly.

Maybe she could convince Trent never to go back to the Faire. But that would go over just about as well as a fart in church. He wasn't the kind of guy who listened to the advice of others—and telling him *not* to do something was about as good as a guarantee that he'd just do it out of spite.

If she warned him about Ludwig the Strongman and the rest of the carnival, he'd laugh her off and call her insane. And she probably was. She didn't have any proof of what had happened to her. None of the photos lasted on her camera. She didn't even have Simon's sunglasses anymore.

Where had they gone, anyway?

She sipped the gin and shut her eyes. If the Faire was asking for her life in trade for Trent's, if that was really the deal on the table? Could she do it? Could she really do it?

Could she lay down her life for her friend?

It was one of those moments where everyone would smile and say they'd do it when asked the proverbial question, because it was only that—proverbial. But this was *literal*. The Faire wanted her to die—or undergo whatever the hell Simon was going to do to her—in order to allow Trent to live. That was her theory, anyway.

What kind of life did she have, anyway? One of pain, and misery, and working as a teller in a fucking bank because her Ehlers-Danlos Syndrome kept her from pursuing anything else she enjoyed. She wasn't happy. She was always in agony and finding new ways to hurt. She was just going through her days, watching Netflix and playing videogames, going to the gym enough to make sure her joints popped out less frequently than they would otherwise, and passing the time.

Until what?

She died?

She didn't even date anymore. Not since the terrible business with Duncan. It'd been five years, but the idea of being intimate with anyone made her sick to her stomach. She just couldn't sit at a table with someone over dinner and pretend that she wanted to try.

Trent had a life. He had a career. He'd get married someday to some lovely guy and probably buy a small dog and have a beautiful home. He'd wear a sweater around his shoulders, host brunches with mimosas, and be happy and adorable.

None of that was in the cards for her.

Pound for pound, his life had more potential than hers. And she cared about him. He was her best friend—one of the few she still could talk to without having to put up walls or lie about how she felt. About the depression, the pain, any of it. He was the first person she went to after she had thrown Duncan out of their apartment. Trent was the one who had held her while she wept in a puddle on the kitchen floor.

"Nothing beats a good old-fashioned kitchen floor reset. They make for the best sob sessions," he had told her. And he was right. After she sat there on the kitchen tile and wept, she had felt better. The giant tub of ice cream he had pulled out of his freezer had also helped.

He was always there for her with a joke, with a good story, or wanting to take her out to clubs to cheer her up. Never mind the fact that clubs had the opposite effect on her, he was always trying to find the bright side of things.

But could she really die for him?

The Contortionist

She never once thought she was afraid of death, until the possibility became very real. She finished her drink and lay down on the sofa, needing some time to let her thoughts circle the drain before she was tired enough to go to bed.

Apparently, she was more tired than she expected.

Because one second, she was laying on her sofa. And the next, she was dreaming.

And once again, she wasn't alone.

And once again, it involved a lot of blood.

15

Cora was standing in a big, beautiful, sunlit room. Windows lined the walls, revealing a sprawling and well-manicured landscape filled with hedges and flowering shrubs. It was the kind of estate people dreamed of living in, and the kind that was very rarely found in America.

There were paintings on easels all around the room. Some were portraits, and some were landscapes. They were all amazing works of art, even the ones that didn't look to be finished.

There was a man sitting on the floor with an easel that was missing its legs in front of him. The stand was dominated by a large canvas. She recognized the man immediately, even though his head was down. The wild, dark hair around his face was hard to miss. Simon.

The floor around him was covered in shards of wood. It looked like the frame of a canvas had been broken into pieces. He had one large piece in his hand like a stake and was digging it violently into his thigh. Blood was pooling around him on the ground. She watched as he reached into the wound with his other hand, smearing blood on his fingers, before reaching up to use the gore as paint on the canvas.

"Simon?"

He didn't answer. He didn't even glance to her. It was like she didn't exist.

"You did this shit the first time. I'm not falling for it a second time."

When he finally lifted his head to look higher up the canvas, but not to her, she noticed his cheeks were damp. He was...crying. Tears were streaming down his face, unchecked and ignored. "Hello, Cora. I'm afraid now is not a great time."

"I'm not the one doing the dream-sessions. You are." She took a step toward him and, keeping her distance, crossed the room to see what he was painting.

"Touché."

It was a portrait of a beautiful woman. Cora knew the girl's hair would be blonde if it wasn't made of smears of red. It was the girl from the photograph. "Who was she?"

"I can't forget, and I can't remember..." he whispered. "Her name was Suzanna. But I can only remember her face in my dreams." He kept painting frantically with the blood, digging the wooden shard deep into his thigh to pool more crimson up to the surface. "Why? Why now? Why with *you*? I had other plans. I always have other plans...and it takes those away, too. The Faire takes everything from me. Even this!"

He was rambling. He had the glassy-eyed expression of a madman. Now and again, she could almost forget he had a few screws loose. He seemed to be so lucid most of the time. She fought the urge to stop him from hurting himself. She had to remind herself that he wasn't a friend. He was going to hurt her.

Or worse.

But watching him dig the shard of wood into his thigh was too much for her. And with him crying like that, something in her couldn't help it. She walked up to him, knelt at his side, and tried to pry the wood out of his hand. She noticed then that he was left-handed, using his right to dig the stake into his leg and the other to paint. "Come on, Simon, stop it..."

"No. It's only when I hurt that I can remember what she looked like." He cringed and tightened his grasp on the wood. But as she tried again, he quickly relented and gave up. She tossed it aside. His eyes slipped shut, and he hung his head in defeat. He looked so forlorn...so heartbroken.

Cora looked at the painting. "She's beautiful."

"She was. She's dead now. Dead and dust." He looked down at his bloody palms.

"You didn't..."

"Huhm?" He glanced up to her, the odd coloring of his eyes startling her for a second. But she was slowly getting used to it, even if it was still eerie. "You think I hurt her?" He sneered. "You think I'm a monster just like they say." He pushed up from the ground. Or rather, he tried. He made it to standing and took one step before his leg gave out and he collapsed back to the floor next to her with a grunt. "Oh, good. I hit a tendon. How charming. Yes, fear me, Cora Glass. Today alone, you've seen me battered, beaten, bloody, and now crying on the floor of my childhood home like a little girl. I'm so utterly terrifying. Run, run and save yourself from my horror and wrath."

She laughed at his deflated sarcasm. She shouldn't. He really was a monster. "I'd be more sympathetic if you weren't trying to kill me." She stood from the floor and offered him a hand. He eyed her warily, then shrugged, and

The Contortionist

let her help him up. She supported his weight as he walked to a sofa near a wall. It was a beautiful piece, all embroidered upholstery and carved wood.

When he collapsed onto it with a thankful groan, he looked down at the sofa. "I'm going to muck the fabric. Oh, well. I suppose none of this is real, so none of it matters." He leaned his head back on the wood, and his black-red-white eyes gazing at her. "Why?"

"Why what?"

"Why help me?"

"You were bleeding on the floor and miserable. I don't know. It seemed like the right thing to do."

"You said yourself that you believe I'm trying to kill you. Which I'm not, by the by." He pointed at her defensively. "That is an assumption, and you should feel bad about it." He managed to hold a serious expression for a few seconds before it cracked into a grin.

She stared at him flatly for a moment. "You're extremely confusing."

"That's the nicest thing anyone's called me in a long time." He patted the sofa next to him. "Sit, Cora dear. Let's chat."

What else was she going to do? This was a dream. She was stuck here until she...she didn't know, woke up or he let her go. One of the two. With a beleaguered sigh, she sat on the sofa, as far away from him as she could.

He rolled his eyes and scooted over until his leg was touching hers. At least it wasn't the bloody one. He slung an arm around her shoulder and pulled her to him. "I'm confusing, and you're stubborn."

"Maybe I don't want you touching me."

"Maybe." He smiled. "Or maybe you do." He laughed at her glare and leaned in and placed a kiss atop her head. "I'm sorry tonight went so poorly for all of us. This wasn't at all what I had planned."

The kiss did something strange to her. It should have been revolting. It wasn't. She shivered. What was wrong with her? She shifted away from him as much as he'd allow. "What did you have planned, exactly?"

"Well," he took in a deep breath and let all the words out as a rush, "I-had-a-few-different-options-and-would-have-been-happy-with-any-of-them."

"What were the options, then?" She fought the urge to stab her finger into the wound on his leg.

"Too many to list." He stroked his thumb over her shoulder. She shivered again from the touch, and her face went a little warm. He let out a low hum at her reaction. "This wasn't on the list, but I'll take it."

She shoved his hand off her. He put it right back where it was. "Don't be difficult."

"Difficult and confusing. You're displeased with me, aren't you, cupcake? What've I done to deserve this cold shoulder?" He pouted comically.

"You want to turn me into one of your dolls. What does that mean?"

"Don't believe what those fools say. They hate me, and they're jealous. They would ruin anything of mine just to make me miserable."

"Were they lying?"

He looked off for a long moment before muttering his answer. "No."

She elbowed him in the ribs. He grunted and laughed at the same time, but still didn't move his arm from around her shoulders. If anything, he pulled her against him in slight squeeze. "Simon."

"What?"

The Contortionist

"What're you doing?"

"By God, you really are a slow one, aren't you?" He leaned closer, and before she could react, he had grabbed her legs and pulled them across his lap. She was now sitting sideways on the sofa, and he was caging her in with his arms on either side of her. His face hovered close to hers.

The smell of an antique store and cologne came over her again. A thousand different scents of old things, of leather, of dust. Of places and things to explore. He was warm. She could feel the heat from him against her. It was something she hadn't experienced for five years—being near someone.

Stunned, she didn't know what to do. He was a madman. He wanted to turn her into one of his dolls—whatever that meant—but he was captivating. God help her, something about him caught her breath in her throat.

He was monstrous. He was wicked. He was beautiful. He watched her with those fiendishly colored eyes, and she saw desire in them. She saw mischief. She wanted to know what he was planning...because she might want it a little bit, too.

He watched her like a cat with a wounded bird that knew its victory was sealed, but was still dragging out the moment for a bit more fun. He lowered himself just a little closer, forcing her to lean back against the armrest. His lips ghosted over her cheek and wandered to her ear. His breath pooled against her, and goosebumps rushed down her arms.

"I want you, Cora," he murmured. "I want you in every way you'll let me have you. There. Is that more direct?"

Her stomach felt like it dropped off a cliff. She didn't know what to do. Her hands were tangled in his vest, and she couldn't find the strength to push him away. She could only hold on for dear life.

"I can take away all your pain. All the agony you wake up to in the morning from that poor shoulder of yours, I can remove. I don't want to kill you, my sweet, tasty little cupcake. I want to keep you. You will live on for a long time...somewhere you belong. Somewhere you'll be cared for. Somewhere you'll be protected. And you won't ever be alone." All his words were barely more than a whisper. "You will save yourself...and your friend. It isn't a curse. It's a trade."

He moved back just far enough to look down at her, bizarrely colored eyes boring into hers. She felt like she had forgotten how to breathe. And any hope of fixing the situation was crushed when he kissed her.

His hand laced into her hair at the back of her neck, cradling her head as he pressed his lips to hers. It was slow. It was sensual. It felt like the definition of sin itself. It wasn't rough, and it wasn't harsh. It was gentle and passionate. But all the same, the embrace was possessive. It was stealing a part of her, just as the Faire had done. It felt like he was taking a part of her soul with every second he worked his lips against hers.

When he finally broke away from her, she was trembling. She had her hands pressed to his chest, but she was shaking too much to decide if she was trying to pull him closer or push him away.

"Cora..." He slid his hand from her hair to cradle her face. He stroked his thumb along her cheek. "That was...that was glorious. That was delectable. Yes, in fact, I think I shall have another, thank you for asking..." He leaned in, and she pushed against him. He hesitated. "Hm?"

"No." She struggled to fill her lungs. How could a person be out of breath in a dream? "Please."

He pulled a little farther back. He furrowed his brow in confusion. "Am I a bad kisser? No one's ever complained before. What did I do wrong?"

The Contortionist

"Nothing—I just—I can't."

He sat back. "Did I misjudge? Or did I simply get ahead of myself again?"

"No, it's..." She pulled her legs off his lap until she was sitting next to him cross-legged. She felt like she was shaking like a leaf. "It's too much all at once."

"I've been told I am that." He smirked and lifted her hand and kissed her knuckles. "I don't want to hurt you, Cora. I don't want to do anything of the sort. I'm trying to give us both what we want. You will be cured of your pain, and your friend will survive. And I...get you." He wove his fingers into hers and kissed the side of them, slower than the first time.

"I'm not special. I'm not interesting. I don't understand..." *Stop kissing me. Don't stop kissing me. I need serious therapy.*

"Ah, but you are. There is a bright fire that burns within you. You were made to fit into a life that is not worthy of you."

She finally pulled her hand from his. She chewed her lip. She felt as though there were butterflies in her chest. His touch did something to her. Something that was dangerous. Something she hadn't felt in a very long time.

"I don't want to die." She tried to hide her face.

"It isn't death." He caught her chin with the crook of his finger and turned her back to look at him. "Come see me tomorrow. I will show you. I will let you decide. This choice will be yours to make. If you don't want freedom from the pain—if you don't want to save your friend—you can walk away."

"How can I trust you? How do I know that...that becoming one of your dolls will save Trent? The two don't seem connected. Explain to me how they're linked."

Simon went silent for a long moment. He was clearly debating telling her something. He watched her. He shrugged, seemingly coming to a decision. "Clever. No, Cora. They aren't."

"So...you admit you're lying."

"No. Not quite." He slowly combed his fingers through his hair. "The Faire wants you. It whispers to you. It has never done that to anyone. The Faire is what is threatening your friend. It is doing so to draw you in. This is at odds with what I want, Cora dear. I want you for my own. It wants to take you from me. I am trying to ensure this doesn't happen."

"What does it want with me?"

"I only have a theory."

"Which is?"

"I don't want to worry you needlessly."

"Uh-huh. Sure." Cora narrowed her eyes at him. "So...if you turn me into one of your dolls, which I still don't understand what that means, Trent might still die. Because it's the Faire threatening him, not you."

"Once you're no longer available to the Faire, your friend will be useless to it. It will have no reason to hurt him."

"Do you know for sure, or is that just a theory?"

He laughed at her turning his words back around on him. "Clever. Yes." Simon smiled sweetly. It was a bad attempt. "But my theories are generally accurate."

She pinched the bridge of her nose. He was frustrating. She wanted to slap him. "You'll tell me one theory, but not the other?"

"Correct." When she groaned in frustration, he laughed. "Come see me in person, my sweet. Let me show you what I offer. This dream is lovely, but...I want to see if you taste the same in person."

"No."

"You don't? Or you won't let me find out?"

She growled. "No. I won't."

He sighed wistfully. "For shame. I'll have to try to convince you." He reached out and placed his hand on her shoulder. He cringed. "Oh, poor thing. I can feel it through the dream how much pain you're in."

"It's normal for me."

"It doesn't need to be." He shifted to move closer to her. He leaned in again and this time kissed her cheek. "Come see me tomorrow, Cora dear. I can make it all go away."

He pressed his hand into her shoulder, and it began to burn. She cried out as her dream shattered. It wasn't Simon who had caused it—it was just her normal kind of pain. She had fallen asleep on the sofa. That never went well for her. She rolled over on her side, clutching her sore shoulder, and blinked back the tears that stung her eyes.

She needed a hot shower. She needed some real sleep. She looked at the clock and sighed. It was one in the morning. When she finally crawled into bed, she was sore, she was exhausted, and she was emotionally wrung out.

But at least her dreams were quiet.

16

CORA WOKE up feeling like she had been rolled down a hill in a trashcan. There was no other way to put it. Her shoulder was barely usable. She'd loved to blame it on Harrow Faire, or on Simon, or on anybody, but the truth was that this kind of morning wasn't unusual. Oh, sure, the reason she had dislocated her shoulder was new and exciting, but the act itself wasn't.

It was just another sore morning, sore shower, and sore breakfast. Usually, that was enough to make her want to give up and lie on the floor all day. *People have it worse than me* was what she always tried to tell herself on the bad days. People lost limbs and kept going. People went blind. Or survived major burns. She just had fucked up tendons that made her joints forget how to do their damn job. Even with her own illness, it could be much worse. Prolapsed organs, living in a wheelchair, spontaneous death, and so on.

Didn't mean that it didn't suck. But now, it was also coupled with the fact that she had to come to a decision on whether she was willing to die to save her friend. It was injury on top of injury, forget insult.

Simon said it wasn't death. She snickered at her own hopeful stupidity. *Like I can trust that fucker.* She ran her left hand through her hair—the one she could actually lift higher than her shoulder—and scratched her scalp. She shut her eyes at the memory of the kiss. It had only been a dream, but those visions were so real it was uncanny. He might as well have been there beside her.

She shivered. Just the memory of the embrace twisted a knot in her stomach and sent anticipation and excitement rushing through her. No, he wasn't a bad kisser. Far, far from it. *All right, fine. He's sexy. I'm attracted to him. But he might actually be Satan, for all I know, so it's not a smart thing to feel.* She laughed again, sadly, and rested her forehead on the table. *Since when have I been smart?*

Either way, the Puppeteer was trying to *keep* her. That much was clear from his own words. He wanted to turn her into a doll—whatever the fuck that meant. Whereas the Faire wanted to do "something terrible" to her. If Simon was to be believed—and he probably wasn't—what the Faire wanted to do was far worse.

If only she knew what it was.

But, in the end, it didn't matter. She was trading away her life, one way or another, to save Trent. It was a bonus that she would get rid of the pain she lived with every waking moment—and most sleeping ones—but that wasn't the point anymore. That might have been where Simon had wanted to start his bargain, but the pot had grown much bigger since then.

She called out of work a second time. Three, and she'd have to get a doctor's note if her boss followed the rulebook, but she had the feeling it wouldn't be a problem tomorrow. Either she'd be back at her desk...or she'd be a "doll." Either way, she really wouldn't care about getting written up at her stupid job.

She picked up her phone and called Trent. She wanted to hear his voice. It was still fairly early, but she knew he was usually up at this time, anyway, or he hadn't gone to bed yet. One of the two.

It rang a few times. She was worried he wouldn't pick up, but then she heard the click. "Hey, Cor. Good morning, sunshine. How's it going?" Trent sounded way too awake for this hour in the morning. He was such a perky bastard.

She smiled. She felt a glimmer of hope at the sound of his voice. Maybe she could talk her way out of this. "Hey! I wanted to see if you wanted to meet up for dinner tonight. You and me. It's been a while since it's just been us."

"What've you got against Emily?" He snickered. "That would be great, but I actually have plans today. Ludwig asked me to come by again tonight. He said he has something important to tell me." Trent sounded giddy. "I wonder if he's going to pop the question." He was joking. Mostly.

He also sounded thrilled. Whereas she felt nothing but dread. *Oh, no. No, no, no. Please, no.* "That'd be a bit fast, don't you think? C'mon, ditch the lug-head and come out to dinner with me, just for the night."

"Don't you judge me, Little Ms. Totally-banging-the-freak-in-the-red-getup," Trent teased. "I saw the way he looked at you yesterday after you two pulled that stunt. Y'know, you didn't have to scare me away to get me to give you some private time. I would have cheered you on."

"That's not—he and I aren't—"

"Uh-huh," Trent goaded her. *"Suuure."*

She sighed. There wasn't any use trying. If Trent suspected something naughty was going on in any situation, involving absolutely anyone, it was always locked in as fact

The Contortionist

in his head. It usually made things funny, but in this instance it was frustrating. "C'mon. Dinner, you and me."

"I can't. But let's get dinner at the Faire together, then. The four of us. You, me, and our freaky circus lovers."

She fought the urge to argue with Trent about either him not going to the Faire, or the fact that she wasn't screwing Simon. Either argument wasn't going to work. He'd made up his mind. She might as well have been yanking on Excalibur. "Sure. That sounds good."

"So...you admit it, then? You and puppet guy?" Yup. He was ever the gossip hound.

She figured she should give him something to entertain himself with. And besides, it was normal, right? He was the one screwing Ludwig, after all. He couldn't exactly shame her. "He kissed me."

"Yes!"

Cora had to pull the phone away from her head, he shouted so loudly. She laughed and put it on speaker phone, setting it down on the table. It made it easier to drink her coffee, anyway, what with only having one usable hand. "You're terrible. It was just a kiss. And I had nothing to do with it."

"Was it good?"

She went silent.

"Coorraa!" Trent whined. "Was it?"

She rolled her eyes. "Yeah."

"I'm so excited for you! Even if you do have really bad taste in men, at least he's somebody. Anybody. I was going to buy you a gigolo for your birthday."

"You wouldn't have dared." Still, she smiled and chuckled at the idea. "I'd have kicked the guy out."

"Psh. Not with the quality I would have hired. I was about to start a GoFundMe for your love life." He really did sound overjoyed. It was touching. "Oh, Cor, I'm so happy for you!"

If only you knew. "It was just a kiss. I wouldn't get too jacked up about it."

"But kissing leads to other things. Then other things lead to you finally getting laid. I can't wait to actually meet this guy now. He seemed a few crayons short of the full set. I never figured you for the kind to like the crazy fucks. They are the best in bed, though. I can attest. There was this one guy, nuts as a bag of cashews, but he could do this thing with his tongue, that—"

"Stop, stop." She melodramatically gagged. "Too much info, Trent."

"Prude."

They laughed. She smiled sadly and looked down at the image of him that showed up on her phone. It was a picture of them all together. And right then and there, she made up her mind.

She didn't have a choice. He was like her little brother. And she was going to protect him like she had on the playground as kids.

This really was goodbye. "All right, T-bag. I'll see you for dinner at the Faire." *No. I won't. I'll probably be dead...or a "doll."*

"Great. Seven? Maybe they'll let us talk them into leaving the Faire for once. I can't get Ludwig to come to my place to save my life. Oh, well."

I don't think he could if he wanted to. She rubbed her hand over her forehead. "Maybe he's shy."

"He really is. He's such a sweetheart. I wonder what he wants to talk to me about that's so important. I can't wait to find out. Oh. I hope he's not breaking up with me. That'd be terrible."

The Contortionist

"I'm sure that's not what it is." *I think the Faire is going to make him kill you. It's not exactly the same thing.* "Who would ever want to break up with you?"

"Plenty of people. Trust me. Well, I have to finish my omelet and head to the office. I'll see you later."

"Talk to you later, Trent." *Very later. Afterlife-style later.* "Bye."

"Toodles!" *Click*.

She put her good arm down on the table and rested her forehead on top of it. She felt tears sting her eyes, and she didn't bother fighting them. She couldn't let Trent die. She knew—just *knew*—that it would happen today if she didn't intervene.

How could she let him die? How could she throw him away, knowing she could have stopped it? She couldn't live with herself if she did. That was the simple, sad fact of it. She had no choice.

She'd finish her coffee. Shower. Dress. Put the vacation feeder on her fish tank and hope someone found them before it ran out. She debated writing a goodbye email to her friends and letting it send on a delay in a week, but she didn't know what she would say. The idea of writing it hurt too much to try.

It was at around eleven in the morning that she finally became too anxious to wait any longer. She was pacing her apartment uselessly, like waiting to go in for surgery. It was time to rip the bandage off.

Going into her bedroom, she picked out a few pieces of jewelry. They were all things that had been given to her by her family. She shouldered her camera, said goodbye to her fish, and...left her apartment. It was the last time she was going to see any of it.

She chewed on her lip as she drove down the road

toward Harrow Faire. Half of her expected to find it totally abandoned again. She could only hope. That was the best possible way any of this could go. Sadly…it was still intact. The gates were open, although the Faire didn't open for another hour or two.

Simon hadn't said when to come by. She was certain he didn't really care.

She parked in the lot and got out, looking at the entryway façade and its ticket booth. She picked up her camera and flicked it on. "What do you want me to do? Help me understand. How do I save Trent's life?" She took three photos of the façade. *Click, click, click.*

She reviewed the images. A normal one. A second normal one. And a shot of the entrance of Simon's tent. The Faire wanted her to go to him. That was what it had shown her last night in the mirror maze. But if Simon and the Faire were caught in a competition for her life…why would it want her to go see him? Didn't the Faire want her instead?

It made no sense. But none of this made any sense. "Fine. I'll go." She sighed, turned off her camera, and headed up to the gate.

There, at the counter, was Aaron, the Barker. He looked at her and blinked in astonishment. "Cora? What on Earth are you doing back here?" His face fell. "Oh. I know. You're here for your friend."

"Huh?" She blinked. "Trent?"

The man raised one shoulder in a dismissive shrug. It was clear he couldn't give two shits about the name. "Twinkle Toes is about a half an hour ahead of you. He's off with Ludwig."

"Oh, no…" She cringed. She thought she had more time. "Oh, fuck."

"Mmmhm. Exactly." Aaron stood from the counter and

The Contortionist

opened the little door to the booth. He strolled out, cracking his back loudly. "C'mon, toots. I shouldn't do this, but I'll let you in the service door. Turk'll be pissed, but it is what it is."

"Why? Why help me?"

"Something's going on. I don't know what, but it's going to be interesting." He looked at her curiously for a moment, as if pondering what kind of secrets she had. She wished she knew. "If the Faire is putting your friend in danger, then you're here to save him. And if you're here to save him, you're giving the Faire what it wants. Who'm I to get in the way?"

"Thanks. I think."

"Don't thank me, toots." He pushed open the door that was hidden in the paint of the façade. "Now, go on in after... whatever it is you're after." He pondered her for another long moment. "It isn't for your friend, is it? You didn't even know he was here. Why?"

"I like cotton candy." She glared at him flatly. She tried to walk around him, but he grabbed her by her upper arm. She yanked out of his grasp.

He didn't care about her annoyance. "No, really, why are you here, Cora?"

"I need to save my friend."

"But how? You didn't know he was here, so how is coming back going to do that? What do you know?" As she started to walk away, he followed her. "You didn't tell us the whole story last night, did you? What is going on, Cora? What has the Faire told you to do?"

"It told me how to save Trent."

He sighed heavily. "I want to help you, Cora. I really do. But I can't if you don't tell me what's going on."

"I don't know what's going on, Aaron. That's the problem." She stopped walking to turn to look at him. "But I think today is the day I die." She was scared. No, she was far past scared. She shook her head and tried to keep her hands from shaking. She did it by shoving them into her pockets. As she did…she felt a pair of glasses. She knew what they were without looking. They would be red and black antique sunglasses, of course.

They were gone. Now they were back. Add it to the list.

Aaron's eyes went wide. "What do you mean? Cora. What do you know?"

"I have to go. I'm sorry. It might already be too late." She turned and walked away, not glancing back over her shoulder as Aaron called after her. But she needed to do this. She needed to get to Simon's performance tent and get this all over with before Trent was murdered.

When she reached her target, she looked at the flaps and felt nothing but dread. Her stomach fell into a pit to Hell. This was the end of it all. Whatever game the Faire was playing with her…this was it. She should turn and run. She should literally run for her life.

But she was trapped, wasn't she?

She rubbed her sore shoulder. The one silver lining to this whole disaster was that if she was dead or Simon's "doll," her constant pain would at least be over. She was never one to try to find the bright side of situations. Finding it now made her laugh sadly.

No point in lurking on his doorstep. She didn't even know if he was inside. Taking a deep breath, she slowly let it out. One step in front of the other was all it took, and it was all she could manage. As she walked inside, the sunlight transitioned quickly into darkness, and it took her eyes a few seconds to adjust.

The rows of benches in front of the stage were all empty. Props sat on the edges of the wings, along with rows of flat

The Contortionist

and painted scenery, all stacked up and waiting to be used. The overhead lights were dim—the old-fashioned amber filaments giving the room strange shadows. It gave them the illusion of movement, like the shadows themselves were creeping toward her. Maybe they were. She wouldn't have been surprised. "Hello?"

Silence reigned for a long moment before a voice whispered in her ear. "You came."

She screamed.

17

THE VOICE HAD COME from right behind her. She whirled and looked up at Simon, with all his sharp angles and shadows. His bizarre, black-red-white eyes were unhidden. He smiled at her slowly, the expression going from friendly to decidedly hungry. He would be gorgeous if he weren't looking at her like she was a ham sandwich and he was starving.

"Hello, Cora."

"Your face healed." She winced, remembering what he had looked like the day prior. She had seen through to where Ringmaster's whip had split his face down to the bone. His face looked like nothing had happened. There wasn't even a mark. It was just more proof of the impossible. More proof of magic.

"Hum?" He touched his face. "Oh! Yes. Right. That. I nearly forgot." He chuckled.

"You forgot about your face being ripped open?"

"Oh, yes. It happens."

"I...um...okay." She chewed her lip for a moment. Reaching into her pocket, she retrieved his sunglasses. She

The Contortionist

held them out to him.

"I was wondering where they went to!" He took them from her and, flicking them open, examined the lenses. He cleaned them off with his handkerchief and placed them back on his face. "Thank you, dear."

"They disappeared when I left here, then reappeared when I came back. Why?"

"Hm? Oh. Simply because outside this place, we don't exist. Only in the fleeting dreams of others. And even then, if they are to dream of us in their nightmares, we only exist as who we are after we came here."

"That makes no sense."

He smiled. "I know. It doesn't matter. Now, I *assume...*" He drew out the last word for way too long. He folded his hands behind his back and leaned forward, as if he needed to tower over her even more than he already was. "You're here because you've chosen to save your friend who is currently getting stuffed like a Thanksgiving turkey."

"Yes. And don't ever describe it like that again." She made a face.

"Have a problem with your friend's proclivities, do you?"

"Not in the slightest. I just don't need to think about him mid-action, that's all."

He straightened back up and laughed. "I thought it was quite clever! Although you should be the judge. You have such a colorful use of language."

She took a step back. He was too close to her, and he really was tall. He was all long lines, and it was unsettling at best. She didn't know if she would ever get used to it. She didn't know if she would have the chance to. "Thanks..."

"I still very much enjoy your invective about the pogo stick. I opted not to follow your instructions, though." His smile grew. He was almost always smiling—it was just a matter of degrees. "Hope you don't mind. It's not my style. Maybe your friend might want to give it a go." He sniffed dismissively. "It'd clearly fit."

She fought the urge to laugh. Fought, and lost. She shook her head at the man's terrible joke and let herself chuckle. That seemed to please him, and his smile split into a grin for a moment. "Simon...what're you going to do?"

"A complicated question with an equally complicated answer, I'm afraid!" Every once in a while, his British accent flared up, and his words flowed out of him effortlessly with a smooth flair. She remembered their kiss, and her face went warm. He really was handsome.

For a monster.

I'm about to die, and I'm standing here wondering if he'd wait an hour so I can go out with a bang. She laughed at her own stupid pun.

"What?" He blinked quizzically.

"Nothing."

"Something was funny." He stepped toward her. "What was it?"

She took a step back. "Nothing I'm going to tell you."

"Fine. Be that way." He smiled. "I don't mind. Now, Ms. Cora. We have a deal to broker, don't we?" He stepped closer again, backing her toward the stage and away from the exit. He had that fiendish, wolfish grin on his face, even if his unnatural gaze that she could see just above the edge of his glasses looked more sultry than dangerous. "Unless you came for something else..." The way he purred the innuendo sent a shiver down her spine.

"Let's make this perfectly clear. I'm here to save my friend. That's all. I'm not here because of you."

"A shame." He shrugged dismissively. "No matter. You'll have plenty of time to change your mind, although we'll be

The Contortionist

relegated to the worlds in our dreams after today." He strolled toward her again, and she dutifully retreated. "I'm a sick bastard, no doubt about that, but having *relations* with one of my dolls is too twisted, even for me." He wrinkled his nose. "And rather uncomfortable too, I imagine. Splinters, and all."

"You said you weren't going to kill me..."

"Cora dear, come now." He backed her into the lip of the stage. She jolted at the impact, grabbing it with both hands as he closed the distance between them. He leaned in, and she was forced to tilt back over the stage to keep the few remaining inches she had. He pressed his palms to the stage on either side of her. "I told you I'm not. And I wouldn't lie to you."

"Then what are you going to do?"

That dangerous, fiendish smile split his face. Once more he was the cat and she was the canary, and he couldn't be happier. "I tasted a piece of you. Such a small, delicate shard. And I decided I could not live without savoring the rest of you. I don't plan to kill you—I plan to consume you. Bit by bit. Little by little, until there's nothing of you left..."

Her heart was pounding her ears. "You're insane."

He was watching her, lidded eyes dark with lust as his gaze flicked to her lips and lingered there. "Mmhm. We've covered that. But don't worry. It won't hurt. None of it will. You'll have many, many years of pain-free existence. You won't even feel yourself fading away. I'll drink you slowly, sip you like a fine wine, over the many years to come. You'll join my family. You'll be mine. I'll protect you, care for you, even...play with you, pretty doll." He tilted his head, and she wondered if he was going to kiss her again.

"Holy fuck." She wanted to cry. "Please, no."

"It's the only way to save your friend. And that's the most

important thing, isn't it? The release from your illness is just a secondary benefit." He chuckled. "I know you're afraid. But think about it. No more pain. My children last for a long time—I take very good care of them. Some of them fade away faster or slower than others. You? You burn so bright. I think you could last for centuries. There's so much of you to eat." His face split once again in a sadistic smile.

That was it.

I'm sorry, Trent. I can't do this.

She turned and scrambled up onto the stage, desperate to get away from him. Looking up, she tripped over her own feet at what she saw and wound up sprawled on the wood surface. They weren't alone. But what she saw didn't quite qualify as people, either.

Dolls.

Puppets.

Full-size human figurines stood on the stage, arranged in a line, all looking at her. Some men, some women, all with painted faces and empty, lifeless expressions. Some were porcelain, some were wood, some were fabric. Each one was a work of art. She could see the joints of their limbs, and the small linkages that held them together. Some of the figures were faded and old. Some looked almost new. One of them, a woman, was missing an arm.

There were no strings attached to them. They all stood there on their own. But they weren't living people. They weren't costumes. They were too thin, too weightless. They all looked as though they were hovering on invisible wires.

There was a figure sitting in a chair in the middle of the stage, covered by a white cloth. But that it was the figure of a woman under the fabric was unmistakable.

"What the—what the—" Cora scrambled back up to her feet.

The Contortionist

Hands settled on her shoulders, and she screamed. She tried to run, but he shifted one arm to snap around her waist and yank her back against him. He might as well have been made from steel. She struggled, but it did no good.

"Let me go!"

Simon shushed her, his head close to her ear, his breath hot against her skin. "Look at them. My children. Aren't they so pretty?" He reached an arm over her shoulder and, with the twist of his fingers, beckoned one of the dolls forward. It was the one of the lady who was missing an arm.

The marionette lurched and stepped forward, the movements jerky and unnatural. *"Don't be afraid."* The voice came from the woman, but the face didn't move. It was just painted on. It wasn't a mask. Speakers, maybe? The sound had to be piped in. That was all.

Her mind scrambled for purchase. Magic might have been proven to be real, but these were monsters. And he was going to turn her into one.

"Aren't I pretty? I wanted to be beautiful forever. And now I am."

"Each one of them came to me with something I could fix. They were afraid of aging. Of dying. Of disease. That one there had terminal cancer." He pointed. "He could barely breathe. Now, he's cured forever. Suzie, here, was such a pretty flower, and now that flower has been preserved. Think about it—no more pain. Wilbur, over there, murdered his family and wanted to escape justice. Sasha was a drug addict, seeking a reprieve. And now, they're mine…and you will be, too."

"You're insane!"

"You keep saying that. It isn't news." He chuckled and rested his cheek on her temple. She tried to recoil from him, but he was impossibly strong. "You'll be my new main attraction, Cora. My masterpiece. Look." He dragged her toward the figure under the sheet. "It isn't quite done yet, but I think it will be my finest work yet. I had to rush a little. I hope you don't mind." He pulled the sheet away, and Cora felt her knees go weak. If he hadn't been holding her up, she would have collapsed.

It was her.

The face was an artistic rendering of her, but she recognized herself in the features. The eyes looked like they were made of painted mirrors. A wig of long, wavy dark hair fell around the shoulders of the life-size doll that was made to her proportions. It was even wearing similar clothing to what she had been wearing a few days ago.

"Oh, God..."

"No. I won't be your God. I will be your creator, though. Although please don't call me 'Father' like the others like to do. It'll make my attempts to woo you in your dreams a little too strange, even for me." He chuckled. "I'm especially proud of the eyes. I painted on mirrors so they might change in tone like your beautiful gray eyes. Sometimes dark, sometimes light...I'm quite pleased with how it turned out. I need to finish the details, but we can work on that together, hm? You can pick your nail color."

"No, please, please, no—" She was shaking. Tears were already flowing down her cheeks. She wanted to go home. This was worse than death.

"Don't be afraid, Cora dear. It won't hurt. I'll take your life and store it in a piece of art. My masterpiece. You will be safe." He shushed her, wrapping his other arm around her to hold her, as if he were trying to console her. "It will be all right, I promise."

"You freak, let me go!" She stomped on his toe. He snarled in pain, and his arm loosened enough that she

The Contortionist

whirled and kneed him hard in the groin. That doubled him over.

He grabbed himself as he groaned. *"Ow."*

She ducked around him and bolted for the exit. She was going to get out of here as fast as she could. She was going to get in her car and drive as far away as humanly possible. *I'm so sorry, Trent. I can't. I can't do it. I can't. I'll go to hell for this, but I can't!* Fuck this place, fuck Simon, fuck his freaky monster dolls, she—

Something wrapped around her throat, and she gagged as the sudden stop yanked her back. It felt like fishing line. It burned, and she wondered if it had cut into her skin. She went to grab at it.

Her arms didn't move. He had her in those terrible, invisible, and impossible strings of his.

She screamed.

"Shut *up,* will you?" Simon snarled from behind her. "Such a noisy one, you are."

Suddenly, she was moving. Sliding backward across the packed dirt of the center of the tent. She wailed in fear. She wasn't moving her legs.

She could see the exit. So close, and yet so far. And getting farther. She struggled, but nothing in her seemed able to obey.

"So much needless fussing."

The movement stopped, and she was standing still again. But still nothing obeyed her commands. She couldn't even turn her head. Suddenly, she was bent over backward, looking up at the ceiling of the tent. She should have fallen —that wasn't a natural position to maintain. But she couldn't do anything. She hovered like that, bent back at a sharp angle, and winced in pain. She could bend that far— but that didn't mean it was comfortable.

Simon appeared in her vision, upside down and standing at her head. He smiled. The fingers of his right hand were bent at odd angles, like he was holding the strings of a puppet. Every now and then, she thought she could see the amber light glint off strings that ran from them, to her.

"This—this can't be real—" she whispered, her heart pounding in her ears. "Please, don't do this. Please."

"This is very real. These are my gifts, beautiful girl." He leaned down over her a little, the dark curls of his hair falling alongside his cheeks. "I'm afraid you're mine now. Commit willingly, and it'll be so much more pleasant for you. Don't you want to save your friend Trent?" When she only sobbed, he tutted. "You're just afraid. When you take the leap, when the fall is over, you'll be glad I made you change your mind and turned you into one of my dolls."

"You said I could say no—"

"I'm afraid I changed *my* mind."

"You can't do this!"

He smiled. "Oh, but I can. Usually, I don't take unwilling children. I hate the *whining*. And I have plenty of people who come to me because they want me to solve their problems. But for you, tasty, sweet, delicious Cora—for you, I'll make an exception." He grinned. "Are you ready, cupcake?"

She felt tears streak down her cheeks. She was shivering.

"I want to go home..." It was a childish wish. But it was the only thing she could think of to say. "Please."

He shushed her and stroked her cheek, the other hand still holding the strings that controlled her limbs. It was a gentle, tender touch. He leaned down to kiss her. But she knew it wasn't a simple embrace.

These were the fangs of the spider, ready to fill her with poison. He'd wrap her in his cocoon and drink her dry. She sensed the danger. Something inside her was screaming, even if she couldn't make the sound.

"Please—" she whispered, feeling his lips ghost against hers. She might as well have been begging a demon. She might be doing just that. She knew it was hopeless, but she had to try. "Let me go home..."

"Oh, sweetheart." He hesitated before sealing the embrace. "But you are home."

Her life was going to end.

She thought she would just waste away over the years. Wind up in a wheelchair like so many people with her disease. She thought she'd live her boring, painful life, and die a boring, painful death. She had dreaded it.

Now she realized how much better that option really was.

His lips pressed against hers. Her heart hitched in her chest.

A booming voice interrupted her racing thoughts.

"Enough!"

18

CORA HIT THE DIRT HARD. Simon released her from the horrible invisible strings in the least gentle way possible. She groaned and held her head, squeezing her eyes shut against the pain. She could barely register the shouting that was going on over her for the second time that week.

And it was the same two people shouting.

"Get out, Ringmaster. Now is not the time for your constant meddling! We had a deal."

Simon's voice reminded her how much danger she was in through the fog of pain in her head. She scrambled away from him, staggered to her feet, and ran full-tilt into a giant, squishy wall. A hand settled on her shoulder.

"Our deal is void. You lied. I shouldn't be surprised. But you acted in bad faith, and now things have changed." Why was everybody in this stupid circus so fucking *tall*? It was a strange and irrelevant thought to have, but it came to her anyway. The source of the voice was Turk, the Ringmaster. He was looming over her. When he smiled down at her, his expression was warm and sympathetic. "I warned you not to come back here. But now I understand why you did. You should have told me what the Faire showed you."

"How do you know...?"

"I spoke with Mr. Harrow. He told me what the Faire had said to you. He told me what it wants with you. What it *really* wants with you." He kept his heavy hand on her shoulder. "I am very sorry for Simon's mistreatment of you."

"Mistreatment!" Simon was furious. "I was going to give her all that she ever wanted. All she ever needed! A home—a family—freedom from her pain. She is *mine,* Ringmaster. We had a deal. You're ruining my plans. Get out!"

"I'm afraid your plans no longer matter." The Ringmaster was still smiling down at her, even if he was talking to Simon. "You broke them when you didn't tell me that the Faire wanted her to fill the empty slot."

"Turk, I need to go, please—" She tried to squeak around the double-wide man who was taking up most of the aisle.

The grasp on her shoulder grew harsher, and he pulled her back to him. "I'm very sorry, Cora. But I can't let you leave."

"What? Why?" She felt her heart drop into her stomach. "You can't keep me here."

"Yes, I can. And sadly, I have direct orders to do just that."

Something snatched her wrist. Something thin and tight. It yanked her around, so she was facing Simon. The invisible and impossible string started to pull her back to him. But before she could go far, Turk was in between them. His hand caught whatever was holding her and yanked. He tugged Simon forward instead, and it sent the Puppeteer staggering to keep himself upright. She wasn't moving toward him anymore, but she also couldn't pull her hand back. That meant she couldn't run, either.

Simon's expression, always smiling, was now twisted in rage. "She belongs to me. I saw her first—I tasted her first—she's mine. You have no right to take her!"

"I may not have the right, but Mr. Harrow does. We have a vacancy. One that you made empty, Puppeteer."

"So much grief over a waste of life." He laughed. "Hernandez was such a disappointment. We're all better for his absence, and you know it. The only good he ever served was in becoming my plaything! Even if you make her take the zero—even if Mr. Harrow makes this stupid mistake—I'll still eat her whole, just like I did to the last one!"

Take the zero? What the fuck are they even talking about? "Please, just let me go—"

Ringmaster glanced back at her and smiled sadly. "I'm so sorry, Cora. I really am." The huge man looked back to Simon, and his expression instantly hardened. "She shall take the zero, as Mr. Harrow wishes. And you will not harm her. Not now, not ever."

"You can't stop me." Simon's expression twisted back into a sick smile. "You can't ever stop me. I can't kill you—but you can't kill me either, can you, fat man?"

"Oh, but I *can* stop you, Puppeteer. You have a price to pay. Your tab has been open since you mutilated Hernandez." Ringmaster wrapped the invisible string around his arm and yanked Simon forward a few more steps. The Puppeteer dug in his heels, but the bigger man was clearly stronger.

"Release me, you tub of lard!" Simon yanked, but the Ringmaster kept reeling him in like a fish on a line. She was still trapped on the other side end. Simon snarled and pulled again, but it did no good. "You have no right—"

The Contortionist

"I have every right! Mr. Harrow has decreed that Cora is to take the zero. The spot you emptied."

"Then I will eat her like Hernandez the next moment."

"You won't. Because it will be *you* who is going to be the one to Sponsor her. You are going to do your part to fill the void that you created."

None of this made any sense. It was like a bad fever dream. She pulled on her wrist, but she was still caught by whatever held her. *Take the zero. Sponsor.* None of it made any sense. It was all insane.

Simon laughed. "You're a fool. I have no reason to do anything of the sort."

"You have never *once* sponsored anyone to join the Family. Not once. And because you're responsible for our loss, you'll be responsible for the replacement. The fact that you're too selfish to endanger yourself once the deed is done will ensure you don't harm her." Ringmaster tugged Simon closer, and as soon as the other man was within arm's reach, Turk snagged him by the front of the shirt and pulled him in.

Cora pulled on her wrist but knew she was either just going to yank her joints out of her sockets or rip off her hand. The string wouldn't let go.

"You can't make me." Simon grinned up at Turk. "You can't force me to Sponsor someone."

"Oh, yes. I can. I just never have had a reason to. Now, I do."

It was only then that Simon's smug smile flickered and faded. Suddenly, he looked almost afraid. "You...you wouldn't."

"All you ever do is *take,* Simon Waite. It's time you finally give something back."

"I'll let her go. I'll let her leave the Faire." Now the

Puppeteer was the one begging. "I'll do whatever you say, just don't—don't do this!" He grabbed the big man's arm and tried to pull himself free, but now he was the one who was stuck.

"No."

The Ringmaster turned to her and put his hand on her shoulder. It might as well have been snapped around her throat for how firm it was. It was clear she wasn't going anywhere. He smiled sadly at her again. "Welcome to the Family, Cora. I'm sorry it had to be like this."

Something stabbed into her mind like knives.

Simon screamed.

She did, too.

Her world went white. Then it promptly went black.

At least the pain stopped.

———

Simon slammed to the ground on his knees, and he would have cared if it didn't also feel like someone had drilled a hole out of his chest and yanked out part of his lung. Unfortunately, this wouldn't be so easily solvable as a bit of good, old fashioned, bodily mutilation. That'd heal. It always healed.

What the fat *fuck* had taken out of him wouldn't ever grow back. "Damn you!" He wheezed. He leaned on the nearby bench hard and tried to push himself to his feet. He didn't quite make it on the first attempt.

"You did this to yourself, Puppeteer," Ringmaster said from over him. "If you hadn't made Hernandez into one of your abominations, this never would have come to pass. Now you're responsible for her." Ringmaster sighed and put

Cora down on a long bench. She had fainted when the fat fool pulled out part of Simon's seity and shoved it into her.

Simon wasn't surprised that she had blacked out. It hurt to have one's whole being rearranged. As it was, he felt like he was going to throw up. And he wasn't the one having her body remade into something new.

Ringmaster straightened and turned to him. "You took a piece of her. And now, she has a piece of you in return. You're bound together. If anything happens to her, it happens to you. You're a selfish, egotistical, self-centered waste of air, Simon. I trust that your dedication to self-preservation outweighs your indignance." Turk smiled derisively.

"You're a bigger idiot than I gave you credit for if you think I'm not going to find a way to get back what you just stole from me." Simon finally pushed himself to his feet and brushed the dust off his clothing. "I will be whole again, and I'll leave her desecrated remains on your doorstep as a reminder that you're to blame for what she'll suffer."

"No, you won't." Ringmaster turned to leave. "You'll try, but you won't succeed."

"Wait. Where are you going?" He furrowed his brow and pointed at the unconscious Cora. "Take her with you!"

"She's your problem now, Simon. You made this mess. You deal with it when she wakes up. You wanted her, so you deal with her. I expect she's going to be very frightened and hideously angry at you." Ringmaster turned to smile over his shoulder. "Enjoy."

As the big man left his tent, Simon roared in frustration.

Cora woke up and felt like she had been hit by a truck. A very large, very angry truck that was filled with bees that someone had been shaken up a few times before letting them loose. She felt feverish. She felt like she wasn't inside her own body anymore.

She could hear the noises of the carnival going on around her, but they were faint. It took every ounce of her strength to open her eyes against the incredible desire to just lie there and not do anything at all. But whatever happened to her, she knew she was still in danger.

It was dark. Hours must have gone by, but it was hard to know exactly how many. She felt grass underneath her as she struggled to come back to reality. When she could finally sit up, the world abruptly spun around her, and she lay back down.

"Oh, hey, take it easy, there." Someone was next to her and had their hand on her arm. She didn't recognize the voice, although she thought she might have heard it before. "Easy. Don't rush. You're okay."

Somebody else whistled. "Hoo-boy, Ringmaster did a number on you, eh, toots?"

"Not like him to just dump her in the grass."

"I don't think he's the one who left her here."

Cora listened to the conversation going on over her, and she wanted to make it all stop so she could try to get her own thoughts straight. But she couldn't ask them to shut up, so she lay there and had to listen.

"Who would've Sponsored her and left her here like trash, then?"

"Take a flying guess."

"No." The first male voice laughed. "No. No way. Bullshit."

"You saw him. He was after her the moment she went through the gate. He wants her bad."

"Sure, like one of his pets, but not like this."

She really needed them both to stop talking. "Guys..." Unfortunately, they didn't seem to hear her. They were too busy debating.

"But here she is. You can feel it. She's Family now." Now she could recognize that voice. It was Aaron. "We're whole again, at least."

"I don't know about this, Barker. Something feels wrong. Very wrong. You think she came willingly?"

"Fuck, no. Look at her. It doesn't hurt that bad if she chose this. I bet she didn't even know what was happening. She came here to save her friend—the Faire was threatening to hurt the sprite who was dallying with Ludwig. I don't think she had any idea this was what the Faire and Mr. Harrow were after."

The first man sighed heavily, and she felt someone settle down in the grass next to her. It might have been Jack, the Rigger. "Great..."

"You gonna sit there with her like an idiot and hope she doesn't decide to take this out on you? You know she's going to be pissed as a cat in a bag when she comes around."

"Better she tries to claw my eyes out than be alone."

"Suit yourself, kid."

She pressed her hands to her eyes and took a deep breath. "I really need both of you to shut the fuck up, please."

Aaron laughed. "Feels like the worst kind o' hangover, doesn't it, toots?" He nudged her foot with his. "You'll come 'round in a few minutes. I'll tell you what. You sit here with Jackie, and I'll go get you something stiff that'll help."

Silence. She assumed he walked away. She finally lowered her hands and blinked. There was a tree over her. When she turned her head, her vision moved out of sync with the rest of her, and it all felt disjointed and nauseating. As she blinked a few more times, things started to clear up. She was on a little grassy spot between some paths. She could make out the boxcars with the numbered doors nearby. She was back in the "staff area." Rolling on her side, she fought the urge to retch.

Jack rubbed her back. "Deep breaths'll help. I didn't come here willingly either. You'll be okay in a few minutes."

She struggled to sit, and Jack helped her until she was leaning back against the tree. But at least she was finally upright. Rubbing her face, she shivered. She felt like she kept breaking out in a sweat like she had a fever. She finally managed to look at him. "Hi."

He smiled and sat by her thigh. "Hi there, Cora with the nice car and the bad luck."

"It's a shit car."

"It's been a while since I've seen one." He shrugged. "I'm sorry about all this. Especially with how it probably went down."

"What happened? One second I—" She jolted in fear as she remembered Simon. She went wide-eyed as her heart instantly started pounding again. "Oh, God, he's going to kill me!" She started to scramble to get up, but she failed on two counts. One, because her legs weren't working, and two, because Jack caught her arms and held her still.

"Hey, hey, simmer down. Calm down. It's okay. You're safe. Nobody's gonna kill you, not anymore. Simon can't touch you. Well. He could, but I'm pretty sure now that he won't." He shook his head and winced. "Sorry. That's not helping. That's not the important part. The important part is that you're safe."

The Contortionist

"I need to get out of here—I need to go home. I need to find Trent and get out of here. I need to convince him never to come back and—" Her head spun. Her body wasn't ready for the adrenaline she had just pumped through it. She felt dizzy, and she groaned.

"What'd you say to get her all riled up?" Aaron walked back up to them and crouched in the grass next to her. He held a flask toward her. "Take a sip, toots."

"Nothing. She's just putting it together." Jack sighed. "Simon was going to turn her into one of his dolls."

"No shit." Aaron rolled his eyes at the other man. "Please excuse Jack. He's a sweet face but dumb as a brick."

Jack glared. "Asshole."

"Yeah. Drink up, toots." Aaron shook the flask at her when she hesitated. "No cooties, no drugs. Nothing but good, old fashioned moonshine whiskey."

"I wouldn't take his word on the cooties bit," Jack interjected. Aaron snickered and reached out to slap Jack in the arm.

She felt unsteady. She felt dizzy and sick. The moonshine might help. It might make it much worse. It was worth the risk. She took a swig from the flask. She coughed. It burned like rubbing alcohol. "Holy shit," she coughed. "That's not whiskey, that's goddamn paint thinner."

"Yeah, burns going down, but it'll straighten you right out."

Not wanting to try it again, she handed the flask back to him. He took it with a small chuckle and stood back up to his full height. To his credit, she wasn't shivering as badly. But a second swig of that paint thinner was going to knock her out for a different reason. She wasn't a lightweight by any means—but neither was the moonshine.

"What...what the actual fuck just happened to me?" She

felt fuzzy. "I don't think I can remember everything. It all went black."

"We'll get there. Start at the beginning. Talk us through what happened, toots. It'll help." Aaron slipped the flask into his vest pocket.

"No. I need to get out of here. I need to get to my car, and I need to leave."

"Right, right. As soon as you get your legs under you." He waved his hand dismissively. "We've got a couple minutes before you can speed off into the night." When Jack furrowed his brow in confusion and opened his mouth to say something, Aaron cut him off with a glare. "Fill us in while we wait. What happened? What did the Faire tell you?"

"I...shouldn't have come back here." She put her head in her hands. There was no point in lying anymore. "It showed me Trent, dead. I asked it what I could do to stop it. It showed me the hall of mirrors, then Simon's tent...then one of those boxcars with a zero painted on the door. When I went to the hall of mirrors, it...showed me myself. But I wasn't me. I was a contortionist. And I was covered in blood."

Aaron swore a few times. "It picked you, then. Not Mr. Harrow. Shit."

"I thought Mr. Harrow always picked the new Family members," Jack said from beside her. "What's this mean, Aaron?"

"I don't know yet. What was Simon's deal in all this, Cora?"

"He wanted me to be one of his dolls. Said he could take away all my pain. I didn't know what he meant. When I saw...what he was going to do to me, I tried to run. I shouldn't have listened to him. He's going to *eat* me."

The Contortionist

"Never listen to the Puppeteer. But now, you know. It's always the same story with him. He's a conman of the highest degree. And trust me, it takes one to know one."

Aaron rubbed his chin. "Then what happened?"

"Turk showed up. Said that…said Mr. Harrow told him I was supposed to 'take the zero,' or whatever. It doesn't make any sense. Simon said he was still going to kill me anyway, but Turk said that if Simon 'Sponsored' me, then he wouldn't dare hurt me. I don't know what any of this means. Something hurt, like something stabbed into my head, and I must have passed out. Please, I want to go home."

Aaron and Jack groaned in unison. Aaron followed up with a few more vivid obscenities.

"What? What does it mean?" She looked up at them.

"It's a long story, toots." Aaron reached a hand down to her. "Come on, let me show you where you'll be staying, and you can sleep it off. We can talk to Turk in the morning."

"I'm not staying here! I'm going home."

"You aren't. I'm sorry, but you aren't going anywhere." Jack reached out to put a hand on her shoulder, but she yanked away. "This is your home now."

"No. I'm out of here." Cora pushed up from the ground and wavered, but finally managed to stay standing. "Screw this. Screw all of this!"

Jack reached for her. "Cora—"

"Go fuck one of the carousel horses!" She shoved his hand away from her. "I'm not doing this. I'm not."

As she walked away, she heard them talking behind her.

"You're just going to let her go?"

"She'll figure it out soon enough."

"You really are an asshole, Aaron."

"That ain't news, Jackie. That ain't news to anybody."

19

Cora staggered her way through the carnival. She felt weak. She felt like she'd been in a car accident. She needed to get out. She needed to get to her car. There were psychopathic, undead serial killers after her. People around her cleared out of her way, thinking she was either drunk, or sick, or crazy.

She felt like a mix of all three.

Her phone was missing. *Great.* She wanted to call 911. She wanted to call her friends. But she did have her car keys, and that was the important part.

It was on the main drag that she found someone she recognized. He was walking out of the Strongman's tent with a broad smile plastered all over his face. Hope and relief blossomed in her. Suddenly, there was a chance again. *It was Trent!*

"Oh, thank God! Thank God you're okay." She raced to her friend and grabbed his arms. "We have to go. We have to get out of here! They're all murderous freaks. This place is trying to kill you. I don't know how to explain, but we need to—"

The Contortionist

"Holy *shit*, lady! Get off me!" Trent shoved her back, sending her sprawling painfully to the pavement as he caught her by surprise. He was staring at her wild-eyed in a panic, his hands up. "What the fuck is wrong with you, you fucking weirdo?"

"Trent, what're you talking about?" She stood, brushing the gravel off where it clung to her hands. "They tried to kill me. They tried to kill you, too! I came here to try to save you, but—"

"Whoa, how do you know my name?" He took a step back. "Stay the hell away from me, you psychopath!"

"Trent, it's me, Cora."

He shook his head. "I don't know a Cora, lady. I don't know you."

She stood there, stunned, staring at her friend in dumbfounded horror. Maybe she had died. Maybe this was a nightmare. None of it made any sense. She wanted to cry. She tried to stop the tears, but they came anyway. She'd been through too much.

There had been so much hope in her heart at seeing him, and now it all felt ripped away. And she didn't know why. "Trent, now's not the time to play games with me. We need to get out of here, please."

"Then go." He pointed toward the exit gate. "I don't fucking know you. And I don't know anybody named Cora. Now get away from me before I call the cops for assault." He hurried away from her. "Bitch."

"Trent!" she cried and went to follow him. A massive hand caught her upper arm and pulled her back, leaving her to watch her friend beat a hasty retreat.

"Please don't bother."

Terrified that it was either Ringmaster or, worse, Simon, she looked up at who had spoken. The voice was low, rough, and gravelly. It was the Strongman, Ludwig. He was looking down at her with nothing but kindness, sorrow, and regret.

"Let me go." She yanked her arm out of his grasp and knew it was because he had allowed it. He was too big and too strong, otherwise.

"He won't know you. None of them will. Not anymore. You're not real anymore. Not like you were. Not in their world. Cora Glass doesn't exist anymore. Not to them." His voice was as deep and broad as he was. "Only here. Only to us."

She shook her head and took another halting step away from him. "You're lying. This is all just a stupid prank. Now you have Trent in on it. I don't—I don't know what's happening." She wiped at her face. Tears were rolling down her cheeks. She didn't know why she bothered wiping them away, because more were eagerly replacing them. Panic was welling in her like bees, and the sound of the swarm was starting to drown everything else out.

Ludwig hung his head and shook it sadly, as if he were standing at the grave of someone whose death he couldn't prevent. He turned around and walked away without another word and back into his tent, disappearing into the shadows.

Enough was enough. She'd get home, call the cops on her landline once she was safe, and sort all this bullshit out. Magic might be real, but maybe she could shut this place down. Get them to put cement barriers around it. And Trent was going to get an earful from her when she cornered him for playing along with this terrible prank. Or whatever the *fuck* was happening.

She made her way to the exit gate. It led straight back into the parking lot. Every step brought her closer to her car and to safety. She was half-running. But she could see her

The Contortionist

freedom, just there. Hope was starting to blossom again in her heart.

Right when she ran into a wall.

She grabbed her face and howled in pain. Looking down at her palm, she saw blood. Great. A bloody nose. That was all she needed! But what had she hit? Nothing had been there.

She looked up and, sure enough, empty air was right in front of her. Empty air that people were walking through without a problem. Two people in clown outfits stood on either side of the gate, making sure nobody snuck in. She couldn't see their faces through their freaky vintage masks, but she knew they were both looking at her.

She reached out to the empty air.

And pressed her palm against a wall that she couldn't see.

It was like a barrier had somehow appeared in front of her. But one that other people could walk through without a problem. She ran her hand along the surface, trying to find a gap or a seam. But there wasn't anything she could find.

"Nice job, mime. Where's your makeup?" some asshole shot at her as he walked into the parking lot. He walked right through the space where she had just tried to find a hole in the barrier that was keeping her *in*.

She was too busy having a panic attack to care about his stupid remark. Her nose was still bleeding, and she reached into her pocket to find a scrap of a napkin and pressed it to her face with one hand, as she searched desperately for a hole with the other.

Nothing.

Now she was sobbing. She threw her shoulder into the barrier, but it didn't budge. She smashed into whatever it was again, and again. It didn't budge. She wailed and threw herself at it. "Let me out!"

People were giving her a huge clearance as they tried to avoid her. She was acting insane, after all. But she was bashing herself into something that didn't exist. "Please, somebody help me, please!"

"Neat trick."

"Wow, what's her problem?"

"How's she doing that?"

It all blurred together. She was too busy trying to break down whatever it was that was holding her back from freedom.

How long it went on, she didn't know. When she was panting too hard to continue, she collapsed to her knees. Her hands were sore. Her shoulder was sore. She had been bashing herself against nothing, and "nothing" really didn't want to move. At least her nose had stopped bleeding. That was fast. Small favors.

Freedom was right there in front of her. But it felt like it was a universe away.

She was so *close.*

She could see her car. But the rest of the parking lot was empty. The park was closed now. She must have been at it for hours. Everyone had left. Everyone had *left her there.* The realization that a whole park's worth of people had walked right past her while she was desperate for help settled on her like a bag of bricks.

Cora doubled over, put her head in her hands, and wept.

She'd never had a mental breakdown or a panic attack before, but here she was. And she was pretty damn sure she was having both at the same time.

A hand settled on her shoulder. "C'mon, toots. It's not worth all this."

The Contortionist

"Don't touch me!" She shoved Aaron away.

"Okay, okay." He took another step back and raised his hands. "But come on, let's get you inside, make you some hot tea, and—"

"Leave me alone." She put her head down and laced her fingers into her hair, shutting her eyes tight. "I just want to go home, please...please let me go."

"I wish I could, Cora. But I can't. Nobody can. Not even Mr. Harrow. Once he or the Faire makes a choice...that's that. There's no going back. C'mon now, get up off the ground. Let's take you to your boxcar, and you can get some sleep."

"I'm not going anywhere with any of you." She lifted her head to glare at him. She realized he wasn't alone. Ten paces behind him was a small crowd. She blinked and looked at them all in astonishment. She recognized Jack, Ludwig, and Turk. She saw the old fortune teller, Maggie, and the bearded woman, Bertha. Everyone else was new to her. There must have been almost twenty of them.

They were a rainbow of bizarre oddities. Each one seemed to be strange in a unique way. They ran the gamut. There was a short, dark-haired woman standing next to the beautiful blonde woman Cora had seen performing on the metal hoop. Both of them were wearing bedazzled leotards. The short woman had a man next to her, who had an arm around her waist.

She saw a man and a woman who were standing very close to each other. It took her a second to realize they were literally joined at the hip and the shoulder. Which was messed up, because she knew that wasn't how conjoined twins worked. But there they were anyway.

Another man smiled brightly at her, his teeth white

against dark skin. He was shirtless and covered in tattoos and piercings. An unlit torch hung at his side.

A clown with the painted face of a crying skull watched her, his face twisted into an overblown frown.

A beautiful woman with a long silk gown was looking at her with all the compassion of a statue.

A man with strange, somewhat blunted features watched her through eyes that caught the light very oddly. There was something feral about him, but she couldn't put her finger on what was exactly *wrong* with him, either.

There was one person missing. Simon.

More small favors.

It was all too much. "Go away…all of you. Leave me alone." She wanted to scream at them. She wanted to sound firm. Instead, her voice sounded small, broken, and afraid.

Aaron started walking toward the pack of people and gestured with both arms for them to turn around and go the other way. "Shoo. All of you. Let's go. We can all introduce ourselves later. Give the girl some space to breathe. She's had an absolutely shit week, and she's not going anywhere."

Everyone obeyed, murmuring quietly to each other while they broke off and began walking away. All except the Ringmaster, who patted Aaron on the shoulder as he passed. When everyone else had gone, Turk walked up to her but kept a respectful distance.

"Let me go," she begged him. He seemed like the guy in charge. He had to know how to let her out. "Please."

"I can't, my dear. You were chosen for this the moment you walked through the gate. It was only a matter of time. But you're safe. No one is going to hurt you anymore."

"Simon was going to *eat me,* or whatever the fuck he was trying to do."

"That was then, and now things have changed." He

sighed and took off his top hat to run his hand over his slick black hair. "Simon can't hurt you now without hurting himself, and he's very keen on keeping himself in one piece. He's the most valuable thing in his life."

"Why can't I leave? I don't understand." She was shaking. She was exhausted, she was starving, and her shoulder felt like it was on fire from bashing into the invisible barrier so many times. "This isn't possible."

"You've really taken a left turn out of all the things you think are possible, Cora. I hate to break it to you, but...well." He gestured at the gate. "That world is gone to you now. And you're gone from it."

"I need to use your phone. I need to call the police."

"The only phone we have won't work for you unless the Faire lets it. The same reason you're not allowed outside. The Faire takes who it wants, and it keeps who it takes. It doesn't trust you yet."

"I don't know how much you paid Trent to pretend he didn't know me."

"We didn't do a thing. You don't exist in that world anymore. Every trace of you is gone. Your own mother wouldn't recognize you. They don't know you...no one will. You're one of us now, Cora, and this is your home. There is no going back."

"This can't be real." Tears welled in her eyes again, and she let them fall. Whatever. "Please, make it stop."

"I wish I could. I really do wish I could." He shook his head sadly. "Take as much time as you need to get your thoughts together. When you have questions, come talk to me."

And with that, he turned and left.

She wanted to get up and try climbing the gates. Maybe she could find a forklift and drive it through the wooden barrier. Fuck "magic," she was going to get *out* of here. But she felt small, she felt weak, and she felt *exhausted*. Whatever had happened to her—whatever the Ringmaster had done to her—it had already left her in a heap.

She knew she should keep fighting.

Maybe the fact that she couldn't bring herself to do any of those things made her weak. She didn't know.

She hung her head and cried.

It was another twenty minutes of that when the world decided it wanted to officially make her night even worse. The skies opened up, and rain began pouring down on her. Instantly, she was soaked.

She looked up at the dark skies over head. "Oh, fuck you!"

She had officially devolved into yelling at the sky. Great. She really was losing her mind. She lowered her head again and was glad at least she didn't have to bother crying anymore. The world was doing that for her.

What was she supposed to do? Get up and keep fighting? She had thrown herself against an invisible barrier until she couldn't stand anymore. Was she supposed to give up? Claw out her eyes with her car keys? Go find somebody and threaten to slit their throat until they found a way to set her free?

Nobody seemed to be thrilled she was there. Every face in that crowd was looking at her with a mix of curiosity, pity, and sadness. It was like they all felt *bad* for her. Like they didn't want this to happen, either.

But why? What had they done to her? She had no answers to anything. All she knew was that through the rain she could see her car, but it might as well have been a mirage on the desert sands.

So close, and yet...so far.

The Contortionist

The early spring rain was cold. She was shivering, and she was soaked to the bone. She couldn't give a fuck. She sat there for what could have been hours. She was going to wait until the first person came through those gates the next day, and she would fall at their feet and beg for them to call the police.

She had seen Jack on the other side of the entry gate out in the parking lot. She knew they could go out there. But not her.

"It doesn't trust you yet." That was what Turk had said.

Whatever.

She was so lost in her thoughts that she didn't notice when it stopped raining. Well, more accurately, it had stopped raining on *her*. It was still pouring, but the spot around her in a circle was no longer being hit by the rain. Neither was she.

She blinked.

She went to look up just as something slipped over her head. She yelped and grabbed at it. It was fabric. Were they sticking her in a bag and dragging her off to—

It was a towel. It came off easily in her hands. A white cotton bath towel. She looked down at it in confusion, then up to find the source of whoever had dumped it over her head like they were playing with the family dog.

A man was standing over her with an umbrella above his head, his expensive red and black suit looking more crimson in the dim light. His eyes were covered by sunglasses, despite the darkness. And he was smiling down at her.

Simon.

She shot to her feet in record time. When she tried to run from him, he held out his hand in front of him, his fingers at odd angles.

And suddenly she couldn't move at all.

"Don't run, my dear, sweet, darling cupcake. I'm out here in the rain for you, after all." He pulled in a deep breath, and when he let it out, all the rest of his words ran together in one quick stream. "I was sitting in my boxcar, and I was thinking we better not start all this off on the wrong foot, what with me trying to eat you and all, so I figured I should come and apologize." He coughed as he ran out of air toward the end. He smiled a little broader. "And when I saw you out here, crying in the rain, I thought—how sad. How perfectly tragic." He scrunched up his nose. "You look awful. Like a drowned rat."

"Fuck you."

"Later." He tilted his head to the side slightly, as though thinking. "Now? I could do now."

She tried to pull herself free, but his strings were impossible. "Let me go. I can't take being manhandled anymore. Please. Stop this."

"Don't run away from me, then, and I will. I don't want to watch you get rained on like a stray cat, and I don't terribly want to ruin my suit, either. This is very nice velour I'm wearing."

She gritted her teeth. Where was she going to go? She couldn't escape. Not yet, anyway. "Are you going to kill me?"

"No, sweetheart. Killing you means killing me. Maiming you means maiming me. And I very much like not being mangled." He smiled with what she assumed was supposed to be an innocent expression.

It wasn't. Not in the slightest.

"Fine. I won't run."

"Very well." He lowered his hand, and she felt the bindings around her drop away. She stood there, wondering if she should break her word and take off anyway. But he could likely just snatch her again before she had made it ten feet. And she was so tired and sore, she knew any attempt on her part would be pathetic. "Now, be good."

So, like an idiot and a loser, she used the towel to dry off her face and her hair.

"Silly girl, sobbing at the door, like anyone will care." He chuckled. "Come on, let's take you to your boxcar. You need a warm shower and to get some rest. Things will look better in the morning."

"I doubt that."

"Well, they certainly can't look worse, now, can they?" He laughed, clearly pleased and proud of his joke. She glared up at him, and that only made him laugh harder. "Oh, don't look at me like that. We're friends, aren't we?"

"I'm not going to magically forgive you for trying to kill me."

"I don't suppose you would. And for the *last time,* I wasn't trying to kill you, cupcake. I was trying to trap your life force inside a puppet of my own creation so I could slowly consume you over the course of the next few decades." He leaned in closer. "Do try to keep up."

She stared at him angrily and tried to see if she could burst him into flames with her mind. Sadly, no dice.

"Come along, now!" He straightened and turned from her, starting to walk back into the park. She was quickly back in the rain, and she shuddered at the sudden cold. He looked back at her, stopped, tipped his head back, and let out a loud and beleaguered sigh. "Why do you have to be so *difficult?* You can't get sick and die anymore, but you can be miserable. Heel, Contortionist." He whistled and patted his thigh like she was an animal.

"What did you just call me?"

He smiled. "Contortionist. That's who you are now. I'm

Puppeteer. You have already met Ringmaster, Barker, Rigger, and Strongman. I believe you also met Soothsayer and Bearded Lady." He shook his head. "You really are adorably dense." He moved his hand, and she jerked forward and back under his umbrella. Invisible strings had pulled her there. "And you're just getting soaked again. Now, stay close."

He began to walk, and to her sheer horror, she was walking alongside him. Entirely against her will.

Puppeteer. Right.

"Stop it. Stop it! I'll walk. Just—please—" She felt panic creeping up on her again. She was going to hyperventilate. "Just no more."

"Okie-dokie, darling." He released her, and she staggered a few steps as she tried to regain control of herself. She straightened, clutching the bath towel tightly, and was shaking as she walked alongside him in the rain.

He was whistling a waltz, seemingly as happy as he could be.

Meanwhile, she was on the verge of a nervous breakdown.

And now that she wasn't actively in the rain, she was cold, miserable, and exhausted. They walked down an abandoned path through the carnival, between the rows of switched-off rides, food carts, game booths, and attraction tents. All the lights were off, save for those that ran up the massive observation tower in the center of the park. Those always seemed to stay lit and twinkled through the rain.

It felt like the whole place was staring at her, and she wrapped the towel over her shoulders out of a need to feel some kind of comfort.

"What's happened to me...?"

"I'd tell you, but you wouldn't believe me. I bet a few

The Contortionist

people have tried already." He pushed his glasses up his nose with the press of a ring finger to the silver bridge. "So, I won't bother. Not until you've had some proper sleep and maybe breakfast. You look like you're one good startle away from going into a coma as it is."

"You're probably right."

"I have half a mind to test the theory, but...eh...you're pathetic looking when you're crying, and I don't like it."

"Asshole."

"Mmhm. Be more creative if you're going to insult me. I know you're capable of it."

They walked past the small gate that said *Staff Only* on it in large letters. There she saw the rows of vintage train cars, arranged in lazy arcs. Some had lit windows, and some didn't.

She read the numbers as they passed. Sixteen. Four. Twenty.

Simon's words that he'd shouted at the Ringmaster echoed in her head. Something clicked together. "Is this what you meant when you said something about me 'taking the zero'?"

"Ah! You aren't a complete idiot. Hallelujah!" He cackled. "Devils be praised."

She wanted to punch him in the face.

He was oblivious to her glare, or he just didn't care. "Yes, sweetheart. That's exactly what I meant. But it means a lot more than a number painted on some lousy old boxcar that hasn't moved in...eh...at least a two hundred and fifty years. Wait. What year is it, again?" He paused to look down at her. "You told me, but I'm afraid I forgot."

"Are you kidding me?"

He pointed a finger into her face. "Don't look at me like I'm the moron here, missy. I've been very busy. We only just got back the other day, and apparently newspapers aren't a thing anymore."

"It's 2020."

He tipped his head back and laughed. "Yes! Right. How *droll.*" He began walking again, and she hurried to stay underneath the reach of the umbrella.

"What does it mean, then?"

"Hm?"

"You said it means more than a number painted on a train car."

"A story for tomorrow. Ah! Here we are." He stopped at the base of a little wooden set of stairs that reached up to a door. It was the one with the zero painted on the door, although she didn't recognize it from when she had seen it previously. Just yesterday, it had looked abandoned with weeds and vines growing up the stairs. But now it looked freshly painted, and all the overgrowth had been cleared away.

Simon placed a hand on her wet hair, and she jolted at the contact. "Get some sleep, Cora Glass. Rest. You've had a rather trying day, I might say. And I know I'm to blame for it. Well. Mostly." He gestured at her to go up to the door.

Without any other plan and wondering if every second was going to be the moment she died, she didn't know that she had much choice. She walked up the stairs and opened the door. Swinging it into the dark space, she fumbled around on the wall for a switch. Luckily, she found one in a few seconds, and flipping it, she looked around.

It was a train boxcar, all right. But it had been converted into a single-room apartment. It had a bed in the far back with a sliding door to separate it from the rest of the room, a small kitchenette, a door to what was probably a bathroom, a few closets, and a desk. She had far smaller, far crappier

The Contortionist

places in college. It wasn't...bad. It honestly looked kind of cozy. Like one of those tiny homes they made shows about.

It also probably looked cozy because she was exhausted and as worn out emotionally as she was physically.

At least there weren't any knife-wielding maniacs. That she could see, anyway. There was still time for them to come leaping out of nowhere.

Simon cleared his throat to get her attention through the rain. She turned back to look down at him. "Welcome home. It's yours. Have a good night, Contortionist." He began to walk away, leaving her standing in the doorway in the shelter away from the rain. He paused, turned to look back at her, and smiled. It would have been the kind of smile that would have melted her heart, and maybe something else, if he wasn't such a psychopath. "If you get lonely tonight...or any other night, I'm in fifteen. Ta-ta for now, cupcake!"

He turned and left, whistling, barely audible through the patter of the rain.

She walked into the train car and shut the door. She leaned on the back and looked around the little space. It was dated and vintage, like everything else. But it looked to be in good condition.

And the bed...it looked shockingly large. At least a queen, if not a king. And, man, it looked comfortable.

She felt woozy, dizzy, and like cold garbage. She needed to sleep. There was sense in the idea of trying to rest and sorting out her problems when she didn't feel like she was going to pass out or puke at any given point in time.

She locked the door. She threw the deadbolt she found on it, and even the dumb little chain. She checked every window in the space to make sure they were locked. Opening the two sets of doors she could find, she discovered a bathroom behind one and a closet behind the other.

A closet with clothing in it. Clothing that was clearly meant for a woman.

The previous person who had this car was a man, though. Didn't they say that? She shook her head. She didn't know who had owned the clothing, but she hoped they didn't mind if she borrowed something to sleep in that wasn't soaked through.

Picking through the rack and the drawers set into the bottom half of the closet, she found a t-shirt and cotton pants.

Peeling off her soaked clothing, she tossed them into the tub in the bathroom. For a train car home, it really was shockingly roomy. Sure, it was efficient, but it had all the necessities.

This isn't home. You don't live here. This is one night. Then you're going to break down the fucking gate with the closest vehicle you can hotwire.

She flicked off the lights. She curled up under the covers.

Sleep came for her, hard and fast, for the first time in a very, very long time.

20

Simon watched as the lights in the boxcar across the way flicked off. She hadn't taken him up on his offer to come to his bed, although he wasn't surprised. He wondered if they would dream together tonight, but he doubted it. He wouldn't try to make the link between them work. She was too tired. She had suffered a panic attack and had an all-around terrible day. She would need her rest.

He would leave her be. Just the once.

Simon scratched at his chest. It felt like someone had stuck needles into him and were wiggling them around. It was annoying. It was irritating. It stung.

I hate this.

He paced around his train car for a while, back and forth, scratching his fingers on his scalp. It was the needling pain that had sent him out into the rain with an umbrella and a towel to fetch the girl and try to talk some sense into her.

She had been suffering. And so, therefore, had he.

I hate this so much.

This was precisely the reason he never Sponsored

anyone. Why he never shared a part of his seity with someone else in order to make them part of the Family. He'd heard from all the others how wonderful an experience it was to share their life with another.

No, this was anything but wonderful. This was shit.

He had found her weeping on the ground, looking for all the world like a stray cat in the rain. He hated seeing her like that. And *hated* that he *hated* it. It should have amused him. Instead, it made him anxious. And so, he paced.

He knew precisely the moment she must have fallen asleep, because it was when the itching in his chest finally let up. He sighed and slumped down onto his bed. Pulling off his sunglasses, he tossed them onto the shelf that served as his nightstand. Rubbing his hands over his face, he snarled in annoyance.

Damn Ringmaster and his meddling. Damn him to the fires of hell! Since when had he been able to force a Sponsorship? Simon couldn't recall it ever having been done before. But that was what the big fat fool had said—that he hadn't ever needed to do it before.

He rubbed at his chest over his thin nightshirt. The itching had gone, but the memory of it remained. He wondered idly what part of him she had received. He tried to check off all the things he knew about himself in his head down in a line but couldn't find anything missing.

That's how this works. You don't know what's gone because you don't remember having it.

This was a travesty. This wasn't fair. He was going to have to find a way to fix it. He would have to find a way to tear out his stolen seity from her and get it back. He would kill Ringmaster for this. He'd find a way to rip that man to pieces and eat him whole.

In the meantime, she is a pretty thing, isn't she?

The Contortionist

He chuckled to himself, stretching his limbs out wide. His bed had always been devoid of company. He liked it that way. Let the others dally and cavort with each other. He never felt the need. They were all revolting, weak-minded, insipid creatures. This space was his. If he ever played with a guest who came through the gates, it was in his tent. Not here.

Poor, pretty little cupcake.

Cora had thrown herself at the barrier to the Faire for three hours, by his count. And she had sat there in the rain weeping for another two before he finally had to put a stop to the itching he felt in his chest.

That wasn't someone who was weak-minded, although her frustration at her eventual surrender had been written clearly on her face. Exhaustion had broken her down, not her will.

Surviving the kind of pain she clearly suffered on a daily basis took a resolve that he had wanted to consume. She burned brighter than most of the souls he had seen come through the gates in the past century and a half. It should have been a clear warning that the Faire wasn't going to let him win this one.

Not when it came to someone like her.

I never win. I never get anything I want. I try, and I try, and it always finds a way to take it away from me!

At least for now, he was going to be denied the meal he had wanted to make of her. He'd find a way to get what he wanted, but it would take some time. And now that she had taken over the empty slot in their unnatural coterie, time was something he was going to have in abundance.

Play the slow game. Take the scenic route.

But maybe there was another game he could amuse himself with while he waited for the chance to kill Ringmaster, reclaim what had been stolen from him, *and* consume Cora. He smiled. There were other things he could think of to do with her while he waited.

Lifting a hand, he spread his fingers, watching the threads appear and span between them. They shone in the dim light of his train car. He never understood why others had such a hard time seeing them—they were so obvious.

They're fools, that's why.

He turned his hand over thoughtfully. Cora had a piece of him. He wanted it back. But in the absence of that, he could keep that part of him close. Even if it meant she had to come with it. At least she was easy on the eyes. At least she tasted so sweet on his lips. He remembered their kiss, and he was eager to find the chance to have another.

Someone would need to show her the ropes. Someone would need to teach her about her new reality and help her fit into the slot she had been chosen to fill. When he had dumped her off in the grass, he had intended to let her become somebody else's problem.

Jack the Rigger was an overly sympathetic lout, and he had already tried to console her.

Aaron the Barker was always a sucker for a beautiful face. He'd try to sleep with the girl within the week, he was certain.

The thought of either of those men touching her turned his stomach. Jealousy, unexpected and unwelcome, surged up in him. He snarled. He was forced to share her pain. Who knew what else he would have to split with her? He grimaced at the idea of sitting by himself and feeling her happiness in the arms of one of those idiots.

Oh.

This isn't a passing fancy or a little spot of lust, is it? I really do want her, don't I?

The Contortionist

This is problematic.

He laughed hard. "I never cease to disappoint myself." No one was there to hear him—his dolls were never let inside his private car. And his ever-present, ever-mocking shadow couldn't talk to him. He placed his hands over his face and growled low again. His stolen seity had to be to blame for this surge of *need* that he had for her. It had to be. Yes, he had kissed her before that was the case, but it felt so much worse now. This wasn't simple attraction; this was something more. The girl was beautiful, with her long and flowing dark hair and her bright, big gray eyes. Like smoke from a candle.

And now she's more than a little flexible, isn't she?

He smacked his hand against his forehead. "No! Bad, bad Puppeteer!" But the images that flashed through his mind wouldn't clear. The idea of her, dangling from his strings, bent into all sorts of seemingly impossible angles. And oh, how he could enjoy those positions.

Snarling, he flew up from his bed and threw open the door to the bathroom. He needed a shower. He needed to clear all of that out of his head. Killing Ringmaster and regaining his seity was his priority.

But I will have some time to kill while I scheme.

He climbed into the shower and smacked his forehead on the white tile.

And someone does need to show her the ropes, don't they? Why let it be one of those shit-stains? No. Better it be me. I want her in my hands, not theirs.

It was a few minutes of standing there with his forehead whacking against the tile, feeling the water pour over him, before he realized something. He'd forgotten to take his night clothes off. He laughed, the sound turning into a cackle. Now he was just as soggy as she had been!

He was never one to deny himself something he wanted. Ever. If there was a cookie in a jar, it was his. And Cora was a tempting morsel, indeed.

You have a piece of me, Cora. It's only fair that I get an equal value in exchange, isn't it?

That settled it. The girl belonged to him. He was going to take her under his wing, show her the ropes, and entertain himself with her while he figured out how to consume her and reclaim his missing part. And if he could convince her to be his in the process, all the better.

He laughed. "Seems like I'll get to find out what you taste like after all, Cora dear."

THEY SAY that the very worst thing a man can be denied is love. This is not true. The very worst thing anyone can be denied is not the respite to be found in another's arms—but that which is to be discovered in the embrace of the grave.

Death is a mercy.

Humanity would be wise to learn this.

It is the greatest gift mankind has ever been given by any God, new or old. To deny death is a curse. And humanity, like children, are always scrambling to find a way to achieve such a terrible end. For we fear that silence of the beyond, where we should look at it as nothing more than the rest of sleep.

As a wiser man once said, "To sleep, perchance to dream."

And in these dreams of death, what dreams may come, indeed? For if we were to forever hold on to this mortal coil, what would come of us then, I ask? What madness and blithe malice might form in the vacuum left behind, believing ourselves to have ascended to some greater form?

We would become beasts of cruelty, as we were paid the same.

The laws of the universe must still hold true. There is no action without equal and opposite reaction. If death is denied, then more death must be caused.

For to die is to be mortal. And mortality is a requirement of mankind. I say to you, then—that if we are denied death...we are no longer of the human race.

Take these matters together into an account, and simple arithmetic leads us to the answer of what an inhuman creature we might become in the absence of our own deaths.

We become an instrument of death instead.

-M. L. Harrow

To be continued in Harrow Faire: Book Two
"The Puppeteer"
Order Here

A Sneak Peek of Harrow Faire: Book Two
"The Puppeteer"

MADNESS IS AN INSIDIOUS DISEASE.

We do not see the danger until it is too late. It creeps into the cracks and crevices of the mind and makes itself at home, like carpenter ants in the framing of a home. We do not know the floor has rotted away until one ill-timed step destroys the façade of normalcy.

But carpenter ants do not destroy a home. They change it. As matter cannot be destroyed, they consume the structures we have built and rearrange it for their own use.

While a home beset by such insects might seem uninhabitable for those who look at the situation from the outside, to the ants it was the intended outcome. We might inspect the foundation and find it derelict and dilapidated. We might scoff and say that anyone who lives within such a place is idiotic, and that they should have not neglected it in such a way. And, in extreme cases, they should move.

Consider this metaphor in relation to one's mind. That place in which we spend the entirety of our mortal lives. What happens when your home is beset by insects then?

One cannot move out of one's own mind, try as we might. We are trapped within these structures of ours, for better or worse and come what may. We must make do with what we are given and what we have left. Whereas you or I in our daily lives might seek new a homestead in such an infestation, in this labyrinth of the psyche, we cannot.

There are different ways that a consciousness, once gnawed and riddled with holes, might come to adapt to such a state of being. Consider three men with this dilemma, if you will.

The first man may seek to repair the damage—replace the eaten portions and shore up the foundations. This man is pragmatic, but shortsighted. He treats the symptoms, but not the cause.

The second may seek to exterminate the infestation—to seek the illness at the root and rip it out. This man is wise, but must need act quickly before the house collapses around him.

The third man merely laughs—he accepts his new state of being and does nothing to repair his home. He declares himself King of the Ants, lifts up hammer and sledge, and tears the remaining walls apart with his own two hands.

You might think that man the fool. You might think him a harmless, laughing lunatic.

It is a mistake that leads to ruin.

For that man is the most dangerous of them all.

-M. L. Harrow

CORA WOKE up from a dreamless sleep. She had expected to be troubled by nightmares or at least her usual tossing and turning. Or, which had been the pattern the past few days more often than not, to be pestered or terrorized by Simon. But it seemed she had been so exhausted that her mind couldn't even summon up nightmares from her day. Which was pretty damn impressive, as she had plenty of fuel for her mind to burn.

Being haunted by a man-eating murder-circus, almost being turned into an inhuman and monstrous meal-via-porcelain-doll by an undead psychopath, and now being trapped inside said man-eating murder-circus with said undead psychopath.

An undead psychopath to whom she was mildly attracted, but that was another stupid problem entirely.

It took her a solid couple of seconds to remember where she was. The linens smelled fresh and clean, but not like home. Despite a slight chill in the air from the early spring weather, the blankets were thick and warm. She could hear the click of a heater going on and off occasionally.

The room was streaming with morning sunlight. It hadn't even occurred to her to pull the blinds around the large bed at the back of the boxcar. But the light didn't bother her. She was lying there…basking. And it took her a long time to realize why.

She didn't hurt.

She was…comfortable.

There was no ache in her back or her hips. There was no tenderness in her joints. There wasn't that background hum of pain that had plagued her for the past decade of her life.

She stretched and waited for the pain to start. It was too good to be true. She waited for the familiar pang to stab into her hips, her shoulders, her elbows, anything.

Nothing.

She rolled her wrists. She arched her back. She waited for the sound of popcorn and crunching and the mild ache that went along with it. Nothing happened. She rolled onto her stomach and pushed up onto her hands, waiting for the agony to start. There was none.

She fell onto her stomach and let out a small, disbelieving laugh. She flopped onto her back, stretched out her arms and legs wide, and let out a long, contented groan.

She didn't hurt. For the first time in years…she didn't hurt. She felt like she had slept. Really, honestly *slept*. She

The Contortionist

wasn't exhausted, beaten down, and feeling like she had woken up after being dragged behind a runaway truck. She felt good. Honest-to-god good.

It wasn't possible.

None of this is possible.

She looked up at the wood paneling of the ceiling. It was stained a rich cherry, and it was clear the whole space was very old, but well maintained. *No, this place is alive. The Faire is keeping it this way with the bits and pieces it eats from people. Remember?* She sat up and ran her hands through her hair. It felt stringy and gross from having been out in the rain last night for hours.

She looked down at her hands. She remembered nearly tearing off her fingernails clawing at the invisible wall. She should at least have bruises from what had happened. She bruised so easily ever since she was a kid. But nothing was there. Touching her nose, she remembered bloodying it when she ran into the invisible wall. But it wasn't even sore.

Simon healed.

I healed.

I...Am I really one of them now?

No.

No, she refused to accept that she was trapped. She refused to accept that she was trapped in this damn place. A monster and a circus freak. This was all some wild illusion. It was a trick. She'd get dressed and get the hell out of here. Simple as that.

She slipped out of the bed and the little demi-room in which it was partitioned in the back of the boxcar. Going into the bathroom, she pulled the t-shirt up and over her head to look for the purple blotches she was certain would be on her shoulder.

After spending hours trying to get through the invisible

barrier that was holding her prisoner, she should have *something*. Some mark of what she had done. She should hurt somewhere. She always hurt *somewhere*.

Nothing. She didn't even have bags under her eyes. She looked…better than she had in a long time. She furrowed her brow at her own reflection, confused. Letting out a sigh, she didn't know what to do about it. Be mad that she wasn't in pain? That she didn't have puffy marks under her eyes? That she looked…healthy?

Glancing over at the tub and shower combo with the old-fashioned brass wall-mounted showerhead, she was too tempted. If she were going to try to escape this place, she might as well do it not feeling gross. She pulled her still-soggy clothing out of the tub and threw them over the towel rack and flipped on the shower. It got hot after a minute, and she stripped out of her borrowed nightclothes and stepped in.

It was amazing how cathartic a shower could be. Hot water seemed to make everything better. She found some shampoo and went about scrubbing her hair. She had a lot of it—it went down well past her shoulders—so it took a while. It didn't help that she had knotted sections while being out in the rain having a breakdown.

Combing conditioner through her hair with her fingers gave her time to think.

She played over the events of the past few days in her head, right from the very beginning, and tried to piece it all together. No matter how many times she thought it through, it all came down to one thing.

Black magic was real. Or at least some kind of dark supernatural power. It certainly didn't seem benign.

The Faire was alive. It ate parts of people's "seity," and so did the men and women—the *things*—that lived inside it.

The Contortionist

But what she couldn't accept was the possibility that she was now one of them. That was where she drew a hard line. But all the evidence pointed to the opposite. The invisible wall that had kept her trapped last night. And then there was what happened with Trent.

He hadn't recognized her. They had been best friends since grade school, and he had looked at her like a stranger. There wasn't even a flicker of recognition in his eyes when she had desperately begged him for help. Nothing.

Even if they had paid him off, she wasn't sure he was that good of an actor.

She decided it didn't matter what was real and what wasn't. She could sort it all out when she was safely at home, in her own bed, and talking to the cops filing a report about kidnapping and harassment. She'd leave the "black magic, occult, man-eating murder-circus" out of the police report.

Her thoughts swung back to Simon. Those puppets of his...what he had said he was going to turn her into. She shivered despite the hot water and went about scrubbing herself with a washcloth and soap. Now Simon claimed he couldn't hurt her without hurting himself, and so therefore, he was safe. She didn't know if he would ever be *safe*. He was a lunatic.

Why had he come out in the rain for her? It didn't make any sense. He was all over the map with her. His compass spun wildly and without warning. One moment, he was kissing her. The next, he was terrorizing her, screaming in a rage about how she was his property. If Aaron and Jack were to be believed, he had dumped her out in the grass like garbage. Then he...came out into the rain to drag her inside. North, south, north, south, and back again.

It didn't matter. Simon was dangerous. It was more than

a little likely that everyone else in the Faire was just as murderous, but they just hid it better.

Her next steps were simple. Get dressed, find a car, and drive it through the invisible wall. Get home, call the cops, then cry into a bottle of whiskey. Simple. Right?

Probably not. Nothing had been simple all week, and something told her that it sounded easy, but she might as well be trying to climb the outside of the observation tower with two suction cups.

I will not accept the fact that I'm trapped here. I'm not going to just accept this.

She turned off the shower and dried herself off. Her clothing was still soaking wet, so she dug around in the closet until she found what she needed. She wound up with underwear that thankfully fit her, along with black jeans, socks, boots, a tank top, and a simple gray linen coat. It was all stuff she would happily wear.

As though someone had picked it out for her.

She shuddered at the idea that this could all have been planned in advance. More and more evidence piled on the half of the scale that said she was now part of this place. But on the other side was an ounce of hope. And hope was very hard to kill.

When she had finally finished brushing out her hair, there was a knock on the door. She blinked and debated not answering it. She went through the options of who it could be. Best case scenario, it was a pack of cops coming to rescue her. Worst case, it was Simon coming to kill her.

Santa Claus, Darth Vader, and Einstein could also be standing there, with how her goddamn week was going. After the second knock, she went to the door and cautiously opened it.

And immediately had to jump back as two women plowed into the room. "Wh—"

"Good morning!" the first one exclaimed. She was about Cora's height, with shoulder-length blonde hair and a bright, shining smile. It was the woman she had seen performing on the metal hoop the other day. She was effortlessly beautiful. She was also carrying a tray with a plate heaped with scrambled eggs, bacon, and hash browns.

It wasn't until Cora noticed how good it smelled that she realized she hadn't eaten since breakfast the day prior. Her stomach grumbled, not caring that the invaders might be dangerous. "Uh..." She just watched as the other woman followed the first.

The second woman was a tiny thing. Maybe five foot even, or just a smidge more, with short dark hair. Both women looked like athletes. The blonde looked like she could rip off a car bumper with her bare hands.

Cora blinked. "Hello?"

The blonde with the tray put it down on the table in the little kitchenette. "I'm Amanda. This is Donna. You missed breakfast, so we figured we'd bring it to you." Amanda shot her another award-winning smile. Weirdly, it didn't seem faked, like those kinds of smiles usually did.

"I...um..." Cora shook her head, not sure what to do. The two women were just standing there smiling at her. Amanda was looking at her with happiness and excitement. Like it was Christmas morning.

Donna, the little dark-haired one, waved Cora over to the table. "I know this's been rough for you. Come on, sit, eat. You'll feel better with something on your stomach."

"I, thanks, but..." Cora chewed her lip and shook her head. No, she shouldn't feel like the awkward one. These people were kidnapping her. "I need to go home. I need to find a way out of here."

Both women sighed and cast knowing glances at each other. Donna moved from the kitchenette to Cora and put a hand gently on her shoulder. "I didn't come willingly either. I didn't know what was happening. Juggler just picked me out of the crowd, and before I knew it, I was trapped here too. Just like you. I spent *days* clawing at the walls, trying to get out. I snapped off my fingernails and didn't understand why they just grew back. It took me a month of running through the Inversion before I realized I wasn't going to get home. I don't want to see that happen to you."

"The Inversion?" Cora brushed off the woman's hand. She didn't want to insult the woman, but she was a little confused at how touchy everyone at Harrow Faire seemed to be. "I don't know what you're talking about."

"So, sit, eat, and let us explain." Amanda smiled and motioned to the chair. "Please. And then, when you don't believe us, you can go back to running at the gate trying to get out."

Cora rubbed a hand over her face and sighed. "Fine." She went over to the kitchenette table and sat down. It only had two chairs. Donna took the one across from her while Amanda propped herself up against the counter.

She picked up the fork and began to eat. It was good. Very good. And she was starving. After taking a bite, she remembered her manners. "Thank you. I'm Cora."

"We know." Donna smiled. "I'm the Flyer, and this is Amanda, the Aerialist. And now, you're our Contortionist."

Amanda sighed happily, almost dreamily, as if she was picturing something grand in her mind. "It's so nice to have a woman in the role. Imagine the triple acts we can do now! Hernandez was great, but he was afraid of heights. He was

The Contortionist

so skittish. So jumpy." She chuckled. "Are you afraid of heights?"

Cora hovered her fork over the pile of hash browns. "No?" She felt like she was standing on the side of the road just watching traffic fly by. "I don't think so."

"Great!" Amanda clapped, giggled excitedly, then motioned for her to keep eating. "Don't let me interrupt. You must be starving."

She wanted to escape. But she could at least ask a few questions while she ate, she supposed. Maybe try to make sense of the madness they were all trying to get her to believe. "Everyone here has the weird titles?"

"Everyone. There are twenty-two of us," Donna answered.

"There are definitely more than twenty-two employees here." Cora pointed out the immediate hole in the story. "I've seen dozens more than that."

Amanda chimed in. "They're not real. Not...really real, anyway. They're more like ghosts. People we collect or dream up. Zookeeper and Bertha the Bearded Lady both take in people who come to see them. But they aren't...I don't know. Big enough—full enough—to be one of us. I don't know how to explain it. They're not complete. You met Simon's puppets, right?"

"Seeing as he tried to turn me into one against my will?" Cora cringed. "Yeah. I have. Are they really...people he's trapped like that?"

The expression on the women's faces were a mix of disgust and anger. "Yes," Amanda muttered. "They're very real. He's a sicko."

What a horrifying way to live. And a horrifying fate she barely escaped. She didn't know if she should exactly thank Turk for stopping Simon since it had landed her here, but she still felt like she had dodged a bullet.

But maybe she had side-stepped a small projectile only to get hit in the face by a cannonball. "I might have a hard time believing a lot of this, but Simon being a sicko I won't argue with," Cora said with a faint smile that didn't stay for long.

They sat in silence for a long time. She finally couldn't let it last any longer. "Are you all really trapped here?"

"Yes. And you are, too. I..." Donna looked out the little window for a moment. "I hope you don't think about it as being trapped. I know you're scared. I know you want to go home. But this is your home now. We're Family, and we can be friends. You can be happy here."

Cora snorted incredulously. "After the week I've had? Have you *met* Simon?"

The two women laughed, and Donna nodded. She reached out and gently put her hand on Cora's. "Ask us anything you need to know. And anything we can do to help you, we're here for you. We're Family."

It was the second question she was dreading to ask, because she didn't know if she could accept the answer. Not if accepting it meant she was never going home. "What happened to me last night?"

Donna combed her hand through her hair, scratching her scalp and ruffling the short, dark strands. She was beautiful, in that I-could-probably-break-your-arm-without-trying-but-I'm-just-so-cute-you-won't-be-mad-about-it kind of way. Like a spunky bartender. "There are twenty-two of us. We're not complete unless someone is in each slot. It doesn't feel right for any of us when someone is missing. It's like there's...a hole. The zero—the Contortionist—had been

The Contortionist

empty for a long, long time. Thirty-eight years. Longer than it's ever been empty before."

"Why?" Cora kept eating. The hash browns were amazing.

Donna's expression was troubled as she talked. She fiddled with a little saltshaker on the table. "We weren't sure until this morning. After Simon mutilated Hernandez—after he turned him into one of his dolls—we were sure we'd get another Contortionist the next time the Faire returned. But we never did. It wasn't until Simon killed what was left of the old Contortionist that...you came to join us."

"Why did Simon kill Hernandez?"

"Which time?" Amanda grunted in disgust. "Doesn't matter. Sorry. He claims Hernandez asked for it. The poor man wasn't cut out for this life. He...wasn't ever happy here, no matter how many years had gone by. He wanted to be free, and he got desperate. And Simon takes advantage of desperate people."

Cora could attest to that. She ran her hand over her face and thought it all over.

In the silence, Donna continued. "So, when we have a gap to fill, another one of us can opt to Sponsor a new Family member. We can take a chunk of ourselves—our seity—and give it to the recipient. It makes them like us."

"Simon didn't want anything to do with it." Cora sipped the coffee again. Thank God for caffeine. "Ringmaster made him."

"Yeah." Amanda shook her head. "We didn't even know that was possible. It's one thing when the new Family member doesn't want to be here. It's another thing with the Sponsor doesn't want to be a part of it. Simon's been sulking in his boxcar all morning. No one's seen him since he dumped you in the grass last night."

He came out in the rain to get me. I still don't understand why. "So, he...can't hurt me, without hurting that part of himself?"

"Right. He could make you into one of his dolls, but he'd permanently lose that part of himself in the process. Ringmaster's betting Simon won't do it for that reason alone. My guess is the mad fuck thinks he can get that bit of himself back someday." Donna rolled her eyes. "Egotistical shit hasn't ever once Sponsored anyone."

"Why not?" Cora asked. "I mean. I lost a piece of myself when I came here. Ugh...I can't believe I'm actually saying that." She pinched the bridge of her nose. "But whatever. I don't feel any worse for it."

"You lost a tiny bit of yourself. Like a hair." Donna spun the saltshaker idly. "He lost a finger. It's a much bigger part, and...we only have so much to go around. Think about seity like a wick on a candle. We can add to our wicks with what we take from patrons, but once we're out? We're out. We start to fade away like poor Ludwig."

"What's wrong with Ludwig?" She furrowed her brow. "He's still alive."

"But not for long." Amanda let out a sad sigh. "The poor man. He's been here so long. He's Sponsored so many people. He just doesn't have the will for it anymore, and he has so little left to him. If you talk to him for too long, you'll notice that there's...just not much there. He used to be such a big, loud, boisterous man."

Trent said he was calm and quiet. "That's heartbreaking." Cora chewed her lip. No wonder Simon didn't want any part of it. He seemed to very much have the will to live. She didn't blame him for not wanting to "Sponsor" her.

The two other women nodded. Amanda seemed the most upset. "It is. I'm not looking forward to when he goes."

The Contortionist

The blonde folded her arms across her chest and leaned against the side of the fridge. "But he's been with the Family since, what, 1826? It's his time."

Cora blinked. It was all still so hard to believe. "How old are you two?"

Donna smiled. "I came here in 1977. Amanda's been with us since 1859. The youngest of us is Firebreather, who joined the Family in 1992."

Cora looked up at the woman with a raised eyebrow. "The Faire was here in 1992? That was two years before I was born. I remember my dad taking me here when I was little, and it looked like it had been abandoned for years. He never mentioned it being back."

"It always looks abandoned when we're Inverted." Amanda said it like it made perfect sense. "And a lot of times there's no record of us coming or going. It's only when we're here for a long time that it leaves enough of a mark that people remember. Otherwise, we're wiped from their minds."

"I...don't...understand." Cora was going to get a headache from this.

"I know. Not yet. But you will." Amanda gestured for Cora to keep eating.

Cora took another large swallow of her coffee. She hoped it wasn't drugged. But the caffeine was worth the risk. "Magic is real. I accept that. I can't deny it anymore. I've seen too much weird shit this week. But I...I can't accept that I'm trapped here. I need to try to get out. I'm not one of you. I can't be. I just *can't*."

Amanda and Donna looked at each other for a long moment.

Amanda nodded.

Donna shook her head. "No. It's too gruesome."

Amanda shrugged. "It'd get the point across."

"What'd be too gruesome?" Cora shifted back in her chair.

"Oh, it's an old trick to break people in. Coming back from the dead usually does it. I was going to see if you wanted us to break your neck." Amanda smiled sweetly, like it was no big deal at all. "It's not so bad. Doesn't hurt."

"No!" Cora shot up from her chair and went for the door. "That's it. I'm out of here."

"Wait—"

She didn't know which of them shouted for her to stop. She didn't care. She threw open the door and bounded down the stairs. They were going to hurt her! Everyone here *was* a murdering psychopath—

And she ran right into a tall, skinny wall of red and black stripes. "Good morning, cupcake!" He beamed cheerily down at her, a smile plastered on his face. But, like it always was, it was filled with cruelty and edged in madness.

Simon.

"Fuck, no!" She pushed away from him and went to run. She made it ten steps before her limbs froze in place midstride. She sobbed in defeat.

"Where're you going, Cora dear?" He sounded honestly confused.

"Let her go, Simon!" Amanda shouted from behind her. She twisted her head to watch.

Simon bowed. "Oh. Hello, ladies. I didn't know you were here. I see you beat me to it. I was going to take Ms. Glass to breakfast."

"Let her *go,*" Donna snarled angrily at him as she stormed down the steps. The little woman stood close to the Puppeteer, trying to get as much in the face of a man who was well over six feet tall as she could from more than a foot

The Contortionist

lower. Simon only smiled like he found it adorable. "Whatever sick games you think you're going to play with her, I won't allow."

"Sick games?" He put his hand to his chest in mock hurt. "Me? Hardly. I can't touch her now, as well you both know. Someone has to show her around. Teach her about her new life. I figured it might as well be me. She is mine, after all."

They were talking about her like she wasn't there, stuck in mid-running-stride, frozen like she was only a frame of a piece of film. "Hey, ass-clown!"

All three looked over to her. Simon sighed. He flicked his hand, and whatever was holding her like that—his strings—dropped her to the ground in a heap. She groaned from the impact. When she got up, he was already standing there next to her. He placed a hand on her shoulder. "I'm not the Clown, darling. I'm the Puppeteer. Did you hit your head last night in your pathetic attempt at escape?"

She yanked free from him, and backed away slowly, not turning her back on him. "I'm getting out of here. Screw this. Screw you. Screw all of you."

"Careful what you ask for. They'd probably take you up on that offer." Simon shrugged. "All right, well, I'll find you when you tire yourself out." He gestured like he was shooing a child out of the room. "Go on. Do your best."

She didn't need to be told twice. Ignoring the calls from Donna and Amanda to stop, she turned and ran. Again.

She was going to find a way out of here.

She was going to go home.

To be continued in Harrow Faire: Book Two
"The Puppeteer"
Order Here

ABOUT THE AUTHOR

Kat has always been a storyteller.

With ten years in script-writing for performances on both the stage and for tourism, she has always been writing in one form or another. When she isn't penning down fiction, she works as Creative Director for a company that designs and builds large-scale interactive adventure games. There, she is the lead concept designer, handling everything from game and set design, to audio and lighting, to illustration and script writing.

Also on her list of skills are artistic direction, scenic painting and props, special effects, and electronics. A graduate of Boston University with a BFA in Theatre Design, she has a passion for unique, creative, and unconventional experiences.

Printed in Great Britain
by Amazon